Readers everywhere are in love with the new series
by Lisa Renee Jones

THE SECRET LIFE OF AMY BENSEN

"Intoxicating, intense, and deeply seductive."

—*RT Book Reviews* (Top Pick) on *Escaping Reality*

"Suspenseful and packed with questions."

—*Fiction Vixen*

"The slaps to the face, the sucker punches, and the too-good-to-be-true moments will have you audibly gasping and wondering if you're going to get your HEA and still be in one piece."

—*The Book Vamps*

"Suspense, suspense, suspense . . . all over the place and within every page."

—*Cristina Loves Writing*

"It has everything anyone could want. Mystery, intrigue, suspense, enough heat to melt an iceberg, and characters with depth. Do yourself a favor and start this one now!"

—*The Book Hookers*

"A great story that's wrought with tension and fear of kidnapping and murder."

—*Diary of an Eager Reader*

"An amazing storyline with twists and turns; a roller coaster of highs and lows; and at no point could you sit back and relax.

Lisa Renee Jones has stepped forward and claimed her place in the new adult category and *Infinite Possibilities* will leave you breathless and wondering where it will all end."

—*The Reading Café*

"Lisa Renee Jones will have you gripping the edge of your seat, biting your nails, and leave you with a book hangover."

—*Lisa's Book Reviews*

Praise for the "passionate, all-consuming" (*PopSugar*)

INSIDE OUT SERIES

"If you haven't started this series yet, run to grab the first book and dive in! This easy-reading series is compelling—sucking the reader into a dark and seductively dangerous world of art, BDSM, and murder."

—*Fresh Fiction*

"Lots of dark, suspenseful twists."

—*USA Today* (A Must-Read Romance)

"Great characters, angsty and real, that draw me in to their worlds, and storylines that hook me every single time."

—*Smut Book Junkie Book Reviews*

"Darkly intense and deeply erotic. . . ."

—*RT Book Reviews*

"Intimately erotic . . . Jones did not hold back on the steam factor."

—*Under the Covers Book Blog*

"A series that will completely captivate you—heart, mind, and soul."

"Powerfully written. . . . A tumultuous journey."

"A crazy, emotional roller-coaster ride. . . ."

"Brilliantly beautiful in its complexity. . . . This book had my heart racing."

"Breathtaking in its suspense and intrigue."

"Leaves you begging for more!"

"Dark and edgy erotica that hit all my buttons just right."

"If you haven't read Lisa Renee Jones's Inside Out series then you are seriously missing out on something fierce! It's a great blend of sexy, suspense, and kink."

"These stories just keep getting better and better. . . . Every single one of them leaves you wanting more!"

Also by Lisa Renee Jones

The Inside Out Series

If I Were You

Being Me

Revealing Us

His Secrets*

Rebecca's Lost Journals

The Master Undone*

My Hunger*

No In Between

My Control*

I Belong to You

All of Me*

The Secret Life of Amy Bensen Series

Escaping Reality

Infinite Possibilities

Forsaken

Unbroken*

*Ebook only

denial

LISA RENEE JONES

GALLERY BOOKS

New York   London   Toronto   Sydney   New Delhi

G

Gallery Books
An Imprint of Simon & Schuster, Inc.
1230 Avenue of the Americas
New York, NY 10020

First Gallery Books trade paperback edition November 2015

GALLERY BOOKS and colophon are registered trademarks of Simon & Schuster, Inc.

For information about special discounts for bulk purchases, please contact Simon & Schuster Special Sales at 1-866-506-1949 or business@simonandschuster.com.

The Simon & Schuster Speakers Bureau can bring authors to your live event. For more information or to book an event contact the Simon & Schuster Speakers Bureau at 1-866-248-3049 or visit our website at www.simonspeakers.com.

Interior design by Davina Mock-Maniscalco

Manufactured in the United States of America

10   9   8   7   6   5   4   3   2   1

Library of Congress Cataloging-in-Publication Data

Jones, Lisa Renee.
Denial / Lisa Renee Jones.—First Gallery Books trade paperback edition.
          pages cm — (Careless whispers)
I. Title.
PS3610.O627D46   2015
813'.6—dc23
          2015024192

ISBN 978-1-5011-2285-9
ISBN 978-1-5011-2286-6 (ebook)

To my readers:
Thank you so very much for your constant excitement in
Ella's story. Every single one of you gives me a reason to
smile daily, and I am forever blessed to have your support.

Dear Readers:

I'm so thrilled to finally share Ella's story with you. For my new readers, the Careless Whispers series can absolutely be read on its own, despite its being a spinoff of my Inside Out series. Keep in mind that everything is for a reason and everything is a clue!

For my Inside Out readers who have come to find out what happened to Ella, I know you have so many questions and I promise they will be answered throughout the series. I know you're going to have even more questions as you begin to delve in. Some things may not align perfectly with what you were told during Chris and Sara's books, but what may seem wrong or incorrect is not. They are actually clues that will unearth the secrets you're searching for! I just love to play with your minds like that. I hope you don't mind?!

To my loyal and new readers, I hope you enjoy the journey, and thank you for taking it with me!

Lisa

denial

one

I blink and open my eyes to stare at the unfamiliar white
ceiling, a dull throbbing at the back of my head. My throat
is dry and I swallow with effort, waiting for something familiar
to come to me, but there is nothing—just the white ceiling
and more of the throbbing beneath my scalp. I decide I must
be having a weird dream, and I'd really like to wake up now.

Shifting, I roll to my side to find myself staring into a pair
of pale blue eyes so striking and pure that they seem inhuman.
I blink again and bring the gorgeous man directly in front of
me into stunning clarity. Thirty-something, with thick, longish light brown hair. His cheekbones are high, his chin dim-
pled.

"You're beautiful," I murmur, admiring my mind's work. I
like this dream.

His deliciously full and sensual mouth curves with my
comment. "I've been called a lot of things, sweetheart, but
beautiful isn't one of them. And this isn't a dream. How's your
head?"

"It hurts," I say, my brow furrowing as I digest all he has
said, and I realize I muttered that last thought aloud. "And

wait. What? This isn't a dream?" I lift up on one elbow, and I'm punished for my effort with the pounding of my head. "Okay," I murmur, squeezing my eyes shut. "Maybe I want to wake up now, after all."

"Easy," he warns, his hand coming down on my shoulder, his touch oddly familiar even if he is not. "Lie back down," he urges, and when I obey, he leans over me. "Sleep is a good idea. It'll help you heal."

I stare up at my beautiful stranger, and just the sight of him tells me he's wrong. This *is* a dream, and I follow along where it's taking me. "What's wrong with me?"

"You have a concussion," he explains, settling back down onto some sort of stool. "A pretty bad one, which is why you're in the hospital."

"Hospital?" I repeat, putting together the pieces of the puzzle and deciding that he must be my fantasy doctor. Fighting against the discomfort of moving, I roll to my side again, trying to confirm this assessment. The result is the certainty that every part of this man is hot; his black jeans and matching tee are hugging a lean, muscled body that absolutely fits my "fantasy" assessment. The doctor part, not so much. "Shouldn't you be wearing scrubs?"

"Last I heard, that isn't a requirement for a visitor."

My brow furrows again. "So . . . you're not my doctor?"

He laughs. "No. I'm not a doctor. I'm the man who found you in the alleyway passed out."

"Alleyway?" I repeat. This dream is getting a little strange.

He gives me a curious look. "You don't remember?"

"No." Considering I seem to have no memory except for the here and now, my answer is easy.

"Hmmm," he murmurs thoughtfully. "Well, I'm sure it's just the pain and trauma, but we need to call a nurse anyway and let them know that you're awake." He reaches for a remote-control-like device hanging from the edge of my bed and I watch him, thinking that he has very nice hands. Strong, masculine hands. Familiar, I think. Maybe. I'm pretty sure. I'm considering why that might be when he murmurs something into the remote that I can't seem to understand. My head is so murky, it almost sounds like he's speaking another language. Which is crazy.

"Someone will be right in," he announces, returning the device to where he found it.

I open my mouth to thank him and realize something rather important. "I, ah . . . hate to admit this, but I don't seem to remember your name."

"Kayden," he supplies, rolling his stool closer, the full force of his attention landing on me. It's nerve-wrackingly intense. "And you don't remember because I never told you."

"Oh—right. Because I was knocked out."

"Exactly."

"In an alleyway," I say, trying to get my thoughts around that.

"Right again," he confirms.

"What was I doing in an alleyway?"

"According to law enforcement, most likely being mugged."

I wait for the expected shock, followed by fear and bad memories, but still nothing comes to me. "When?"

He lifts his wrist, displaying a watch with a thick black

leather band. "It's six in the morning now. I called for the ambulance just after midnight."

"That's bizarre. What was I doing in an alleyway after midnight?"

"I was curious about the same thing."

"Why were *you* there?"

"Trying to reach the grocery store in front of it, before it closed."

"I see." My brow furrows. "I just can't imagine myself making the decision to go to a dark, deserted place alone that late at night."

"Maybe you didn't. Maybe you were forced."

"That's a horrible thought," I say, and while I mean the words, I remember nothing, therefore I feel nothing.

"But a logical one, considering you ended up in the hospital."

There is a flickering image in my mind of an ambulance and cobblestone pavement, and I can almost feel the cold ground against my body. And it's then that fiction becomes reality. "I'm not dreaming, am I?"

"You didn't really think you were, did you?"

"I thought . . . because I can't remember anything . . . it just seemed off. I'm off."

"Because you have a head injury—and from what you've indicated, a hellacious headache. That's no dream I want to experience."

He's right, of course. *He* might be dream-worthy, but nothing else about this is. Definitely not the blank space in my mind that I try to access now and fail. I don't know what is happening to me. Panicked, I jerk to a sitting position, a mistake I'm punished for as the pain bleeds from the center of my skull left and right, seeming to draw a circle.

Groaning, I curl forward and grab my head. "It feels like my scalp is being detached."

"You need to lie back down," Kayden insists.

"No," I say, grabbing my legs to support myself. "No, I don't need to lie down. I need to remember what happened to me."

"I'm raising the bed for you," he says, and a low hum fills the air as the mattress comes to life.

I force my head up and look at him. "Kayden," I say, clinging to what I know. "Your name is Kayden."

"Yes," he confirms, his hands encasing my waist as he eases me against the mattress. "My name is Kayden."

"Thank God," I breathe out. "I have present-time memory." He starts to move away and I grab his forearms, holding him to me. "Wait. What's my name?"

"What? You don't know your name?"

"I can't remember *anything* before I woke up. Just tell me my name. Please. I need a trigger for my memories."

He studies me for a beat, maybe two, in which I want to yank a response from his mouth. And then he's standing, giving me his back, one hand running through his thick hair.

"Kayden, *please*," I say, freaking out at his reaction. "What's going on? Why aren't you answering me?"

He faces me, hands settling on his lean hips. "Because I can't. You were mugged. Your purse and identification were missing when I found you."

"You don't know who I am, either?" I feel as if I've been kicked.

"None of us do."

"Surely someone has come looking for me."

"Not yet."

"Not yet?" I choke out, and the news is yet another gut-wrenching blow that leaves me reeling and alone. What kind of person has no one looking for her?

He moves to the side of my bed again and sits down. "It's only been a few hours."

"Please don't do that obligatory make-me-feel-better thing that people do. I am indebted to you for saving me, and I appreciate that you waited here until I woke up—but you don't have to stay here with me." My eyes prickle with tears, and I stare at the doorway, trying to compose myself.

Of course, it's at that poorly timed moment that a woman in green scrubs rushes into the room, speaking in a language I don't understand. I inhale and will away the tears threatening to spill over, only to have her stop at the foot of my bed, her speech pausing expectantly. I blink and realize that she's waiting for an answer I can't deliver. I stare at her. She stares at me, and while the tears might be gone, I have this sense of standing in quicksand, sinking fast, unable to claw my way out.

Kayden rescues me, stepping to my side and answering for me. Confused, overwhelmed with everything but memories, I let my head roll forward, pressing my fingers to my throbbing forehead and telling myself not to crumble. I have to be stronger than this moment in time.

"You don't know Italian, do you?"

At Kayden's question, I look up to find the nurse gone and him standing at the end of the bed. "Why would I?"

"It's the native language."

He's making no sense. "No, it's not."

"You don't know that you're in Rome." It's not a question, and he doesn't wait for an answer. "Of course you don't. Why would you? You don't even know your own name."

"What? I can't be in Rome. I'm American."

"You have to know that's not a logical reply. Plenty of Americans, myself included, live in Rome, while thousands of others visit as tourists."

"I know that—I meant I don't live here."

"So you're visiting," he says, rounding the bed to reclaim the stool. "That's progress. Where *do* you live?"

"I don't know," I say, wracking my brain. "I *don't know*. I just know it's not here."

"That's okay. You know you're American. You know you don't live here. You'll remember the rest in time."

"You have no idea how much I want you to be right."

"I'm right," he assures me, "and for the record, you were right, too. I don't have to stay. But I am."

"I don't want to be an obligation."

"I don't do obligation, sweetheart."

"Well, then, pity."

"Another thing I don't do, so if you're looking for someone to feel sorry for you, I'm the wrong guy for the job."

"There are no other reasons for you to be here."

"Aren't there?" he challenges softly.

"What does that even mean?" I ask, but it's a forgotten question when I hear "Good morning."

A twenty-something woman in dark blue scrubs, her long dark hair tied neatly at her nape, sweeps into the room and offers me hope that I might actually find a way to escape all of this white noise.

"I'm Maria," she says pleasantly, stopping at the end of the bed. "How are you feeling?"

"Like someone turned off the switch to my brain," I say, holding nothing back.

"That's quite normal after a head trauma," she assures me. "How about your back? Can you move okay?"

I flex a bit, and grimace. "I can. I just don't want to."

"I'm not surprised," she says. "You have a pretty nasty lump between your shoulder blades."

I don't care about my back. I care about my memories. "When will the doctor be in?"

"He's on his rounds now," she says, "but he'll be by soon to discuss your recovery. Now let's check your vitals."

She moves toward Kayden's side of the bed and he stands reluctantly—or maybe I'm imagining it because I don't want him to leave. He might be a stranger, and I might hate feeling like a burden, but he's also all I have right now.

Moving into Kayden's spot, Maria reaches for the blood pressure cuff and wraps my arm. "So far, your vitals have been looking good."

It's then that Kayden steps to her left, hovering over her shoulder, seeming to supervise her actions, and I swear the look on his handsome face is intense, almost possessive—which is a ridiculous thought. He barely knows me. I barely know him. He's not possessive. Protective, maybe, of the woman he saved. Yes. That has to be it. That's why he's still here.

"How's your pain?" Maria asks, shifting my attention back to her.

"Fine, unless I move."

"That should start easing up by tomorrow," she assures me, going silent for a moment to operate the blood pressure machine before confirming, "Still right on target." She removes the cuff and picks up my chart by the bed.

"What about memory loss?" I ask. "Is that normal?"

"It happens," she says, her tone matter-of-fact, dismissive even.

"But it's not just a few mental hiccups," I clarify. "It's a complete meltdown."

"It's probably not as bad as you think," she says, "but let's do a little test." Her pencil is poised to write on my chart. "Let's fill in the blanks. I need your full name, birthday, and address."

I laugh without humor. "I'd like to know those things myself."

Her brow furrows. "You don't know your name, birthday, or address?"

"That's what I am telling you. My memory is gone. I don't know my name. I don't know how I got here. I don't remember what happened last week."

She narrows her gaze. "What is the last thing you do remember?"

"Waking up here."

"No," she amends, "I mean, what do you remember before right now?"

"Nothing," I say. "There is nothing but now."

She stares at me, her expression cautiously blank; more beats pass as she says nothing. Then she glances over her shoulder at Kayden and speaks a few sentences in Italian that are obviously about me. He replies rather shortly, almost as if he's reprimanding her. But she is undeterred, launching into more Italian.

"English, please," I plead, unable to take one more thing I don't understand, especially since it's about me, and to a stranger. How is *that* okay?

"I'm sorry," Maria apologizes, setting the chart back on its clip.

"What did you say to him?" I ask, glancing at Kayden. "What did you say to her?"

"I told him I'm going to have the doctor in to speak with you in a few minutes," she replies.

"And I told her we'd prefer sooner than later," Kayden adds.

"Do you need anything before I go?" Maria asks.

"To know what's wrong with me," I say, not believing for a minute that either of them has told me everything that was said. "Why can't I remember who I am?"

"Some temporary memory loss with a head injury isn't unheard of," she says.

"So this is temporary?" I press, hoping for positive news.

"Most likely, but the doctor is the one we need to speak with." She reaches down and squeezes my arm. "Everything is going to be fine. Try not to worry."

"How do I not worry when I don't even know my name?"

"I know it's scary, but I'm certain we'll figure it all out. I'll go hurry the doctor along. Do you want anything in the meantime? Water? Something to eat?"

"Water would be good," I say, dying for a drink, but I

amend my request: "It's not urgent. After you find the doctor, but thank you."

"We have water," Kayden announces, moving to a tray on top of a rolling table at the end of the bed and indicating a pitcher. "I'll take care of it."

"Just a little at first, so you don't get sick," Maria warns, heading to the door where Kayden delays her departure and, ignoring my request for English, says something to her in Italian. Maria gives him a quick, clipped reply and, seemingly satisfied with her answer, he steps aside and allows her to pass.

"I'll be back soon," she calls to me, breezing out of the room.

Kayden fills a cup with water, and I can't help but notice a tattoo on each of his wrists. The left one extends beyond the edge of his watch, but it's the right one that catches my eye: a box with words trailing up his forearm, none of which I can make out. I'm still trying when he sits next to me, and I'm not sure if I'm more aware of his powerful thigh pressing against mine or those piercing eyes giving me an intense inspection.

He hands me the water, our hands and gazes colliding, and I am jolted with the impact, feeling it in every part of me. Afraid he'll see my reaction, I tip up the cup and start to drink. *Oh, God.* The first drop on my tongue is liquid gold that has me gulping as fast as I can.

"Easy," Kayden warns, his hand coming down on mine again, heat radiating up my arm as he eases the rim from my lips. "Remember what Maria said. You'll make yourself sick."

"I'm still thirsty," I object, licking the last droplet of liquid bliss from my lips as he takes the water from me.

"A little at a time," he warns, setting the cup on the table beside the bed, acting more like a friend or family member than a stranger, like someone who cares when I seem to have no one who does.

Nervous energy has me wiping my mouth, aware that this is a moment when I should suggest he has better things to do than stay here. But I don't. I can't. I cling to him, the only person I know right now, embarrassingly worthy of the pity he swears he won't give me. "What did you say to Maria when she was leaving?" I ask.

"That I expect you to get the best care possible."

He makes the statement like he's in charge of my care. For a moment it's comforting, while in the next moment I know it's a façade I can't afford. "As much as I appreciate that, I need the cheapest options, not the best. I have no money."

"Money's the last thing that should be on your mind. Healing comes first."

"We both know that's not true. I have to walk out of here and survive, when I don't even remember where I live or where I'm staying."

There's movement outside the door, and Kayden stands as Maria enters with a tall man in a white coat, his thick hair graying on the sides.

"*Signorina*," the man greets me, crossing to stand beside my bed across from Kayden. "I'm your physician, Dr. Mortello. I've been caring for you since your admission some hours ago. I understand your head injury has left you with extensive memory loss?"

"That's correct," I say. "What does that mean?"

"Your CT scan showed a clear concussion, and most likely you're simply encountering side effects from the swelling of your brain. Still, I prefer to err on the side of caution. We're going to send you for an MRI and draw more blood to run some additional tests."

More tests mean more money, but Kayden's right. I can't think about that now. "If this is from the swelling," I ask, "how long until I recover my memory?"

"There's really no solid answer to that question," he replies. "Each patient is different." A nurse appears in the doorway and speaks in Italian, then he tells me, "They're ready for you now."

"Now?" I ask, shocked at how quickly this is moving. "Why is this so urgent?"

"We're always cautious with head injuries, especially with unexpected symptoms."

"I thought I had normal symptoms."

"You do." Before I can press for a more conclusive answer, another nurse rushes into the room and says something to him in Italian. I wait for the moment I can push him for answers, but it never comes. "I need to go," he announces abruptly. "I'll see you back here after we have the results."

And just like that, he's gone, and one of the nurses steps to my side. "I'm Anna," the woman says. "I was with you when you first arrived and had the CT scan."

I study her, taking in her salt-and-pepper hair styled in a bun, and try to place her. "I'm sorry. I don't remember you."

"Of course you don't, silly," she says good-naturedly. "You were out like a light. Glad to see you're awake for the ride this time. We're going to roll you down to the MRI department."

She kicks the brake free on one of the wheels of my bed, and Kayden steps to the other side of me, kicking his side free as well and speaking to Anna in Italian, his hands resting on the railing. I open my mouth to plead for English again, but for some reason my gaze falls to his watch, to the brand name.

Cartier. The name means something to me beyond being an expensive brand, and I'm instantly frustrated that I know it's high priced, but still know nothing of who I am or why I'm here.

My gaze lifts to find Kayden watching me, his expression unreadable, his continued presence truly unexplainable. "Don't you have a job or something to go to?"

"My boss is good to me." His lips curve. "Some even say he's 'beautiful.'"

I flush with the obvious reference to my compliment. "I thought I was dreaming when I said that."

"Which makes it all the better."

"You aren't going to let me forget that, are you?"

"Not a chance."

I blush and we both laugh, the sounds mingling, soft and feminine, and low and deep. And then the air shifts around us and we are staring at each other. I have no idea why he's sticking this out with me, but without him, I'd be alone and even more scared.

"I don't know what would have happened to me if you hadn't found me in that alleyway," I say, a tremor slipping into my voice. "Thank you, Kayden."

There's a flicker in his eyes, a shadow that's there and gone before either of us blinks. "Thank me by getting your memory back," he says, and while it's a perfect answer, it's somehow imperfect. There's an odd undertone that reaches beyond predictability or sincerity.

It's the last thought I have before the bed is moving and I'm being pushed away from him, and I can't think for the motion setting the room spinning. Another bump, and my stomach churns. Groaning, I roll to my side, curling my knees to my belly, and I will myself to not throw up. The bumps and sways of the bed are pure torture.

"Oh, honey," Anna says, leaning over me as we stop moving. "That ride didn't go well, did it?"

"Sick," I manage, my throat thick, goose bumps rising on my arms. "And cold."

"I'll make sure we have some antinausea medicine waiting for you when you get out of the MRI machine."

"Can't you do it before?" I plead. "I don't want to get sick during the test."

"We'll have you done before I can get you medicine," she says. "If you're okay with it, I'd like to try and just get this over with for you. I'll put a warm blanket over your legs now to stop your shivering." She doesn't wait for my agreement, announcing, "We need to move you to the table," and she and another nurse are suddenly lifting me.

My stomach rolls and the throb in my head intensifies as they set me on the hard platform, which hits my injured back in all kinds of wrong ways. It also has me feeling exposed and very alone in my skimpy hospital gown. Hugging myself, I shiver, my teeth chattering. "Cold," I say. "*Really* cold."

"I know," she says. "Hang in there. I'll get the blanket." She rushes away and comes right back and, as promised, wraps my lower body. "Better?"

"Yes," I say, feeling a bit of the chill fade. "It helps."

"Good. Because once we start the MRI, you have to try to

hold still." She unfolds my arms. "Keep them by your side." I nod, and she adds, "I'm going to put some headphones on you. It'll help with the noise." Before she puts them on, she tells me, "Try to just shut your eyes and it will be over soon."

I grab her hand before she covers my ears. "How soon?"

"Twenty minutes," she says.

"That's a long time."

"It'll be over before you know it." She covers my ears with the headphones and I hear some sort of music playing—classical, I think. The table starts to move and I hug myself again, the air around me seeming to chill from cold to frigid. Too soon, I'm in the center of a giant cylindrical machine.

"We need you to be really still," comes a voice in my ears. "And put your arms back down."

"Okay," I say, willing my body to calm. I need this test to get answers. I need to be well and remember who I am.

The music starts to play again, a soft violin that is moody, almost sultry, and I wonder how I know what a violin is when I can't remember my own name. A roar starts around me and the machine begins some kind of swirling motion. I squeeze my eyes shut. The volume of the music is louder now, the violin playing faster, the notes fierce and defiant, and suddenly I'm running down a cobblestone road, darkness cloaking me, my heart racing, fear in my chest. I have to get away. I have to escape. I look over my shoulder and try desperately to see who's after me, but there's only darkness and then a hard thud to my shoulders that makes me gasp, pain splintering upward into my skull.

I sink to my knees and tell myself to get up. *Get up!* But the pain, oh, the pain is so intense. I feel myself falling, my hands catching the pavement, rocks digging into my palms before my cheek is there too. And then there is blackness. Black, inky nothing. Time ticks and ticks, the pain radiating in my skull, until I'm suddenly on my back and blinking up into pale blue eyes, but I can't focus. Then everything goes black again.

two

I blink, and once again I'm staring into pale blue eyes. "Kayden?"

His lips curve, and those eyes of his, which have a way of stealing right into the emptiness of my mind, light with satisfaction. "You remember me. Progress. The last two times that you woke up, you didn't know my name."

"What last two times?" I try to focus, to remember anything but him. "The MRI machine—"

"You had a panic attack inside it, and they had to sedate you."

My brow furrows, and I flash back to the violin playing in my ears. "No. I was fine, just cold and sick to my stomach."

"Until you weren't fine anymore," he says, running his hand over the dark shadow on his jaw that I don't remember being there before. A bad feeling comes over me.

"How much time has passed?"

He glances at his watch again, and I'm relieved to remember it's a Cartier, relieved by all things familiar. That is until he announces, "Thirty-six hours."

Losing that much time is like a blow; my throat is suddenly so dry it's sandpaper. "I need water."

He stands and finds the pitcher, filling a cup for me. I try to sit, and he quickly abandons his efforts, gently shackling my arm, his touch electric, familiar in a way that no longer surprises me but still confuses me. "Let me lift the bed," he offers, and I nod, allowing him to help me, the way I have so many times before, it seems, when really it hasn't been that often at all.

The bed rises, and I settle against it while he reaches for the cup. He offers it to me, and this time when I accept it, and our hands and gazes collide, I don't look away. I can't look away. "Déjà vu," I whisper, feeling the sensation clear to my soul.

"Yes," he agrees. "Déjà vu." While I could dismiss it as just that, I have this sense that there's more to this moment than a simple repeat action.

I down the contents of the cup, drinking quickly before he can stop me, and when I'm done, he takes the cup from me. "More?"

"No, thank you." I glance down, unnerved to realize my IV is gone. "It's hard to comprehend that I woke up twice and don't remember."

"You not only woke up—the last time you were awake, you ate some soup and had a nurse help you shower."

"Shower? Okay, I'm even more freaked out now. How can I not remember that? How bad *is* my head injury?"

"Your tests were all normal aside from the concussion, which is healing. Your back should be healing as well."

I flex my shoulders and nod. "It feels better, and my head

doesn't hurt the way it did. But I'm not encouraged that I can't remember the last two times I woke up."

"It's the drugs they gave you after you had the panic attack."

"How do you know?"

"Because the second time you woke up and didn't remember the first time, I was worried and asked."

"Could my entire memory loss be the drugs?" I ask, hopefully.

His lips tighten. "No. Sorry. I asked the same as well."

"Of course it's not the drugs," I say grimly. "That would be too easy a solution. At least I showered, I guess."

"As did I," he says. "I was afraid they'd kick me out if I didn't."

It's then that I notice he's now in a light blue T-shirt and faded jeans, which indicates, I assume, that he went home, changed, and made the decision to return here to me. "It's been thirty-six hours since my test, and at least another eight before that, and you're still here."

"Yes. I'm still here."

Reality hits me with gut-wrenching clarity. "No one came looking for me."

He gives a grim shake of his head. "No."

I inhale and then let the breath out, devastated by this news. Kayden is here out of obligation or some sense of responsibility. Whatever the case, he won't admit it, and I'm not going to pathetically drive home the topic. I need out of this place, and so does he.

"Do you know when the doctor will be back around?" I ask.

"Not until tomorrow."

"I can't wait until tomorrow; I need to talk to him now," I insist. "Please call him." I realize I've grabbed his arm and I'm squeezing. "I'm sorry." I jerk my hand back, and it's trembling. *I'm* trembling. All over. "I just need them to fix me. They . . . they have to make me remember who I am."

"The doctors keep saying that you will," he assures me, reaching to the table beside the bed and presenting me with a leather book.

"What is that?"

"A journal. The staff psychologist left this for you. She wants you to write down your thoughts and dreams. Apparently there's reason to believe it will help you regain your memories sooner."

In disbelief, I ask, "That's my medical treatment? A *journal*?" I take it from him, my brow furrowing with a memory that's here and then gone, leaving me frustrated and ready to throw the darn thing. "How is this supposed to help me?"

"It's one part of a treatment plan they intend to present to you on Monday."

I set the journal on the bed, rejecting it along with the "treatment plan." "They seem to believe that your brain is suppressing memories to protect you from some sort of trauma."

"Leaving me homeless and without a name?" I ask. "That's a horrible way to protect myself. And I don't even *have* memories to write in it."

He shifts on the bed, his hand settling on my leg. It's a strong hand, the hand of a man who knows what he wants and goes after it, while I know nothing at all. "Maybe if we talk, it'll help."

"That's no different than writing in the journal. I can't talk about what I don't remember."

"My memories might stir yours."

I sigh. "Okay. But it would be so much easier if there was a pill for this kind of thing."

His lips hint at a smile. "Most of us would agree with that at some point in our lives. Why don't we talk about the night you were mugged?"

"That's exactly why I'm here," says an unfamiliar male voice.

My attention shifts to the doorway, where a man in his mid-thirties leans on the doorjamb, his suit and dark brown hair a bit rumpled and his tie slightly off center.

"What the hell are you doing here, Gallo?" Kayden demands, shoving off the bed to face him.

"My job," the man states, striding toward us. While his features are too hard and the lines of his face too sharp to be called good-looking, there is something about him that refuses to be ignored, and he stands at the end of my bed, fixing me in a steely gray stare. "I'm Detective Gallo. I hear you were mugged, and I want to ask you a few questions."

"You don't handle muggings," Kayden points out.

"I do when your name's on the report," the detective says shortly. It's pretty clear these two don't just know each other; they don't like each other.

"Of course," Kayden replies, sounding amused. "Because I've broken so many laws."

The detective is not amused. "Just because you haven't been caught doesn't make you innocent." He gives me a pointed look. "I'm guessing you aren't Maggie."

I blanch. "What? I . . . no. Or . . ." I look to Kayden for help. "What is he talking about?"

"He's being a smart-ass," Kayden states. "I registered you under that name and told them you were my sister."

My brow furrows. "What? Why?"

The detective takes it upon himself to answer. "Because it gave him access to you."

"Exactly," Kayden confirms, offering no apology or explanation.

He doesn't need to, and yet I want more. More what, though? I don't know. Just . . . more.

"At least he put you up in the ritzy end of the hospital," the detective points out, demanding the attention again, and making a big show of glancing around the room. And as obviously intended, I follow his lead, and for the first time since I've been lucid, I look at it, as well. *Really* look at it—and realize it's larger than expected, with a sitting area to the left and a mini kitchen.

I look at Kayden in shock. "How much is this costing? I don't even know if I have a bank account, let alone money to pay for this!"

"Don't worry about money. I have this," he says softly.

"You mean you're paying my bills. Kayden, I can't let you do that. I don't know if I can pay you back."

"Let him pay," the detective interjects. "He's got a boatload of cash. But I do have to say, his registering you under a fake name, on top of the upgraded security in this wing of the building, does make it damn hard for anyone looking for you to find you."

"The staff know to direct any inquiries that might fit your

description to me," Kayden assures me, flicking the detective an irritated look. "Obviously—since you found her."

"I found *you*, not her." He looks at me again. "And I'd ask for your real name to connect a few dots, but I understand that you don't remember it."

"That's right," I confirm, resisting the urge to fidget, like I have something to hide, when I don't. Do I?

"What *do* you remember?" he asks.

"Nothing before the moment I woke up here."

He arches a brow. "Nothing?"

"Nothing."

"Not even the actual attack?"

I shake my head.

"I see," he says, stroking his clean-shaven jaw. "I was hoping the actual attack wasn't a part of your memory loss."

"I'm completely blank, Detective, and it's really quite terrifying to think about being in that alleyway, passed out and alone. I'm thankful Kayden was there to get me help."

"Right." His hand leaves his face, and he grips the railing at the foot of the bed. "That was *lucky*." His gaze lands on Kayden. "Not often a real hero comes along."

"If you have something to say to me, Gallo," Kayden says calmly, "then say it and let's move on."

The detective's steely eyes fix on Kayden, and the hate radiating off him is so fierce. I'm clearly in the center of something very personal, and very bitter.

"Detective—" I say, intending to ask for the help he swears he's here to give me.

"You and I need to chat for a few moments alone," he says, his hard stare returning to me.

"Let's cut to the chase, Gallo," Kayden interjects. "You're here to badger me by badgering her, and I'm not going to let that happen. Especially while she's fragile."

"I'm not fragile," I insist.

"I can assure you," the detective replies, ignoring me, "this is about her, not you."

"If 'her' is me," I say, certain this one-on-one is going to happen, "I'll talk with you alone." I glance at Kayden. "I get that there are two agendas here. I can handle it. I just need to solve the mystery of who I am."

The detective's approving gaze falls on me. "At least two of us are on the same page."

Kayden's lips thin, but he accepts my answer. "I'll be right outside the door if you need me."

I give him a nod, and he meets the detective's stare, the two of them exchanging what I'm pretty sure are some heated silent words, before he strides out of the room.

Detective Gallo claims the stool Kayden favors and scoots closer to me. "It really was lucky that he just happened to be at the right place, at the right time, to rescue you." His tone says he doesn't think it was a matter of luck at all. "And talk about dedication to a stranger. Forty-eight hours later, he's not only still here, he's paying your bills."

Already he's attacking Kayden, but I'm not foolish enough not to find out why. "What are you getting at?"

"That maybe, just maybe, he knew you before he found you." He holds up a finger. "And maybe, just maybe, he wasn't in the right place at the right time by chance."

My mind flickers with an image of Kayden's hand on my back, and I can almost feel the familiar sensation of his touch spread from my shoulders down my spine. "He says I didn't know him."

"Do you believe him?"

"You know I have no memory."

"You have instincts."

"Which could suck, for all I know."

He rests his arms on the railing, the position eating away much of the space between us. "I'm trying to help you—you know that, right?"

"You are here for him, not me."

"I'm here because of him, but for you."

"I don't know what that means," I say, "and I honestly don't care. I have to find out who I am, before I'm discharged and on the street."

"You won't end up on the streets. There are programs—"

"So *that's* the help you're giving me?" I interrupt. "You'll stick me in some government program and I'll cease to exist before I landed in this hospital room?"

His lips tighten and he leans back, crossing his arms over his chest. "I ran a general check on all missing persons reports, including anyone traveling from outside the country."

"And?" I ask, holding my breath, almost as afraid to hear the answer as I am desperate for it.

"At this point there are no active reports that match your description locally."

"What about internationally?"

"Or for anyone traveling by way of a passport," he adds.

I'm shell-shocked, trying to figure out what this means for me.

"However," he adds, "there tends to be a slight delay in

reports filed for a missing person who lives or travels alone."

"Alone." The word carves a hole in my soul, taunting me with the idea that no one's looking for me because no one cares about me. "No," I say, rejecting that idea. "I might not know who I am, but I know I wouldn't live here without learning the language, which means that I'm visiting. And I wouldn't visit a foreign country alone."

"And as you said, your instincts might suck."

Infuriated at his lack of help, I say, "I don't need instincts to know that I can't wait for a missing persons report that might not come, to deal with my situation."

"And you don't have to. If you are indeed an American citizen—"

"I am. I know I am."

"Well then," he says, "you'd be traveling with a passport, and there will be fingerprints on file."

A ray of hope replaces my anger. "You mean we can cross-check my records?"

"Exactly. I'll pick up a fingerprint kit, and we'll run them through the database. If we get a hit, then we'll know your name, home country, and even your parents' names."

"Why wouldn't we get a match?"

"There are any number of reasons," he says, "but let's cross that bridge if we come to it."

"No. No, I want to know the reasons."

"It's really—"

"*I want to know.*"

He sighs. "You could have crossed the border illegally."

"Why would I do that?"

"There's a black market for American women in the sex

trade. Normally they're drugged, and you have no marks on your arms. But—"

"Enough," I say, not needing anything else to freak me out. "I get the point: there are reasons. What happens next?"

"I'll bring in a fingerprint kit." He glances at his watch. "It's nearly five now, and visiting hours end at eight. So most likely I'll have to bring it tomorrow. In the meantime, I'd like to get a photo that I can show around the neighborhood where we found you. Maybe someone knows you."

A photo—good God, I don't even know what I look like! "I . . . Yes. Okay."

He pulls out his phone. "I'll take a few now, if that works for you?"

"Of course." I've barely issued the approval before he snaps a few shots and is inspecting them.

"Looks good," he says. "Do you want to approve it?"

He offers me the phone and I hold up a hand again. "No," I say quickly, irrationally panicked at the idea of seeing myself, especially when seeing myself, finding me, is exactly what I'm after. "I really don't want to know how I must look right now."

"Far better than you might think," he says, a hint of warmth in his tone as he slips his phone back in his jacket and stands, his hands settling on the railing as he stares down at me. "There's a reason he told them you're his sister."

"What do you mean? You said he did that to be able to be in my room with me."

"A decision he made the moment he brought you to the hospital. That doesn't add up to being a stranger to me."

"Why can't he simply be a good guy helping someone in need?"

"Because this is Kayden Wilkens we're talking about, and Kayden Wilkens doesn't do anything, including you, without an agenda." He's looking at the doorway now.

My gaze follows his, my lips parting with the impact of finding Kayden standing there. If Detective Gallo demands attention, Kayden just plain claims it. He is power, control, beauty, and, right now, anger. The air crackles with its intensity, and when his piercing blue eyes shift from Gallo to me, I have a sense of a wolf who doesn't bother with sheep's clothing, with his sights set on me.

And I'm certain that it's not protectiveness or obligation I see in his face. This time, it's one hundred percent *possession*.

three

I am his.

That is the unapologetic message in Kayden's gaze I know he intends for both myself and Gallo to see. And I do. I see it. I understand it and I feel it in every part of me. Possession. Demand. Control. He wants it all, but I do not know why. Nor do I know why I am not afraid of him or these things. I only know that Kayden Wilkens is one hell of a man, and that it's become necessary to my survival to admit that the woman in me is drawn to him, deeply, completely. To the point that I'm not even close to objective where he's concerned, vulnerable in ways that could be dangerous if his intentions toward me are not as honorable as he claims. And the truth is, my strong sense of my familiarity with Kayden both supports the detective's claims that he might be more to me than he admits and drives my need to believe he is honest, the true light in the tunnel of darkness I cannot escape.

"Take my number in case you need it," Detective Gallo orders, bringing my attention back to him.

I face him to find him extending a card to me. I accept it, murmuring an appropriate "Thank you," but I am not pleased with the glint of satisfaction in his eyes that tells me he knew Kayden was at the door when he issued that crass warning. That also tells me I am indeed a token in a game he's playing with Kayden, rather than someone he is truly here to help, making me question his motives for being here at all.

He glances at his watch. "I'm going to gamble on making it back here tonight with the fingerprint kit."

"I thought it would be tomorrow," I say.

"He can't wait to see me again," Kayden says, claiming his self-assigned place by my side.

The two men tune me out then, facing each other, both placing their hands on the railing. Their gazes collide in an explosion of silent hatred. Gallo spits something at Kayden in Italian, and I don't have to understand the language to know it's downright foul. Kayden, who radiates absolute control, does not reward him with an equal reply but rather with a rumble of deep, masculine laughter that is as musical as it is hard. Gallo's teeth clench and he says something I am certain is even fouler than his prior remark, and most likely far from professional, as his job dictates he should be. Kayden smirks and offers a clipped reply that earns him Gallo's glare and a motion to the door that is nothing short of an order. Gallo heads toward the door, assuming Kayden will follow. Kayden glances at me, giving me a wink before casually sauntering after Gallo, apparently pleased with the reaction he's evoked from the other man.

And then both men are gone. The shift in the air is immediate, leaving me huffing out a breath I didn't know I was holding, hating how I am helplessly at the mercy of two men I barely know, one of whom has seduced me since the moment

I woke up and called him beautiful. All because I can't remember who I am.

I glance down at my hands where they rest on the bedcover, and at least they are familiar. They are *me*—but this bed is not, and neither is my letting these men use me as the rope in a game of tug-of-war. It is a relief to know this about myself. To know I am strong, and a person of action, not inaction. A person who gets up and looks in that mirror. Yes. I have to face myself, and maybe, just maybe, if I *see* me, I'll fully *know* me, and Kayden's motives, innocent or not, will be revealed along with my past.

The idea spurs me into action, and I throw off the blanket and lower the railing. Shoving the skimpy gown down my legs the best I can, I rotate to let my feet dangle off the edge of the bed, grimacing at the buzz in my head, a weakness that forces me to pause to let it pass. The instant it eases, I scoot farther to the edge of the mattress, trying to make the step to the floor as small as possible.

"What the hell are you doing?"

Jolting at the sound of Kayden's voice, I stretch my legs down to the ground to make my escape, only to have my head spin and my body sway. Gasping, I start to tumble forward, saved as Kayden catches me, dragging me forward, my body landing flat against his larger, harder one.

"What are you doing?" I demand, feeling the thunder of his heart beneath my palm where it now rests on the solid wall of his chest. Or maybe it's my heart pounding so hard that it feels like his.

"Keeping you from ending up inside another MRI machine. What were you thinking?"

"That I need to go to the bathroom," I say, his touch humming through my body just as the detective's warnings hum in my mind. "I'm fine now." I try to twist away from him but he holds on to me, and I shove against him. "You can let go of me, Kayden."

"That's not going to happen," he promises, his voice low, as seductive as everything else about this man is, and when I look at him, that wolf is back in his eyes as he adds, "In case I didn't make that point already."

"You have, and I'm not sure how I feel about that." I try to push away again, yelping as he scoops me up and starts walking.

"I can walk," I insist, appalled that my bare backside is hanging out of the gown, and pressed to his forearms. "Put me down, Kayden. Put me *down*."

He complies in front of the bathroom door, and when I would escape, his arms cage me as he opens the door. I try to turn, but his hands come down on my shoulders, and he begins walking me inside the bathroom. The instant the mirror looms in front of me, adrenaline surges through me, giving me the extra fierceness I need to twist around to face him, only to cause a collision of our bodies.

Stunned, I freeze, my hands on his chest, my legs intimately aligned with his, and when our eyes meet, the look in his is unbridled passion, as possessive as it is hot. I'm scorched in every place he touches, and every place I suddenly want him to touch. Desperate to maintain what objectivity I have left with this man, which I've already determined is not much, I shove back from him, hitting the sink, catching myself on the cold surface.

He doesn't move. He just stands before me, power and sex wafting off him like a seductive drug that if tried once would surely become a dangerous addiction. A second passes. Then two. On three, the tension between us is palpable and I can take it no more. "I can't use the bathroom when you're here. You're hovering like you think I'm going to escape through some secret passageway."

He arches a brow. "Escape? Is that what you want? To escape?"

Not from you, I think, but good sense prevails and I instead reply with, "Should I?"

And as if he's read my mind, he says, "Not from me," and just like that, he's backed out of the room and shut the door, leaving me stunned and staring at the spot he's left empty. What did that mean? Not from him? From who, then? Was he being literal? Surely he wasn't. The longer I try to figure out the answer, the more the silence around me grows, and so does my awareness of what I'm avoiding. The mirror. I'm avoiding the mirror.

"Turn around," I whisper, but just thinking about doing it stirs a flutter in my belly that's darn near painful, and I know then that the doctor was right. I'm suppressing my memories. I'm afraid of what is in my own mind, and it's a terrifying realization. What could be so bad that I'd rather leave myself behind than face it?

Inhaling against the pressure building in my chest, aware that I *have* to get past my fear, I mentally prepare myself to just get it over with. Another deep breath and I whirl around to face myself, but chicken out, clutching the sink and letting my head drop forward, my hair draping my face. Brown hair.

A deep mahogany brown that falls to my breasts, and yet I hadn't even noticed the color until now. I pant out a few more breaths and force myself to lift my chin, bringing my image into view.

And then I wait for the eruption that doesn't happen. And I wait some more. Still nothing, and I begin analyzing myself like I'm some sort of a lab specimen. My face is heart-shaped, my eyes a deep green. My skin ivory. There's a smattering of freckles on my nose I'm not overly fond of, but none of this helps me. I'm completely disconnected from the image in the mirror.

Frustrated, I curl my fingers into my palms where they rest on the sink, squeezing my eyes shut and promising myself that when I open them, my reaction will be different. Instead, my mind rewards me with one single memory, and I find myself standing inside what looks like an apartment, laughing with a pretty brunette. And there is no disconnect from her. Just seeing her softens a hard spot inside of me, easing the tension along my spine. She's a friend. Someone I love. I slip deeper into the memory, and the images play like a silent movie. I watch in wonder, reveling in every second. She begins to fade, and I try to pull her back but fail, only to realize that I don't know her name any more than I know mine.

Frustrated again, I open my eyes and stare at myself, feeling as if I know the woman in that memory far more than I know the one in the mirror. "Who are you?"

Leaning closer to the mirror, as if that might actually help me in some way, my eyes catch on a red strand of hair near my nape, and then another, and another, all hidden in the under-layer. Shifting my attention, I examine my eye-brows, and sure enough, I locate several strands of red. Heart racing, and I'm not sure why, I grab my gown, and tug it upward and confirm that I'm either shaved or waxed, but whatever the case, it hides the proof of my coloring. *Hiding.* The word plays in my mind, echoed by another. *Running.*

I drop the gown and lean on the sink, staring at my image again, and I am now officially freaked out. I *am* running. I know it in some deep part of me. The question is—from whom or what?

"Oh God," I whisper, thinking of the fingerprints. What if I'm in trouble? What if I broke the law and I'm giving the proof to a man who can arrest me? I don't feel like a criminal, but how does one feel when one breaks the law? I just . . . don't know.

Or maybe it's not the law that's my problem. Maybe it's a person I'm trying to escape. What if it's Kayden? What if that is why he's familiar?

A knock echoes on the door and I jump, whirling around to face it.

"You okay in there?"

At the sound of Kayden's voice, the detective's words play in my head. *Kayden Wilkens doesn't do anything, including you, without an agenda.* And I remind myself that I don't know Kayden, so I don't know if I can trust him. The same applies to the detective, which leaves me with a devastating conclusion. I can't lean on anyone but myself until I retrieve my memories—which means I can't stay here. I have to leave, now, tonight, and do it with no money or help. And go where? *Think. Think. Think.* And then it hits me. Italy is rich with religious culture. I'll go to a church. Surely one of them will have a place for me to stay and hide.

Abruptly, the door opens, and I gasp as Kayden steps into the room, his big body claiming the small space, his presence sucking all the air from my lungs.

"What are you doing in here?" I demand.

He shocks me by kicking the door shut. "Opening your eyes."

With dread in my belly, I grab the sink behind me, holding on for the blow that I sense is coming. "What are you talking about, Kayden?"

"It's time for you to remember." He closes the small space between us, crowding me, the spicy, warm scent of him with hints of vanilla teasing my nostrils and stirring a flicker of a memory I can't place.

"I was right," I accuse, my chin tilting upward to challenge him. "We aren't strangers, are we?"

"Do I feel like a stranger?"

"*I* feel like a stranger. Why wouldn't you?"

"What does your instinct tell you?" he asks, playing the same card Gallo had earlier.

And again, I say, "I don't trust my instincts."

"And yet you refuse your memories and leave yourself with nothing else to go on, vulnerable to lies I'm not telling you."

Vulnerable. He uses the word like he knows what I'm feeling. Like he knows me. "How do I know that? How do I know anything you tell me is true?"

"Exactly," he agrees. "That's my point. It's time to come out of the shadows and remember who you are."

"You think I don't want to? I can't just flip a switch and make my mind work. And neither can you."

"Maybe not, but I'm not leaving you in those shadows, either." He reaches for me, and I gasp as he twists me around to face the mirror, his hips leveraging my backside from behind.

"What are you doing?" I demand, grabbing the sink while he grabs a hunk of my hair and holds it up to display the red.

"What does this tell us about you?"

"Lots of people dye their hair," I say, afraid of where this is going, of what I'm about to find out.

"You not only colored your hair," he says, "you did it quickly and badly." He turns me around again, pressing my backside to the sink, his hands settling on my hips, scorching me through the thin material. "You were running when I found you, and you almost got caught."

"You can't know that," I say, my fingers curling on the hard wall of his chest where they've landed. "I don't know that."

"Those men chasing you in that alley weren't two-bit thieves. They were skilled, experienced criminals, and they were after you."

"You saw them?"

"Yes. I saw them. And I intervened or you wouldn't be here right now. What I didn't know, when I called emergency and gave them my damn name, was who those men were. Not until I found this." He digs out a package of matches. "Do they look familiar?"

"No," I say, my voice cracking. "Nothing looks familiar but you."

"Because you don't want to remember anything before me and you have to."

"I want to remember."

"Mezonnett," he says, reading the writing on the match-book flap, and then grabbing my palm to press it inside my hand, curling my fingers, and his, around it. "It's a restaurant owned by a man named Niccolo. A very rich, very arrogant man who also happens to be the biggest mobster in Italy."

"Mobster?" I whisper, my fears of criminal connections realized, and then rejected. "No. No, this isn't right. I can't be involved with a mobster."

"I don't care what you did or didn't do with or to Niccolo to piss him off. I just know you did something, and his men won't chase you and forget you, because he doesn't forget those who burn him. And that is not only your problem; it became mine when I gave my name to the emergency personnel and it ended up on the police report."

I feel the blood drain from my cheeks. "He's going to look for me through you."

"Yes, he is, which is why I had a hacker erase my name from the police report. He also amended the 'Jane Doe' version of your records to show you were transported here to the hospital, but never admitted."

"That's why you registered me under an alias. So this Niccolo person couldn't find me."

"That's right. I even had your registration date changed."

"But Gallo found you, and us."

"Because someone who knows how much he hates me heard my name on the emergency radio and told him. He intercepted the paper version of the police report about sixty seconds before it would have disappeared as well."

"He hates you."

"Yes. He hates me."

"Why?"

"It's about a woman. Kind of like now."

"About me, you mean?"

"For me, yes. For him it's about *her*, and she's a bitter pill he refuses to swallow. Which is why I'm here before he draws the attention to us I've ensured we don't get. One of the nurses just informed me that he spent the past two days going room to room, looking for me until finally someone recognized me. He talked to a lot of people. Too many for me to feel safe staying here, with Niccolo looking for you."

"How can you know he's really looking for me?"

"He never leaves loose ends. That's why he's survived."

"Because no one else does," I say, my throat suddenly raw and dry.

"You've got it, sweetheart, but to be clear, no one outruns Niccolo. We're going to attack this and win—and to do that, I need what's inside your head." He pushes away from me and crosses to a long, rectangular cabinet and removes a duffel bag, which he tosses on the floor. "It's time for you to remember who you are. Your laundered clothes are inside. Open it and get in touch with your past, because who and what you are to Niccolo will decide what we do next."

"Don't say that like I'm intimately involved with him," I snap. "I was at the wrong place at the wrong time. I *can't* be involved with a mobster."

"A scenario that makes this easier to fix. So open the bag, grab your memories, and give us both a reason to believe that's true."

Adrenaline surges through me, and my eyes land on the

bag holding my personal belongings. My truth. I begin to tremble, a sign of denial and weakness I can no longer afford. Shoving off of the sink, I take the two steps between me and the bag and lower myself onto the ground in front of it, the hard tile biting into my knees. Unbidden, I flash back to being in the same position, with cobblestone pavement instead of tiles punishing my skin, and I want to know how I got there, *why* I was there. I grab the zipper and try to tug it down the bag, only the stupid shaking of my hand interferes, and I grab it, willing it to still.

Kayden settles to one knee in front of me. "Easy, sweetheart," he says, his voice a low, soothing caress I do not expect, nor do I accept, after all he's just said and done.

"You just told me that I'm linked to a mobster, who now most likely wants to kill us both. Nothing about this is easy."

"Any memories you find within the contents of this bag won't be as bad as what Niccolo will do to both of us if we let him catch up with us."

"Thanks for making me feel better."

"I'm not a feel-good kind of guy. You have to do this." He doesn't wait for my agreement, unzipping the bag himself, and reaching inside to set a neatly folded pile of clothes on my lap.

I stare down at the garments, a pair of dark jeans and a lavender V-neck T-shirt, praying for that switch I told Kayden didn't exist to flip on in my head, but the now familiar white noise remains. "Nothing," I say, unable to bring myself to look at him, but he's not having it.

"Look at me," he orders, and I don't want to, but somehow I do, and I can feel him compelling me to give him a different answer, one I can't give. "There has to be something."

"There isn't. Those clothes might as well be someone else's."

"That's not good enough," he says, and while his voice is low, the undertone of truth cuts like a knife.

I snap back, "You think I don't know that?"

His eyes glint, the wolf back in spades, and he grabs the clothes, tossing them in the bag and shoving it aside, his hands closing around my arms. "It's time to remember."

My anger is instant, fear nowhere in sight. "You can't order me to remember and I just do it."

"I'll take that challenge," he declares, standing and lifting me with him.

"Stop bullying me," I hiss, grabbing two handfuls of his shirt, and giving not even a tiny flip about my gaping gown. "Stop bullying me!"

"I'm trying to save your life," he says, rotating me and pressing me against the hard wall, fingers flexing into my shoulders where he still holds me. "What's your name?"

"I can't tell you what I don't know."

"You do know."

"No," I bite out. "I don't."

"Bullshit."

"It's *not* bullshit."

"Your memories could change everything we do when we walk out of this room—you know that, right? Every move we make that could be wrong, you can make right. Now: what's your name?"

I don't know, but I can't say that to him again. "Let me off the wall."

"After you tell me your name."

"Stop being an asshole!" I explode, shoving against his hard, unmoving body.

"I've been called worse, sweetheart," he says, cupping my face. "Give me what I want."

"I can't give you what I don't know."

"What's your *name*?"

"I told you—"

"What's your damn name?"

"Ella," I shock myself by saying. "My name is Ella."

four

Ella," I repeat, joyful laughter bubbling from my lips. "Ella. Ella. Ella!" I grab his shirt, balling it in my hand. "Kayden, I remember! I remember my name! Thank you for being an asshole." I point a finger at his chest and manage a moment of sternness to warn, "But don't do it again. It won't work next time. I'll know what you're doing."

His hands slide from my face to my shoulders, those blue, blue eyes meeting mine as he says, "Ella."

"Ella!" I exclaim, absolutely giddy. "Oh God. It feels good to hear my name." Even better in his rich, deep, sexy voice, and I demand a replay. "Say it again."

His fingers flex where he holds me. "Sweetheart, I need you to listen to me." His voice is firm, directive. "I know you're happy, but—"

"But?" I repeat, my bubble quickly deflating. "That's not a good word. It prefaces a problem." My eyes go wide. "Please tell me my name doesn't mean something horrible to you."

"I've never heard your name before now. And what it means to me isn't what's important."

"If I'm a crazy person and don't know it, but you do, yeah, I kind of think it does."

"You're about to make *me* the crazy person, woman. Time is not our friend right now. I need to know if 'Ella' is just a name to you. Or did we unlock your memory?"

I inhale on the question that might as well be a knife drawing blood. Ella is as much a stranger to me as Kayden. "Ella is not just a name," I argue, rejecting that this revelation means nothing. "It's *my* name. And I know it's my name, and that's more than I had five minutes ago."

"I understand that," he says. "But—"

"It's not enough."

"Can you remember your last name? Give me that name and I'll find out who you are and how you might be connected to Niccolo."

"A last name," I repeat, willing it to come to me.

"Don't think," he reprimands. "Just answer like before. Yes or no. Time is ticking."

"No, but Ella isn't a common name. Surely there can't be that many of us who've traveled to Italy in the short window tourists are allowed to be in a country."

His eyes sharpen, his tone with them. "I take it that's a no on the last name."

I force out a reluctant, "No."

"And we don't even know if you are a tourist." He releases me, adding a murmured, "Fuck," before diving fingers through his hair and flashing the tattoo on his left wrist, which appears to be some sort of bird, while I can now tell the box on his right has a chess piece inside. I wait for either to mean something to me, like his watch and his scent, but nothing comes to me.

"You're sure?" he presses, his hands settling on his jean-clad hips.

The fact that he's gone from "Don't think" to this says he's desperate, and I'm pretty sure he's not a man who gets desperate often. "I wish I wasn't."

"Not even a possible name?"

I give a shake of my head and his lips tighten, his chest expanding on a breath he exhales with the declaration, "Plan B it is, then."

"Plan B?" I ask.

"That's right," he says, giving me a once-over that has my nipples puckering beneath the thin gown, before he levels a stare at me and orders, "Get dressed. We need to be gone before Gallo gets back."

"Please tell me the extent of Plan A, which is always the best plan, wasn't just you being an asshole to try and jolt my memory."

"Plan A was, and is, you remembering who you are, and that will remain the case. I told you. The details of your relationship to Niccolo are a potential game changer."

My fingers curl into fists by my sides. "I *don't* have a relationship with Niccolo. I'd know if I did. I'd feel it. Like I know you're . . ." My voice trails off while the certainty of knowing this man beyond that alleyway takes root, and reality hits me. I've been swept away by this man so much so that I chose him over a detective, and I'm about to leave the hospital without even knowing where we're going.

"I'm what?" he presses.

"I know there's something you aren't telling me."

He reaches for me, pulling me to him, his hand nestling

intimately over the bare skin under my gown and above my backside. "Please don't do this," he pleads, his gentle tone defying the tension wafting off of him. "I know you're scared and confused, but don't start doubting me now. I am not your enemy, Ella."

The way he's holding me, the way he says my name, weakens my knees and does funny things to my belly, which only drives me to challenge him. "Prove it. Tell me how we know each other."

He walks me backward until I hit the wall, pressing me against it, his hands settling on either side of my face, his arms caging me. "We don't have time for this right now," he says, his gentle tone now hard with demand, but that spicy vanilla scent of him reminds me of why I need the answers he's not giving me.

"*Make* time, Kayden."

"Tell that to Gallo, who, according to my calculations, will be back here with that fingerprint kit in thirty minutes. If we let him run your prints, Niccolo *will* find you, even if that requires torturing or killing Gallo to connect the dots to that police report and us."

My eyes go wide. "What? No. No. He wouldn't—"

"He's a mobster, sweetheart. People say he cut his own heart out when he was born, while his mother watched."

My hand goes to my throat. "I can do without the dramatics, Kayden."

"No. I don't think you can." He softens his voice, but his words are just as harsh and damning. "I can't be gentle when underestimating his evil will get you killed too."

Shell-shocked, I whisper, "This can't be real. It has to be a mistake." Then louder: "I *can't be* the person Niccolo is looking for."

"If it is a mistake, I'll figure it out, but I can't do that if we're both dead." He pushes off the wall and scoops my clothes off the floor to set them on the toilet. "Clothes. Now. I want us walking out of this building in ten minutes." He digs his phone from his pocket. "In the meantime, I'm going to make a phone call. Pray the name Ella leads us where we need to go." He doesn't wait for my reply, crossing to my left to face the far wall, his back to me, assumably his version of giving me privacy. And I don't even care. I just want out of this gown and this hospital that's become a cage. I need Kayden to make that happen, but where he and I go from here, I don't know. I'll decide on the fly, but whatever the case, I will make an educated decision that has nothing to do with his damn blue eyes.

Launching myself off the wall, I dart for the jeans that are supposed to be mine, grabbing them and shoving my legs inside, because apparently the other me doesn't wear underwear. They fit perfectly, but they're still not familiar, and I promise myself I will remember every last part of my life, down to my socks. I will own my world again and I will own a plan to make that happen. And while I don't want to be a person who would be involved in any way with a man like Niccolo, I'll figure out how to fix that, once I figure out how it began.

I squat next to the bag, and hear Kayden say, "I need you to search the passport entry for the name *Ella*," and I pause in the process of digging for a bra, another dash of hard-core reality hitting me. He's asking someone to break the law to help me. He's also openly admitted to hacking police records and knowing Niccolo. Who knows a mobster? I squeeze my eyes shut. *Right*. Who? Maybe me, it appears, and I have to face that possibility to get to the other side of this, wherever that may land me.

"No," Kayden says into the phone, "I do not have a last name," and while the irritation lacing his tone is intended for the person he's speaking with, I feel it like a punch in the gut. Why would I remember my first name and not my last? And the answer is instant. My last name would return me to my real world, and knowing what I know about the trouble I've found, I'm pretty sure that I don't want to go back. And it's unacceptable. I can't fix what is broken if I don't even try.

"Coward," I whisper, scolding myself and refocusing on the urgency to get dressed and the contents of the duffel. I remove a pair of tennis shoes and socks and set them on the floor, my eyes going wide as I retrieve a gorgeous cream-colored bra from the bag, noting the splattering of sparkly jewels over the silk. Searching for the brand, I discover the tag is written in Italian. Or I assume it is. It's sure not English, and while I remind myself that tourists buy lingerie, Kayden's words play in my head. *We don't even know if you are a tourist.* And this time, I start to wonder if I really am.

"Yeah yeah yeah," Kayden murmurs into the phone. "I know all the reasons this is difficult, but you're always bragging about how you do 'magic.' Now I'm paying you to prove it." There are a few beats of silence in which he listens, and I struggle to put on the bra without taking the gown off, only to end up a tangled mess. "Within the hour," Kayden tells the person on the other end of the line, abruptly ending the call, and before I can ask what happens in an hour, he peeks over his shoulder and asks, "Are you dressed?"

"Don't turn around," I order, and once I'm certain he's listened, I tear both the gown and bra from my body, groaning when the hook attaches to the armhole.

"Need help?" he asks.

"No!" I say quickly.

He gives a low, sexy rumble of laughter and holds his hands out to his sides. "Just trying to speed up the process, but I have to warn you. In about sixty seconds you get my help whether you want it or not."

He might have prefaced that warning with laughter, but he's serious, and I quickly hook the clasp at my back and reach for my shirt, only to freeze at the sound of activity in the other room. Kayden hears it too, rotating to face me, his finger pressed to his lips, warning me not to speak. I nod, praying Gallo hasn't returned sooner than expected, and preparing to feign illness to avoid those fingerprints.

Kayden's gaze sweeps low, raking over my nearly naked breasts, and when my nipples pucker beneath the silk in reaction, his jaw clenches, eyes flashing with one part heat, another two parts disapproval. He closes the space between us, snatching up my shirt and pressing it to my belly, mouthing, "Now." It's a small action that tells me he's as concerned as I am that Gallo has returned and he's preparing for a fast departure.

My hand closes over the cotton tee, and I'm about to pull it over my head when a knock sounds on the door, and I fumble it, letting it drop to the ground. Heart thundering in my chest, I hold out my hands, silently asking Kayden if I should answer the knock, receiving a quick, negative shake of his head in reply. And so we stand there, neither of us daring so much as to blink. I assume we're waiting to find out who we are dealing with to decide on a response.

Another knock sounds, and I swear I jump a mile high before I hear, "Are you doing okay in there?"

Relief washes over me at the sound of Maria's voice, and even Kayden's shoulders visibly relax. "I'm good, Maria," I call out, rushing toward the door, fully intending to peek outside and send her on her way. Kayden is there in front of me, though, blocking the door and giving me another negative shake of the head.

I grimace at him, and a silent conversation between us ensues.

Me: "Why can't I open the door?"

Him: "Don't ask questions, just do as I bid."

I surprise myself with a "Fuck you!"

He arches a brow, eyes hinting at amusement, not anger.

"Can I get you anything?" Maria asks.

Offering Kayden my back, I press my hands to the door, preparing to wing this any way I can without his silent bossiness. "No thank you," I reply. "Just brushing my hair and washing my face."

"You really must be feeling better," Maria replies, sounding pleased. "Do you want something special for dinner to celebrate? Maybe chocolate cake?"

I jump on a chance for privacy. "Actually, my brother's bringing me dinner soon."

"Oh, how nice! I'll cancel your dinner tray, then. Buzz me if you need anything."

"Thank you!" I call, holding my breath to await her departure, listening as her footsteps sound and begin to fade. Finally breathing again, I turn around and flatten against the door, finding Kayden standing in front of me, a long, sexy lock of light brown hair brushing his brow, my shirt in his hands. My almost naked breasts between us.

"Put it on this time," he orders, tossing the shirt to me, his gaze sweeping low, brushing over my breasts, where they linger a moment before landing on my bare feet. "And shoes," he says, his eyes meeting mine again. "Quickly." He snaps out the last word, turning away and crossing to the cabinet where he retrieved the duffel bag, while I try to catch the breath he's stolen from me.

Shaking myself, telling myself that I have to find a way to put his impact on me on mute, I tug the T-shirt over my head and grab the tennis shoes and socks I retrieved earlier. Sitting on the edge of the toilet, I ignore the increasing pressure in my head and bend over to put them on, irritated that I know the brand "Keds" when I still don't remember my own last name.

I stand up about the time Kayden shrugs into a sleek, fitted brown leather jacket that matches his boots, not to mention hugs every perfect inch of his torso. I'm irritated that I'm even noticing such things when I'm about to be on the run from the Italian police.

Slipping my hands inside the front of my jean pockets, I say, "So we're really doing this?"

"This?" He laughs. "We're not breaking out of jail, Ella."

"We're running from Gallo," I point out, wondering how he so easily uses my newly discovered name.

"I told you," he says, "we aren't running from anyone. We're making sure things happen on our terms."

"It feels like we're running," I argue, hugging myself. "Isn't he going to come after you to find me?"

"Leave Gallo to me," he says, reaching inside the cabinet again to produce another jacket, this one in black and my size. "It's February and cold. You're going to need this." He holds it open for me.

"It's February," I say, closing the distance between us to rotate and slip into the coat. "I know I'm wearing Keds tennis shoes, but I don't know the month. My brain is ridiculously illogical." I face him again. "What's today's date?"

"The fourteenth," he says, and while I think "Valentine's Day" and glance at my naked ring finger, he doesn't seem to notice, moving on to more important things, like getting us out of here. "Here's the plan," he says. "I'm going to check out the hallway and see if I need to create a distraction for our exit."

"What kind of distraction?"

"I'll pull the fire alarm if I have to, but I don't think I will." He reaches into the cabinet and retrieves a medium black purse, which he hands to me. "I told the clerk to fill it. Once I leave the bathroom, you'll have about three minutes to put on makeup, pouf up your hair, and do whatever you can to not look like a person the staff will recognize."

I gape at what I know to be a Chanel flagship purse with a cool five-thousand-dollar price tag, while Kayden glances at his also ridiculously expensive watch and instructs, "I'll knock three times when I come back so you know it's me. Don't open the door for anyone else and don't talk once you exit the bathroom. We don't want anyone checking on you or recognizing your voice once you're in the hallway."

"Yes. Okay."

"Finally," he continues, "people know me on this floor now, so you're going to exit the room before me and turn left. Act confident and walk slowly and casually, no matter how much you want to run. When you reach the stairs, exit. That'll be about halfway down the hall. I'll meet you on the basement level, which is the parking garage."

"Meet me? Where will you be?"

"I'm taking the elevator to draw attention away from you. There's a cell phone in your purse. Stay at the garage door until I call you. I want you to literally walk out the door and we'll drive away. The phone is programmed with my number. If you run into any trouble, find a place to hole up, lock yourself in if you can, and call me." He shuts the cabinet. "We need to do this now."

Adrenaline surges through me, and my stupid hands start to shake. I shove them in my pockets, and Kayden grabs me, pulling me to him, his hands solidly on my waist. "I know you're nervous, but in ten minutes, we'll be out of here, on our way to ending this."

"You make it sound so simple. We're dealing with a mobster, remember?"

"That's why we have to erase the path that leads him to us." His fingers gently wrap my neck. "I'm not going to let anything happen to you. You have my word."

I don't have time to digest his promise, or why it matters to me so much, before he releases me and wastes no time crossing the room to open the door, glancing over his shoulder to say, "Three minutes," before he disappears.

I waste at least five seconds of the first minute staring at the door he's shut behind him before I dart for the sink and open the purse, setting it on the counter. Searching through the selection, I grab a bottle of foundation, and that's when I realize that I'm avoiding the mirror. Grinding my teeth, I unscrew the top of the bottle and face myself, but rather than see me how I am now, my mind's eye shows me *Ella*. Red hair. Smiling. My eyes alight, my spirit fearless. *Fearless.* I was. I have to be now.

Spurred into action, I slather on the makeup base, and one by one, I apply eye shadow, lip gloss, and mascara, my memory supplying exactly how I like each item to look. Lastly, I finger-fluff as I spray my hair for volume, hating the way the dark shade washes out my coloring. I step back from the sink and give myself a quick, critical inspection. My hair is full and shiny. My lips are a pretty, pale pink that matches the eye shadow I've applied, while my lashes are stroked long and thick with mascara. Satisfied I won't be easily recognized, especially in my street clothes, I toss everything back in the purse, getting antsy about Kayden's return, and almost expecting that fire alarm to go off. Leaning on the sink, I stare at myself in the mirror and try to complete my name. "Ella . . . Ella . . . *what?*"

My mind replies, but not with my name. Suddenly I am in another small bathroom, applying makeup to the pretty brunette in my memory, laughing at her as she complains about a red lipstick I want to use on her. And then I hear my voice speaking to her. *"Don't be a prude, Sara."* I suck in a breath, my chest burning with the memory. *Sara.* Her name was Sara. *Is* Sara. *Is* Sara. She's not gone. I am. And I love her. And miss her. But I don't know how to find her.

A knock sounds behind me, followed by two more that confirm it's Kayden at the door. I grab my purse, throw the strap over my neck cross-body style, and face forward as Kayden decides not to wait for me and enters. "We're clear to leave," he says, his eyes flickering over my face, lowering to my lips, where they linger.

I hold my breath, waiting for his approval. He reaches for me, heat radiating from his palm to mine, as he drags me to him, aligning our bodies. "You're the one who is beautiful," he declares, his voice silky on my frayed nerve endings. "But I want to know who Ella really is," he adds. "And I promise you, I will. Soon."

The compliment sends flutters to my belly, while the promise sends a rush of unease through me that I do not understand, but have no time to analyze. Still holding my hand, Kayden is already leading me into the next room, and while he's focused on our exit, my attention lands on the bed that has been my prison, straying further to the journal on the table, and suddenly I have to have it.

Tugging my hand free of Kayden's, I dash around the bed before he can stop me, grabbing it and stuffing it into my purse, the one thing that belongs to me when I have nothing else. My goal achieved, I don't linger or allow myself time to consider why I so needed this little detour. I rush toward the man I'd declared beautiful only days ago, about to take a huge leap of faith and put my life in his hands.

five

Kayden doesn't look pleased about my detour for the journal, but I pretend not to notice, walking with him to the door, where he holds up a hand stop-sign fashion, opening the door to peer outside. I wait, the reality of what we're about to do hitting me, nerves fluttering in my belly. Too soon, and not soon enough, he's pulling me in front of him, his body framing mine. "Remember the plan," he whispers near my ear. "I'll be right behind you."

I don't even try to find my voice, giving him a nod while the flutter of nerves in my belly turns into an explosion radiating straight to the back of my skull. But there is no time for weakness or mending my body as Kayden orders, "Go now."

I inhale, shoving aside my pain and forcing myself to step directly into a half-moon-shaped waiting area with only three other doors indicating rooms. Thankfully no one is in sight. Taking advantage of the clear path, I double-step, hurrying while I can, and push through a door that buzzes with my exit.

On the other side I find a long hallway, doors lining my path as I continue onward, passing several rooms. A nurse exits one of them, while a man in street clothes enters another. The nurse walks past me, and I manage a smile and a wave without making full eye contact, only to have yet another nurse come out of yet another room. Again, I smile and wave, nervously noting a security guard monitoring a bank of elevators, worried he will ask questions I won't know how to answer. I'm relieved when I spy a sign indicating the stairwell that avoids that problem altogether.

Resisting the urge to bolt for it, I count my footsteps for no reason but to calm my mind. One. Two. Three. Four. All the way to twenty, and finally, I am at the door I need, pushing it open and entering the stairwell. The instant I'm sealed inside the small corridor, I face the door and shove it closed, holding it like it might pop open when I'm certain that I saw a security panel that won't allow entry from this side. Inhaling steadily to calm myself, I turn and collapse against the steel surface, one part relieved, one part listening for any activity around me. There appears to be no up level, and a good number of stairs to reach the bottom level, but with the increased security on this floor, I reassure myself that no one can enter this area from anywhere but the door at my back. Which is why I need to get away from it!

Dashing forward, I grab the railing with a frustrating sway. "Not now, please," I whisper, fairly certain I've overexerted myself. I'm ready to be over this damnable concussion already. Giving myself another beat to recover, I push forward, traveling down one flight of steps, then two; I estimate there are another eight to go. I make it three more when the door above me opens and the rumble of Gallo's voice speaking Italian stops me in my tracks. *No. No. No.* This can't be happening. It can't be coincidental that I'm here and so is he.

Someone must have recognized me and told him I left through the stairwell.

Another voice sounds with Gallo's, and I about fall over at the idea that it's me against not one, but two men. My only relief is the certainty that they aren't moving. But I need to be. Fighting the inclination to run at the risk of the noise it would create, I force myself to tiptoe forward. I've made it one level when the voices stop, the door slams shut, as if it was being held open, and footsteps come briskly at me. Fight-or-flight overcomes me and I start to run, every step a blur. Every second is laced with the fear and adrenaline that rockets me to the door I yank open.

I exit the corridor directly into the parking garage. Cold air blasts me, and I eye the rows of cars in front of me. Fearing the open space between me and them, I cut left toward a row nestled behind the stairwell, rounding the corner at the same instant the door opens. Heart in my throat, I take shelter behind a bumper, squatting and holding my breath. Footsteps sound, and then I hear Gallo talking to someone in Italian, this time on the phone, I think. Time ticks by, each second a bullet that is too near, the cold air tormenting my cheeks. Cautiously, I shift my purse to the front of me, debating the idea of digging for the cell phone to contact Kayden, but instead begin to panic at the idea it will ring any moment.

Anxiously, I open my purse and search for it, shivering as I grab the iPhone. Finding the ringer setting, I quickly switch it to vibrate. Task complete, I hear Gallo still talking away, and I decide I have to warn Kayden, searching the phone for the auto-dial number he said he entered. *Bingo.* I click the message option to text him.

I start to type, pausing as I realize Gallo's voice has gone silent, and I'm ready to shout for joy as I hear his footsteps moving away from me. Tension zips from my body, but I don't kid myself into being too overjoyed. Gallo could return at any moment and Kayden hasn't called. I refocus on typing a message to him, when his voice echoes from just in front of the stairwell. Assuming he's on the phone, I pop to my feet to go to him, stunned when another man starts speaking. Since there was no one else involved in our plan, I am officially worried. I stuff the phone back in my purse and, not for the first time, I wish I spoke Italian, and, also not for the first time, I wonder if I do, and just can't remember it. Kayden and the man go back and forth, and I listen, hoping the words will ring some bells with me, frustrated when they don't.

Deciding I need to assess their body language, I stand and lean against the wall framing the stairs, peeking around the corner, bringing a tall man with curly black hair into view, shaken to the core to realize I don't know how or why, but I *know* him. And I don't like him. I jerk back, flattening against the wall, trying to calm my heart, which has decided it wants to jump out of my chest. Where do I know him from? *Why* do I know him? And why is he with Kayden? Most importantly, why do I fear him? And I do. I fear that man. A memory flickers, an image of that man leaning against a wall, but the image is gone a second later. What wall? Where?

Worried I'll be seen, I squat down between the lines of cars, trying to decide what to do. Stay? Run? Listen, when I can't understand anything being said? And why isn't Kayden worried about me right now? He has to know I'm not in the stairwell because I'd already have exited. Another image flickers in my mind, and I squeeze my eyes shut, willing answers to come to me, and am transported back to the night Kayden found me.

I stuff my hands into my jacket pockets, nervously walking the deserted sidewalk, hoping I'm going to find help ahead and fighting the urge to look over my shoulder. Afraid to look and alert anyone following me—I know that they are there—but just as afraid not to look. So I do it, and I discover two men trailing me by half a block at most. It could be innocent, but it doesn't feel innocent at all, and I turn back around, hurrying my pace without breaking into an outright run. Please don't let them be after me. Please don't let them be after me. *I double-step and look over my shoulder again, and they are closer. Much closer now, and my heart wrenches with the certainty that I am in trouble and have no option but to run.*

"Ella. Ella."

I open my eyes, shocked to find Kayden squatting in front of me, those blue eyes meeting mine, and I flicker back to an image of me lying in that alleyway, and him staring down at me. I woke up. I saw him there. "I told you to wait inside, damn it," he scolds.

"Gallo was in the stairwell. Who was that man you were talking to?"

"He's a friend."

"A friend?" I ask, terrified that I'm about to discover he and that man were the two men following me. "What kind of friend?"

That "friend" appears to the side of us, speaking rapid, urgent Italian, then disappearing again. "Fuck," Kayden murmurs, before announcing to me, "Gallo is headed back in this direction. Hide behind a car." He stands and walks around the wall while I crawl to the back of the bumper I hid behind before, listening as three sets of voices sound this time.

Lowering my head to my hands, I try to see those men following me, but my mind proves to be a brutal bitch that gives me nothing when I truly want and need information. Feeling sick, I press my hand to my stomach. Kayden was not following me. He wasn't. Every instinct I own says I can trust him. He saved me. Didn't he? Unless . . . Could someone have spotted him, leaving him forced to call for help? Cotton forms in my throat, and I go back to the cold, hard conclusion I faced in that bathroom and forgot too soon. I don't know what happened to me or who I am, and I cannot trust anyone until I do. I have to leave, right now, and alone.

I push off my knees and go to a squat, hesitating a split second before I start moving down the line of cars, hoping I'm headed toward the exit. Ten cars later, I find a short stairwell, and I take off down it. A few seconds later, I seem to be at the side of the hospital overlooking another parking lot. It's pitch dark, and thunder is rumbling overhead, with the scent of rain lacing the air. I run left, away from the main entrance of the building from what I can tell, a gust of wind lifting my hair and blasting me with bitterly cold air, but I do not allow it to stop me. Forever it seems I push forward, until I'm at the street separating the hospital from a neighborhood. I turn and look behind me, relieved that no one follows.

Adrenaline and hope mix together, energizing me. I cross the road, running even faster now, and I am rewarded with the sight of a giant church, certain they will shelter and protect me. But it's not as close as I thought, and I find myself winding through the streets, trying to find the fastest way out of the cold. The first drop of rain hits me as I cut down the cobblestone road, my mind flickering back to another cobblestone road, and the night of the attack.

Run. Keep running. Faster. Don't stop. Don't look back. I can't be caught. They can't take me back to him. They can't. I won't let them.

I'm jolted out of the past when a downpour of icy rain rushes over me, and the church appears farther away than seconds before. My entire body hurts and I think I'm crying. I know I'm scared. I don't want to be scared. I want to be brave. I have to be brave and I'm not going to quit.

The rain keeps falling, though, brutal, cold, punishing droplets pelting me, while thunder rumbles above with the fierceness of a beast gone as mad as I feel. I'm numb when I finally reach the edge of the massive church parking lot. I'm discouraged to find no cars, no signs that anyone is present, but I press onward, hoping for any form of shelter. I'm within reachable distance of the massive steps leading to the door when a roar sounds in the distance. My heart skips a beat and I drag my aching body forward. *Don't stop running. Don't stop!* The roar gets closer. Louder. *Don't stop!* I close in on the steps and spot another set leading downward that puts me closer to a door. I cut right toward them, but the roar of the engine is on top of me, and I'm so bitterly cold I can barely feel my toes. Still, though, I push myself, and push some more. Only a few more feet. A few more feet!

Suddenly, a motorcycle is in front of me, skidding to a stop and blocking my path. Stunned, I am forced to stop dead in my tracks, and even with a helmet on, I can feel Kayden's energy, his dominance, and I do not wait for his dismount. I dart to my right, determined to reach a door, where I can try to get help. The bike goes silent, and I know it's a matter of seconds before Kayden catches up to me, but I am so close to those downward steps. So close, but I don't make it. Kayden's strong hand grasps my arm, while I try to jerk in the other direction. "Ella! Stop! It's me!"

"Let go!" I shout, only to be pulled around to face him, his helmet now gone, and already his hair is plastered to his face. "Let go of me, Kayden, or I'll start screaming."

He shackles my wrist and drags me to him, holding me hard against his body. "I told you. I'm not going to let go of you. I took care of Gallo."

"I don't care about Gallo," I hiss, tugging away from him, water running into my mouth. "I don't care about Gallo! You lied to me!"

"What are you talking about?"

"I saw you with that man at the hospital. I know he was there the night I was attacked."

A car pulls up beside us and the driver's door pops open. Kayden curses, releasing one of my wrists to hold up his hand, silently telling our visitor to stay back. I tug against him again and take one look at the man who's standing by the black sedan, and even in the rain, I know he's the "friend" from the night of my attack. Certain I will have no chance if they double-team me, a rush of adrenaline overcomes me, and I jerk hard, the water working in my favor and loosening Kayden's grip.

The instant I'm free, I turn and start running for the stairwell, torn about screaming, both desperate for the police to help and fearful they will expose me to Niccolo. I'm not even sure that Kayden isn't Niccolo, or at least working for him. I wanted him to be a good man. I wanted to trust him, and even when he grabbed me just now, some part of me still did. Some part of me does, and it's terrifying.

I hit the stairwell and a sensor triggers a lantern, a glow of light illuminating what is an alcove in front of the door, and now I scream. "Help! Help!" I stumble into the door and start pounding. Kayden is there then, turning me and pressing me into a corner.

"What is wrong with you?" he demands, water pouring off him and onto me.

My hand hits a holster under his jacket and my gaze drops to a gun he didn't have before. I gasp, my gaze rocketing to his. "Is this where you kill me? At a church? Or are you going to take me somewhere else to do it?"

"The gun is to protect us. I saved you. I'm not here to kill you."

"Maybe you saved me because you had to. Maybe someone saw you that night and you had no choice. Maybe you had to call an ambulance."

His hands come down on my face. "There are a lot of things I want to do to you, Ella, but I promise you, killing you isn't one of them." His mouth slants over mine, his tongue delving deep, and I want to resist. I do. I try. But his lips are warm when mine are cold, and the taste of him, passion and fire, and yes, demand, burns through me, tempting me, taking me. And for just a moment, I can't seem to help myself. I want to be possessed by this man. I want to be consumed, so I kiss him back. I kiss him like it's my last kiss, because maybe it is.

I lean into him, wanting another second, another taste,

but he tears his mouth from mine, and my hands are pressed to his chest, his heart racing as fast as mine, as he declares, "I'm a lot of things you won't like, Ella, including the bastard who has wanted to fuck you since you opened your eyes and called me beautiful despite being in a hospital bed. But I will say it again. I'm not your enemy."

I'm trembling, not from the cold, but the impact of his kiss. While I was lost in the moment, I have not lost touch with why I ran. "I want to believe you. But words and a kiss, no matter how beautiful you might be, aren't enough when I'm fighting for survival."

"As am I. We're linked, Ella. I'm right here with you."

Unbidden, the detective's words play in my head—*Kayden Wilkens does nothing, including you, without an agenda*—and with them a bad thought hits me. "What's to keep you from handing me over to Niccolo?"

"Me. I'm stopping me, and that's the only answer I can give you."

"How's that supposed to make me feel safe?"

He presses his hands to the door on either side of me. "I hate Niccolo. I'd destroy him if I could."

"Why?"

"My reasons don't matter."

"They do matter. And selling me would be self-preservation, which I believe you're very good at."

"Oh, I am, sweetheart, but I'm not giving you to Niccolo," he vows, and the way he says the other man's name is pure acid and hate.

"You hate Niccolo. Gallo hates you. You're a man with enemies."

"Wake up, Ella. Your enemies are mine."

Footsteps sound on the stairwell behind him, and his "friend's" voice cuts though the storm. Any bit of progress he might have made with me washes away. Kayden curses at the interruption, glancing over his shoulder and speaking to the man in Italian. I have a fleeting image of me with red hair, wearing goggles, while firing a gun. I know how to use a gun, and I reach for his. He grabs my hand. "What the fuck do you think you're doing?"

"You're full of shit, Kayden Wilkens," I hiss. "You aren't selling me to Niccolo? I don't believe you. I know your 'friend.' And I know he was there the night I was attacked. You're lying to me, and I won't be kissed into stupidity. I might be alone and desperate, but I'm not that girl."

"His name is Adriel Santaro and he works for me. And you're right. He was there. He also has a sister who depends on him and could be used as a weapon against him or even me. The minute I found that matchbook, I sent him away before he ended up on the police report."

Hope blossoms and expands in my chest. "Why didn't you tell me he was there?"

"You don't trust me, as you've proven by reaching for my gun. I wasn't going to give you someone else to doubt."

"And yet he was at the hospital."

"I asked him to cover us while we left. A safety precaution I thought we needed."

I study him, searching his eyes, looking for answers he's too savvy to let me find. "How can I trust you, Kayden?" I ask, wanting him to say something, or do something, that erases my fears, when I know it's an impossible feat.

He doesn't immediately reply. Both my impossible demand and that steamy hot kiss hover between us, and it hits me that what I call familiar, he calls linked. We are linked. We both agree on this, but I don't think it's the way he claims. Not completely. He pushes off the door and puts a small space between us, his expression all hard lines and dark shadows. One second passes. Two. Three. He doesn't have an answer for me, and I'm shivering again, my heart in my throat, sensing something is coming, dreading it. And I'm right. Something is coming.

Actually, it's here. Kayden reaches into his holster and pulls his gun. And now I know what the kiss meant. It was goodbye.

six

I tilt my chin up and look Kayden in the eyes, not willing to die a coward. He holds my stare, not so much as blinking, and seconds tick by that could be my last until he surprises me and takes my hand. "Let me be clear, *Ella*," he says, his tone deepening on my name. "I never give up control, but I am now, for you."

"You're talking in code," I accuse, my voice remarkably steady considering I'm about to die. "Say what you mean."

He places the butt of his weapon into my palm, closing my fingers, and his, around it. He steps into the barrel of the gun, pressing it to his chest. "*You* have control," he says, his hand falling away, while mine trembles around the heavy steel. "You have two options," he adds. "Trust me as I trust you right now, or . . . shoot me."

But I'm not thinking about me shooting him. I'm thinking about him *not* shooting me. "You weren't going to kill me."

"No. I was *not* going to kill you."

The adrenaline I've been running on this past hour drains away, leaving me weak, aware that my head is throbbing, but

I'm oh so relieved. I laugh, and it sounds a little crazy. I think I'm losing it. "You weren't going to kill me."

"But are you going to kill me?" he asks. "That's the real question. Or are you going to put the gun down and trust me?"

"Neither," I whisper, becoming aware of how fiercely I'm shivering, every quake of my body intensifying the heaviness at the back of my head. "I'm not going to kill you, Kayden, but I won't blindly trust you, either. And now"—I squeeze my eyes shut—"I need to sit." I slide down the door, releasing the gun gently to the ground to pull my knees to my chest.

Kayden kneels in front of me, his fingers wrapping my calves, his touch confusingly right and wrong at the same time, like everything about him and me. "How bad is it?" he asks.

I ignore his question, focused on his hands on my legs, on him sitting in front of me, blocking the rain and the wind. Protecting me. Or is it possessing me? "You touch me like you own me," I say, and I sense that my comment isn't about this moment. Maybe not even about Kayden.

"I touch you like a man who wants you." His answer is unapologetic, showing me that wolf in him that doesn't bother with sheep's clothing, his fingers flexing against me as he inches forward ever so slightly to add, "I don't want to own you, Ella, but I *will* intervene when you're trying to get yourself killed like you did tonight."

"Because protecting me is protecting you," I say, and now it's all about the here, the now, and him.

His jaw clenches, eyes hardening. "In ways you don't begin to understand and you never will."

"I'm the one his men attacked," I argue. "I need to understand. *I deserve* to understand." I've barely finished the sentence when a sharp pain darts through my head and immediately repeats, forcing my face to my knees, and a frustrated sound from my lips. "I hate this. I thought this was over."

"That was before you ran through a rainstorm." His hand settles on my hair, his touch gentle, intimate. *Familiar.* "We need to get you someplace warm and safe."

"That would require going back out in the rain, and I can't do that. Not now. It feels like someone's poking me with a needle over and over."

"Which is all the more reason we need to get you out of here."

I turn my head to rest my cheek on my legs. "I can't move right now, Kayden. And I really can't ride on your motorcycle."

"Adriel left us his car."

"We still have to get to the car."

"Leave that to me," he says, unzipping my purse where it hangs at my hip and placing the gun inside. "Security for both of us."

I shut my eyes. "I'm not sure what that means. I'm not sure of much besides that I'm pretty sure you're very rich and probably even more dangerous."

"Not to you," he promises, stroking my wet hair from my face.

I shiver at the touch, my lashes lifting to find those blue eyes staring into mine, and even in this dim light they are as stunning as ever. "If you're trying to make me feel better—"

"You *should* feel better. Do you really want a saint helping you fight a mobster?"

"Double-edged sword," I whisper, pressure forcing my eyes shut again.

"That's it," he says. "We're getting you out of here." He slides his arm under my knees.

"No," I plead, grabbing his shoulder, the sound of the rain splattering on the pavement promising misery I can't take right now. "Please. Not yet. It's too cold."

"The car is at the curb and the heater is running."

"Yes, but—"

He scoops me up and stands, curling me easily against his body. Some piece of sanity breaks through the pain and I grab his jacket, fighting to even keep my eyes open. "I'm going with you, but I know how to use that gun and I will if I have to."

"That's why I gave it to you," he surprises me by saying, already starting up the stairs, pausing just before we're about to leave the overhang. "Ready?"

"No. No. I'm not. Kayden—"

He steps out into the downpour anyway, and I gasp when the icy water instantly consumes us, huddling against him for the mercifully short run to the curb. Kayden sets me down on my feet, his arm shackling my waist while he opens the door and helps me inside, water pouring all over the expensive leather seats. I expect his quick departure, but despite the storm punishing him from all directions, he lingers by my side, hitting the button to lower my seat, his wet hair draping his face. And it's all I can do not to reach up and shove it from his forehead, to see his eyes and try to understand the man who has become the only person I can depend on in this world.

But I don't, and he's gone, shutting the door, and sweet heaven, the engine really is running as he promised, the warm air blowing on me, offering a tiny bit of relief. Still shivering, I roll to my side as Kayden climbs into the car and shuts us inside, water pouring from his clothes and hair as he shrugs out of his coat.

He tosses it on the backseat. "Your turn," he says. "You'll feel better without that wet leather weighing you down."

"I'd rather not move."

"You can rest when you get it off." He reaches over and maneuvers my purse over my head.

Regret fills me. "I'm sure it's ruined. A Chanel purse is not meant to be drenched in water."

"I'll buy you another one," he says, as if a five-thousand-dollar expense is nothing to him.

"How rich are you, exactly?"

He tugs the zipper down on the front of my jacket. "Not as rich as Niccolo, and that's a problem."

"Because money is power," I whisper, shivering, and this time it's not from the cold.

He gives me a keen look. "That sounds like experience talking."

Images flash in my mind. A white mansion. A huge mahogany bed. A man's hands. "Probably. Maybe."

"Whatever the case . . ." he says, reaching up and brushing hair from my lips. His fingers linger there just a moment too long. "You're right. Money *is* power, and Niccolo's supply of both is limitless."

"How do you know him, Kayden?"

"How isn't what's important," he says, his tone hardening, and I can almost feel a wall come down between us. "Just be glad I know enough to keep us off his radar." He reaches for my jacket. "We need to get you out of this and get moving."

I grab his arm. "You really don't know how to take no for an answer, do you?"

"And here you said you know nothing about me."

"Not enough."

"You do know," he says, covering my hand where I hold him, holding me to him, and I have this sense of a shift in control, from mine to his. "I could say the same of you."

"But I'm the one at a disadvantage," I remind him.

"Are you now?"

"How can you ask that? Of course I am."

"We'll agree to disagree on that one."

I purse my lips but don't push him, sitting up enough to shrug out of my jacket while Kayden reaches down and drags the heavy weight off my back. "You were right." I breathe out, relaxing into the seat as he tosses my jacket onto the backseat with his. "I do feel better without it."

I've barely spoken the words when Kayden leans over me, his arm stretched across my chest, his spicy, almost sweet, scent teasing my nostrils. "You shouldn't have left like you did," he says, his low, angry tone throwing me into defensive mode.

"Because you're my hero and I should just blindly trust you?"

"I gave you a gun to earn your trust because I know you won't need to use it on me."

"Yes. You did. But that was after I saw Adriel and thought he was one of my attackers."

"You mean you thought *I* was one of your attackers."

"No. I don't know, Kayden. You should have told me about him."

"You should have asked before you ran."

"And risked not having the chance to run? If you were me, would you have made that decision?"

His teeth clench, his expression hardening. "You have the gun now. That's me trusting you whether you choose to trust me or not. Don't pay me back by getting us both killed." He grabs my seat belt and pulls it across me, buckling me in and then settling back in his seat.

I sit there, stunned, and the stormy night is not the only thing creating the dark wall between us. There is anger. Lots of anger on both our parts, as he adds, "And just so we're clear. I'm not your hero. I'm just the man trying to save both our fucking lives."

My anger evaporates instantly, and I say, "But you're no monster."

His head cuts sharply in my direction, willing me to look at him, and when I do, he demands, "And you know that how?"

"Because monsters always claim to be heroes."

I expect him to ask how I know this as well, and I have no answer. There is just what I feel deep in my soul, a sense of having trusted the wrong person, who I refuse to believe was Niccolo. I would not trust a gangster. But Kayden doesn't ask me. He doesn't say anything. For several seconds he simply sits there, his body rigid, his jaw set hard. And when he does move, he faces forward and shifts the car into drive. I don't turn away immediately, studying his profile, not sure if his lack of response is agreement or disagreement with my statement, only knowing that before this is over, I will find out.

Turning away from him, I sink farther into the leather seat, my gaze catching on the Rolls-Royce emblem on the glove box. I wait for the car or the brand to ring a bell beyond the obvious, and I'm relieved when it doesn't happen. I don't want Kayden to be lying to me. It's the thought I replay in my mind as silence stretches between us, the rain pattering on the rooftop, the tension in the air between Kayden and me slowly softening to a hum instead of a scream. Kayden must feel it as well, because he leans down and turns on the radio, punching several buttons before an Imagine Dragons song starts to play.

I roll to my side and look at him. "You do know this song is called—"

"'Monster,'" he finishes, giving me a sideways look, his lips hinting at a smile. "I thought it was appropriate, don't you?"

Relieved we are over our argument, I feel a smile cut through my pain and find my lips. "Very," I agree. "I guess Adriel likes American music?"

"Yes. He went to college in the States. And he's a big enough Imagine Dragons fan to drag me to one of their concerts here in Rome."

My eyes go wide. "Wait. *You* went to a concert?"

"I owed him a favor. And why is that so hard to believe?"

"I don't know. You just pressed a gun to your chest. It's

hard to think about you doing something so . . ." I lift a hand. "Normal."

"Normal's overrated."

"I'd take normal right about now," I argue offhandedly, and get back to my main goal: finding out who Kayden Wilkens really is. "Do you ever go back to the States?"

"Occasionally," he says, detouring my mission by offering nothing more.

"How old were you when you moved here?" I ask, digging in another direction.

"Ten."

"So this really is home to you, isn't it?"

"It's where I live. Yes."

It's a curious reply, with a hidden meaning I try to decipher. "Where you live? So it's not home?"

"Semantics."

"That's an answer which I assume translates to you not wanting to talk about this."

"Why do you?"

"Because if I can't know me, I want to know you."

"You mean, you still think you know me and don't remember."

"Do I?"

"No matter how many times you ask me that, the answer's going to be the same."

"Fine," I say, but I'm not ready to give up. "How old are you?"

"Thirty-two. How old are you?"

"Twenty-five," I reply, surprising myself. "And I really . . . don't know how I know that."

"A name and an age. It's progress. Maybe if you write in that journal you grabbed at the hospital you'll know I'm telling the truth."

"I'm sure it's ruined."

"And easily replaced."

"Unlike my memories," I say. "And I'm not calling you a liar, Kayden. I can't help how you make me feel."

We stop at a light and he turns to me, and even in the darkness the blast of his full attention is like fire heating ice, and I'm the ice. "How do I make you feel, Ella?"

A million emotions rush through me, but I cannot name one of them, so I whisper, "I don't know."

"Do you want to know how you make me feel?" he asks, his voice a low seduction that promises hot nights, and hotter kisses. I want those kisses. I want more. He might not be a monster, but he's still keeping secrets.

"Not yet," I say, turning away from him to face the roof of the car, when I'd meant to simply say, "No."

He laughs, that low, ridiculously sexy laugh of his, and I am again taken aback by how right and wrong he can feel at the very same moment in time. We fall into silence, the sound of the radio mixed with the raindrops on the roof filling the air. I start to drift off when "Take Me to Church" by Hozier begins to play. My gut knots, my chest tightening with some dark emotion that I think might be fear. Which is ridiculous. I'm sitting in the car with Kayden. The song is just a song, but the words sweep through me like a blade, trying to make me bleed.

There is no sweeter innocence than our gentle sin . . .

I squeeze my eyes shut, fighting the urge to shove away a memory I don't want to see, but I can't hide. I wasn't a coward when Kayden held that gun on me, and I won't be one now. Cautiously, I let myself slip inside the past, and it's like I'm looking down on myself from above, not fully committed to being in the moment. First, there is just me. I don't see the place I am at. I'm wearing a curve-hugging black dress with sheer, long sleeves. My lips are glossy. My makeup is perfect. My hair is red, vibrant, and this is me. The real me Kayden said he hopes to know. That he swore he would know.

My vision expands, and I can see that I am standing in the middle of a bedroom with expensive artwork on the walls, fancy hardwood floors beneath my strappy high-heeled shoes. To the right of me is a large brown leather chair, and beside it a wooden sculpture of a tiger, and I don't like it. Not at all, but I do not know why, nor do I care to remember. I cut my gaze away from it, shutting out whatever memory it represents.

I refocus on where I stand, a massive mahogany bed behind me. Two gorgeously etched wooden doors are in front of me, and I'm waiting for them to open. And they do, as if my attention has invited them to do so, and *he* enters, stealing my breath, skyrocketing my heart rate. I try to see his face, but my mind is still protecting me. I don't have to know who he is to feel his power or the way he owns the room. No. The way he owns everything, and everyone, around him.

He walks toward me, slow, confident, stopping a mere sway from touching me. He is tall and towers above me, watching me, and I can feel the heat of his stare, but I cannot see his eyes or even what he is wearing. And I don't want to, I realize. That's the problem. I'm hiding when I have to face this, and I force myself to go deeper into the memory. No longer am I watching myself from above. I'm right there in that room, living the experience all over again.

"Undress," he orders.

I blanch. "What? I thought we were going out."

He steps closer, towering over me, his suit tailored, expensive perfection, like his body beneath it. "You heard me. I told you to undress."

"I—"

He twists rough fingers into my hair and drags my mouth to his, his breath a warm tease on my lips. "You like our games. Do as I say. Let me fuck you a new way."

"Yes," I whisper, and while I do like our games, there is something different about him tonight, an edge that frightens me. Or maybe it's my inhibitions, my weaknesses, winning.

But he doesn't let me go with my agreement, the twist of his fingers in my hair tightening, his mouth closing down on mine, the swipe of his tongue rough with demand I should revel in, but do not.

He releases me and sets me away from him, crossing his arms over his chest to watch me. I undress, but he does not, which is never the case, and my unease expands, burning in my chest. Once I'm naked, feeling at his mercy, his gaze rakes over every part of my body, and I expect him to come to me, or to order me to him. Instead, he turns and walks to a drawer, opening it and returning with a long piece of rope.

"Hold out your hands."

*This man has been my hero, and I should trust him, but I
don't want to do it. I want to grab my clothes and run. His gaze
sharpens and I feel trapped, unsure of what to do. He arches a brow
and I offer him my hands. Satisfaction gleams in his eyes as he
binds me.*

"Lie on the bed with your hands over your head," he orders.

*I do it, telling myself he's always made me hot. He's always been
good to me. He will fuck me in some amazing way, and my nervous
reaction is silly. He walks to the headboard and grabs my bound
hands, and somehow, I'm not sure where, he ties them over my
head. And then he just leaves. He walks out of the room and leaves
me tied to the bed. And for the first time since I met him, I feel
alone.*

I return to the present with a flutter of my lashes and a
splintering pain in my skull, and that song is still playing, reminding me of him, whoever he is. I want it to stop. *Please
make it stop . . .* But still it goes on . . .

My church offers no absolutes . . .

I'm pulled back into the past, expecting, and dreading,
seeing that man again, but I do not return to him or his bedroom. This time I'm at the church where Kayden found me
tonight. And Kayden is there too, pressing me against the
wooden door, his big body framing mine, his hands cupping
my face as he kisses me. And I can taste his desire, his passion.
His claim to me . . . the possession. And clearly now, when it
had not been in the moment, I know that he wants—even
needs—to own me. This discovery should scare me, but the
scent of him, warm spice and vanilla, is so damn familiar, both

soothing and arousing. I cling to him, kissing him back, hungry for more of him. And with him, I am not alone like I'd been in that room, tied to that bed. He is the answer I need. *Kayden*.

I open my eyes, and I feel like a hammer is pounding in my head. The song is over. The rain continues. And I don't want to think about why my mind showed me *him* and then showed me Kayden. I just want to go to sleep.

❦

I wake with a gasp and shoot forward, grabbing the dash, panting. The car isn't moving. There is no rain and there appears to be a wall in front of the car.

"Easy, Ella."

Looking right, I find a strange man with brown hair and eyes kneeling at the open passenger door. "Who are you and where is Kayden?" I ask.

"I'm here," Kayden says, replacing the stranger by my side. "That was Nathan. He's a friend and a doctor. You were grabbing your head and rocking back and forth. I pulled over and you passed out."

"I passed out?"

"Yeah, sweetheart, you did. You scared the shit out of me. Nathan just gave you something for the pain."

The man appears above Kayden's shoulder. "And something to help you sleep. I'll come back tomorrow."

"What's wrong with me? I feel like someone is hammering in my head. I can't remember who I am and now I passed out?"

"I saw your medical records," the man says. "You have a

very bad concussion, and from what I understand you weren't kind to yourself tonight. You need to rest."

"I'm not even going to ask how he got my medical records."

"Matteo," Kayden says, taking my hand. "The hacker who's trying to find you by your first name. This is his house. We're staying here until we're ready to deal with Gallo."

"Okay. I don't think I want to know what that means either right about now."

The doctor, Nathan, I guess his name is, says something to Kayden in Italian, and I've given up fighting over speaking English. At least for tonight. Kayden kisses my hand, a gentle, intimate gesture that does funny things to my stomach. "Give me a minute and we'll get you someplace where you can lie down."

He stands and faces Nathan, and I don't even try to listen to their conversation. My pain eases, but I feel kind of floaty and weird now, and I don't like it. In fact, it's freaking me out to have this little control over everything, including my own body.

Kayden squats back down beside me. "Ready to go upstairs?"

"I feel weird."

"It's the drugs, sweetheart." He slides his arms under me. "I've got you."

He lifts me, and I don't fight him. In fact, I'm getting kind of used to this man carrying me around everywhere. I sink against him, my head spinning with every footstep and sway of our bodies as he exits the garage and starts up a stairwell.

We enter the main house, and I manage a barely there

look at the giant, modern-looking living room with light wood floors and stainless-steel railings before we're walking up another staircase, this one a dizzying, winding nightmare for my head and stomach. Finally, at the top, there is a door. In a few long strides, Kayden carries me over the threshold, my gaze doing a sweeping inspection of a loft-like bedroom, with the same light hardwood floor as the lower level, several corner pillars running from the floor to the ceiling, brick walls, and a giant bed with a high-backed gray headboard. That bed is the blast of reality I don't want but need, and the magnitude of what is happening hits me with a force ten times that of the storm I ran through to escape him. I'm in a bedroom, alone with Kayden with no hospital staff, or Gallo, to intervene, after having a flashback about being tied to a bed, followed by one of him kissing me.

"Let me down," I demand. "Let me down, Kayden! Let me—"

He sits me on the end of the bed, planting his hands on either side of my hips. "What part of *you have a concussion* do you not understand?"

"I know I have a concussion. Believe me, I know. It just won't *go away*." A wave of dizziness washes over me. "Oh wow." I press my palm to my forehead. "I'm not feeling so good." I fall back against the mattress. "What's happening?" I try to lift my hand from my face and can't. "I can't move my hand. Kayden, I can't move my hand!"

"You're okay," Kayden promises, lying down next to me.

"I can't—"

"I've got it," he says, removing my hand and holding it between us. "Nathan gave you some powerful medicine to make sure you rest. You're just reacting to it. How's your pain?"

"No pain. I just feel weird. Really weird." My lashes lower, and unbidden, I am instantly transported back to another bedroom. To *that* night. To *his* bed. Deep inside the memory, I'm living it, *feeling it.*

Naked. Cold. I keep watching the clock, willing him to return. Two hours have passed, and the man I thought was my protector now feels like my captor. He is my captor. The doors he'd shut open, and he stands there, still fully dressed, sauntering slowly toward me. I try to see his face. Why can't I see his face? He stops at the end of the bed, and I am angry with him. I am hurt. He undresses, and when I would normally watch him, reveling in every delicious inch of his body, I turn my head, every second that passes more punishment. And when his hands come down on my ankles, and he demands, "Look at me," I don't. I won't.

My eyes fly open, and Kayden is still lying next to me, and when I look at him, I see a protector. I see passion. But I am certain *he* looked at me just as Kayden does now. *Before* that night. "Please don't be him," I whisper, and the darkness follows.

seven

I open my eyes and immediately become aware of being curled on my side, snuggled under warm blankets, rain spattering on the rectangular line of windows before me, dim light breaking through the curtains. Memories rush over me and I start piecing together the events that brought me here. The hospital. The stairwell and Gallo showing up. Adriel. The bitter cold run in the rain through the church parking lot. The sizzling hot kiss with Kayden by that very same church. Then there was the doctor friend of Kayden's who gave me drugs, followed by Kayden carrying me to a bedroom in his friend's house. Finally, there was him laying me on a bed, this one, I assume, where I wasted no time passing out. Because why wouldn't I want to pass out while in bed with a man with a hotness factor off the charts, especially after sharing a scorching hot kiss? Curious about where he is, I try to roll over, only to realize there is a heavy weight at my waist.

"You're finally awake."

At the sound of Kayden's deep, sexy voice, I roll over to face him, my gaze colliding with his at the same moment I realize that not only am I naked but so is he. *Oh God.* Maybe I didn't fall asleep. "Please tell me we didn't have sex and I don't remember."

"If we had sex, sweetheart, I promise you, I'd make sure you remembered." His hand settles on my hip, over the blanket, but I am oh so aware that I'm all skin beneath it. "And I have on pants."

"Oh. I guess I was too busy noticing my nakedness and . . . your chest." I press my hand to my face. "I need to stop talking." He laughs, and I peek through my fingers. "Please tell me I undressed myself."

"You couldn't even lift your own hand after Nathan gave you the pain meds."

My hand falls from my face and I gape. "You undressed me?"

"You were wet and cold, and I couldn't wash and dry your clothes with you in them."

"You *undressed me.*"

"Yes," he confirms. "I undressed you, and yes, I've been aware of just how naked you are every second you've been that way, as I am right this very moment." He spares me a reply. "How do you feel?"

I clutch the blanket to me. "Feel?"

"Your head, sweetheart. Are you in pain?"

"Oh. I . . ." My brow furrows, and I forget my state of undress. "Wow. No. I'm not. It's amazing. It's *wonderful.* What kind of drugs did your doctor friend give me?"

"Nathan is his name," he replies. "And when we first arrived last night he gave you a painkiller and a sedative. About four hours ago, he checked on you and gave you an anti-inflammatory that was supposed to ensure you woke up feeling good. Obviously it worked."

"Wait. He came back and gave me another injection and I didn't know it?"

"You didn't know because you were still heavily sedated, and that was the idea. To get the drugs in you before you woke up."

"He gave me drugs when I was *naked*. How many people saw me like this?"

"Only me."

There's a hard, possessive quality to his voice, and I am suddenly, intensely aware of how close we are. How close our *mouths* are, and I'm now officially thinking about our kiss. I decide I need a change of topic. "How long was I asleep?"

"Twelve hours," he says.

"And it's still raining?"

"It's not supposed to stop until tomorrow."

I decide the rain is as never-ending as my memory loss. "And we're at your hacker friend's house?"

"Matteo's house. That's right."

"He's the one trying to find out who I am using my first name?"

"Yes, and he's still working on it." He pauses. "We need to talk, Ella."

My eyes go wide. "Oh no. He found something bad."

"I'm not interested in what Matteo has, or has not, found right now. Who is he?"

"What?"

"Right before you passed out last night, you looked at me

and said, 'Please don't be *him*.' Who is he and what did he do to you?"

The memory of that man rushes back to me with an image of me tied to that bed, and I try to roll to my back. Kayden's leg latches on to my legs, holding me in place. "Who *is* he?"

"I was drugged, Kayden."

"So you don't remember saying that to me? And before you answer, be clear. I don't like secrets."

"I know *you* have secrets, so don't reprimand me. I'm not a child. I'm not your property. This is my life."

"That has become mine."

"It's the past."

"It's impacting the present," he counters. "Who is he?"

"I don't remember."

"You remember something or you wouldn't have said that to me."

"I told you, it was the drugs talking."

"It was your memory talking."

"Fine," I say. "I had a flashback in the car."

"And he was in it?"

"Yes."

"So we're back to the original question. Who is he?"

"I really don't know."

His eyes glint with dissatisfaction. "You don't know or you aren't going to tell me?"

"I *don't know*."

His lips thin, his expression tightening. "You're afraid of him."

"Yes," I whisper. "I'm afraid of him."

He studies me, his jaw set hard, seconds ticking by until he says, "I'm not him."

I want to tell him that I know, but I can't get the words out.

"I saved your life," he reminds me. "I'm protecting and helping you."

Now I can say it. "I know."

"You don't know, and that's a problem for both of us." He glances away from me, a long strand of his light brown hair teasing his forehead.

"It's not a problem," I say hastily, and without meaning to, I've all but admitted he's right. I don't know. I open my mouth to explain. "I mean . . ."

He cuts a sharp look at me. "I know what you mean, and it damn sure is a problem." And then he's tunneling his fingers into my hair, dragging me close, his breath teasing my lips as he adds, "One I plan to solve."

"I can explain," I say, hating the anger radiating off him, into me, but his mouth is already slanting over mine, tongue pressing past my teeth, a silky caress that has my nipples puckering and my sex clenching. But I need to talk to him, and my hand flattens over his chest, his skin hot, or maybe it's just because I'm so hot, burning up for this man. And again, I mean to push him away, but I can't. I don't. I'm not sure I really want to. My moan says I don't, and I give in to how much I want this man, sinking into the kiss, tasting him, getting lost in him.

He rolls me onto my back, the heavy, delicious weight of half his body on top of me, his leg draping mine, his stomach pressed to mine. The hard prod of his arousal is nestled next to my sex. My hands find his shoulders, holding on, not pushing away, as one of his drags the blanket down to expose my breasts. I arch into the touch, and he teases my nipple, nips my lips, and kisses me again, but his anger isn't gone. I taste it, I feel it vibrating through him, into me, and I want to make it go away, but instead he tears his mouth from mine, staring down at me, our breathing filling the small space between us.

"Do I taste like him?" he demands, his voice gravelly, affected.

"What?" I gasp. Alarm bells go off in my head. "How do you know I kissed him?"

"We both know you did a whole lot more than kiss him, sweetheart, and that kiss was to make sure when you remember him, you know the difference between him and me." He rolls away, sitting on the edge of the bed, giving me his back, his shoulders bunched with tension.

I sit and clasp the blanket to my chest. "Kayden—"

"Not now," he says, standing and scrubbing his hand through his hair as he walks away, disappearing into a doorway I assume leads to the bathroom.

Stunned, I stare after him, not sure what to think or feel. *We both know you did a whole lot more than kiss him.* I do know, but he shouldn't. Unless he's *him*, or I ran my mouth in my drug-induced sleep. And if I did, what did I say? Will it give me a clue to figure out his identity or mine? I have to find out.

I lift the blanket and cringe at the reminder that I'm naked, blushing at the idea of him undressing me, which is absolutely silly. My breast was just in the man's hand. I spot a throw blanket lying across a gray chair by the window, but I'm not getting it unless I walk over there in my birthday suit, which isn't the way I want to have a conversation with Kayden.

And we need to talk. Deciding there is really only one way to do this, I take a deep breath and decide to go for it.

Tossing off the covers, I rush to the chair, snatch the blanket, and wrap it around myself, letting out a sigh of relief when my task is complete without Kayden's return. The shower comes on, and I bite my lip at the idea that those pants of his are not still on, and he too is naked, beautifully naked from what I've seen so far. In light of this assumption, and the obvious open-door invitation that isn't about conversation, I hesitate in my pursuit, but decide the situation could be in my favor if I can resist the temptation to end up wet and at his mercy. I need answers, and while he's trapped and unable to shut me down is the best time to get them.

Giving myself no time to chicken out, I dart forward and enter the magnificent all-white bathroom. I pause inside the doorway, a giant sunken tub to my left and a double shower to my right, with clear glass panels. My mouth goes dry at the sight of Kayden's amazing, tight freaking backside, and further confirmation that I was right. He *is* beautiful and he has a tattoo on his back. Skulls, I think, and suddenly skulls are really, really sexy.

"Did you come to join me or just stare at my ass?" he asks without turning.

"I thought there would be a curtain or smoked glass."

He rotates to face me, and I gasp, giving him my back. He, in turn, gives me one of those deep, raspy laughs. "Careful, sweetheart," he warns. "I could drag you in here with me and you'd never see me coming."

My heart leaps at the threat I have no doubt he'll act on, and I turn around, rushing toward him, and pressing my back against the shower door to hold it shut. "What did I say about that man when I was drugged?"

"Not a damn thing."

I turn to face him, forgetting he's gloriously naked, until of course, he's standing in front of me *gloriously naked*, but somehow I stay my course. "You said we both know I did more than kiss him."

He stares at me, his eyes glinting hard, the pulse of the shower spray the only sound between us. One second, two, ten. He shuts off the water, giving me no warning as he shoves open the door, forcing me to back up. I've barely righted my footing before he steps out of the shower and onto the mat. My mouth goes dry at the sight of all that water clinging to all the beautiful parts of him. I'm spellbound by the drops tracking over his impressive six-pack and lower . . . lower . . . My head jerks up. He arches a brow, his lips quirking in cynical amusement. "I . . . don't know why I just did that. I mean, I do, but—"

"Because you want me, like I want you, but you have questions. Well, guess what. So do I, sweetheart." He grabs a towel off the rack and dries his hair, leaving all his manly hotness on display.

My instinct is to turn, but there is a glint in his eyes that is one part challenge and one part intimidation, and I do not let him win. I lift my chin, refusing to let my eyes wander again. "If I didn't tell you anything about that man, why did you say we both know I did a whole lot more than kiss him?"

He wraps the towel around his waist, his damp hair teasing his defined cheeks, accenting those cutting blue eyes. "Are you saying you didn't?"

"Did I say something that made you think I did?"

"Are you saying you didn't?"

"Stop answering my questions with more questions."

"Then give me an answer."

"I could say the same to you," I snap. "I had one pain-induced memory of that man. One. Just one, Kayden."

"That's not an answer I'm looking for."

"You already know the answer. He was . . ." I stop, not sure how to fill in the blank.

"Your lover," he supplies.

"No," I say quickly, the word *lover* somehow too good for that man. "He was not my lover."

"But you had sex with him."

An image of me tied to that bed has me gripping the blanket a little tighter. "My memory had nothing to do with sex."

"Then what was it about?"

"Control," I say, no hesitation in me. "Power."

His eyes sharpen. "Did he hurt you, Ella?"

"I don't want to talk about this." I try to twist away from him, but his hands encircle my waist.

"What did he look like?"

"I couldn't see his face."

"What could you see?"

"I told you—"

"What *could you see?*" he presses.

"That's private."

"Not when my life is on the line, right along with yours."

"It's private and it's not about what I saw anyway. It's more what I felt."

"Which was what?"

"I told you. He scares me."

He narrows his eyes on me. "'Please don't be him,'" he says, repeating my words from the night before.

"I'd just had the flashback, Kayden, and the drugs and the pain made me feel helpless."

He stares at me, blue eyes like pure ice. "Got it," he says, setting me away from him. "Your clothes are under the sink, and the bag on the counter is hair color. Fix the streaks so it's not obvious you colored it."

"So no red. No going back to me." But even as I say the words, I know it's not possible, no matter how much I want it to be.

"You can't even remember who *he* is. You can't have *you* back until you figure him out. Come downstairs when you're done. We're moving to my house."

"Your house? But what about Gallo? Won't he come looking for me there?"

"I told you. I have a plan."

"But—"

His hands come down on my arms, and he backs me up and sets me on the edge of the tub. "The only thing I'm going to explain to you while we're both half-naked is how easily I could fuck you until you don't remember your name that you just remembered. And I don't think either of us wants you forgetting anything more than you already have."

His hands fall from my arms, leaving me chilled in their wake, and I try to grab him, to pull him back and force him to talk to me, but he's already exiting the bathroom, leaving me stunned and unsure of what just happened all over again. Holding the blanket around me, I listen to his movement in the bedroom, wishing I knew what to do next. But I don't know what he wants from me. I don't know what I want from him. Actually, maybe I do. I want to be able to trust him and he wants me to trust him. That's why he shoved a gun into my hand at the church. I'm pretty sure he thinks it didn't matter at all. But it did. I just can't be a fool and pretend that couldn't have been a gamble that went his way. I don't know how to get to a place of true trust until I get my memory back.

I stand up and decide I have to try to talk to Kayden again, though I really don't know what to say. I walk to the open door, pausing in the archway to find him fully dressed and sitting on a chair to put on his boots. He stands at the sight of me, and we stare at each other, the look in his eyes downright chilly. He doesn't speak. I think he's waiting for me to say whatever I came in here to say, and I toss around possible ways to clear the air, discarding every option. I'm pretty sure anything I say will be wrong no matter what.

Finally, he walks toward me, each step a loose-legged swagger, all confident, sexy male, every part of him lean, hot, and, right now, mean. He stops in front of me, towering over me, taller than I think I realized until this tension-laden moment. "You know," he says, his voice a soft taunt, "since you're so against putting clothes on, maybe I should just rip that blanket away and fuck you before you decide I'm him. Or maybe I need to fuck you to make sure you know I'm *not* him." His lips thin. "Or maybe that's exactly what *he* would do and why I need to just walk away." He turns and leaves, crossing to the doorway, and disappears into the hallway. I straighten and consider going after him, but one look at my blanket and I turn toward the bathroom. It's time to put clothes on and keep them on.

⧉⧉⧉

Coloring my hair requires that I let a messy mixture sit on my head for forty minutes, giving me plenty of time to replay every part of my conversation with Kayden. I also have a conversation with myself, in which my good ol' voice of reason returns and I promise myself that it, not my hormones, will dictate my interactions with Kayden. Still, by the time I finish rinsing my hair, I decide Kayden gave me a gun as an offer of trust, which earns him the cautious benefit of the doubt.

Once I'm out of the shower, I bundle myself and my hair up in towels and kneel in front of the sink, opening the cabinet to find my clothes neatly folded, smelling of fabric softener, and nice and dry. With them is my Chanel purse, and a new toothbrush and toothpaste, both in unopened packages.

"He got me a toothbrush and washed my clothes," I whisper, and I can't imagine the man in my flashback being thoughtful enough to do these things. At some point, though, that man in my flashback had to have been good to me or I wouldn't have been shocked when he tied me up. And I am certain that night was the night he'd shown me he was a monster. *Monster.* It's a word I used with Kayden last night, and I don't like what this connection implies.

Shaking myself, I grab the pile of my items, stand up to set them all on the ledge of the giant garden tub, and start to dress. I quickly tug on my jeans, only just now realizing a very slight heaviness in my skull, but it's manageable for sure. I reach for the bra and stare at the label again, willing a memory of buying the fancy garment, but there just isn't one. I put it on, and I'm pleased that even my tennis shoes have been dried. Fully dressed now, I give myself a once-over in the mirror and decide I'm too skinny. I need to eat, but I'm pretty sure, despite decent breasts, I'll never be lucky enough to sport Beyoncé curves. I grimace. *Right.* I know Beyoncé but not my own last name. It's infuriating.

"Ella, Ella, Ella," I murmur, willing my last name to come to me as I squat at the cabinet again and locate the blow-dryer, doing the best that I can with my hair with no styling products, and when I find myself hating the dark brown color, I know the reality here. I don't hate my body or my hair. I hate looking at a stranger in the mirror.

Giving up the struggle with my hair, I locate my purse, surprised at how well it survived the rain. Unzipping it, I set the ruined journal aside and freeze at the sight of the gun, not even sure how it and the journal fit inside in the first place. Wetting my suddenly dry lips, I remove the gun and set it on the counter, recalling the moment Kayden had drawn it and the blow it had been to believe he really was my enemy. I ran from Kayden last night because of Adriel, but if I'm honest with myself, I also ran from my fear that I'd trust him no matter what. A fear I still haven't conquered.

Leaving the gun behind, I snatch up the purse and move back to my spot in front of the mirror, and do a fast job with my makeup. I slide my purse strap over my head, wearing it cross-body, and then I have to face that gun again. Dread fills me at the idea of touching it, and I don't know why. I just had it in my hand, and, impatient with all these weird feelings, I reach for it, only to jerk my hand back and grab the sink as my mind thrusts me into the past. And Lord help me, I am back in *that* room. *His* bedroom. I can see myself from above again. I'm dressed in jeans and a T-shirt, and I'm pacing, tears streaking my cheeks. And then I'm there. I'm in the past, living the hell all over again.

I stop pacing, my hand trembling as I shove my fingers through my long red hair, trying to calm myself, but I know that he'll be back soon. If I'm going to do this, I have to do it now. "I have to do this," I say, and my voice is strong and sure. I turn and stare at a tall mahogany dresser that matches the bed I so hate at my back. My chest expands on a huge breath, and I walk to the dresser and sink to my knees. I dig through lingerie, beautiful, delicate lingerie, and uncover a black box. And I don't let myself think—I open it and display the gun I'm after.

The image fades, and I gasp with the impact of what I just felt, shocked to find I've sunk to my knees, as if I was in front of that dresser all over again. And I'm trembling, like I was that night. I remember that night. What I felt. What I thought I had to do. I shove off the sink and reach for the gun, checking the ammunition chamber to ensure it's loaded, and I do it with the ease of someone familiar with weapons. Someone who would know how to use one to kill if she so chose. Or *needed* to.

I place the gun in my purse and zip it up, folding my arms in front of me, a burn in my chest as I look at the woman in the mirror, and I was right. I don't know her. "What did you do, Ella?" I whisper, and then grab the sink again to yell, "*What* did you *do?*"

eight

I begin to pace the bathroom the way I had *his* bedroom that
night, my hand pressed to my forehead. "I killed someone.
I killed *him*." I stop walking and face the mirror, reprimanding
myself. "Stop saying that. You didn't kill anyone." I look to
the ceiling. But what if I did? My knees go weak, and I sink
to the edge of the tub and press my hand to my belly. It makes
sense that it had to be something this bad for my mind to shut
down as it has.

I bury my face in my hands and think of Gallo and the
fingerprints. My hands drop to the ledge of the tub. How
does Niccolo connect to this? Did he know the man I think
I killed? Is he hunting me for revenge? Or is *he* the man and I
didn't kill him? I just tried? No. I wouldn't be with a gangster.
Unless . . . did I not know who, and what, he was? No. I didn't
kill him. My stomach rolls. I might have killed him. I have to
tell Kayden. Now. Before the truth is exposed and Gallo finds
some way to take Kayden down with me. I push to my feet
and stand there. I don't want to tell him. I have to tell him. I
have to tell him.

Stiffening my spine, I face the door and start walking, and

I don't stop. I exit the bedroom and start down stairs that in daylight I can tell are some sort of frosted glass, the railing stainless steel. Reaching the bottom level, I step across shiny white tiles and enter a living area that feels modern and chic, with light gray furnishings. I step farther into the room, finding no one around, amazed to find a walkway running above my head and the entire length of the room, also made with the etched glass-looking material.

There is another stairwell leading up to that second level, but I choose a door to my left that I'm gambling leads to the kitchen. Once I'm there, I consider knocking, but it's a kitchen, not a bedroom, and Kayden did tell me to come down when I was ready. I push open the door, and, holding it open, I bring another white and gray room into view, with three men gathered at a round, all-white island.

To my left, Nathan, Kayden's doctor friend, sits on a high-backed gray bar stool, his brown hair styled neatly, his blue suit and tie obviously expensive. To my right sits a man who is his polar opposite, with wavy, longish dark brown hair, his features chiseled, the slogan on his obviously worn black T-shirt in Italian. And standing in the center, directly across from me and the only one of the three I truly care about right now, is Kayden.

My eyes meet his, and I feel the connection punch me in the chest. His expression is tight, his eyes hard, and everything that happened between us an hour before is in the air between us now. The kiss. His hand on my breast. Him naked in the shower. But mostly, his anger. "Can I talk to you alone, please, Kayden?"

"Nathan's on a tight schedule," he says. "He wants to check you out before he leaves."

"I'm fine," I insist. "I feel a lot better."

"Not for long if we don't get some additional medicine in you," Nathan assures me. "And I need to evaluate you before I give you additional drugs."

That gets my attention, and I look at Nathan. "The pain is going to come back?"

"Not if we keep you medicated." He pats the stool. "Come sit."

My lips clamp together, and I bite back everything I want to say to Kayden and cross to the island, claiming the seat and giving Kayden my back in the process. "Let me get a few supplies out of my bag," Nathan says, and I nod, glancing at the dark-haired man in the seat across from me.

"*Ciao*," he says, giving me a two-finger wave, surprising me with a fleeting glimpse of a box-shaped tattoo on his wrist, with script up his forearm. "I'm Matteo."

"Hi, Matteo," I greet him, trying to figure out why he and Kayden have matching tattoos. And what do they mean? "Thanks for letting me stay here."

"Always happy to help a pretty woman," he assures me, motioning to Kayden. "And as a bonus, now Kayden owes me a favor."

"You owe me at least ten," Kayden reminds him.

"At least it's not eleven," Matteo rebuts, winking at me, and I like him. Actually, I like Nathan as well, but neither of them feels even remotely familiar the way Kayden does.

"Okay," Nathan says, "I'm ready for you."

I rotate to face Nathan, who's now to my left, which means I'd be eye to eye with Kayden if Nathan wasn't standing between us, us holding up a small light. "I just need to check your pupils." He flips it on and tilts my chin up, giving each eye a check and popping the light into his pocket. "They look good," he says, his hands sliding to his hips under his jacket. "On a scale of one to ten, what was your headache like yesterday versus today?"

"A ten yesterday. A one today."

"Excellent," he says. "Let's get some vitals and I'll give you some more drugs."

"So as long as I take the drugs, I won't relapse?" I ask, as he removes supplies from a leather briefcase.

"Not unless you run through a church parking lot in a thunderstorm," he says, a smile ghosting across his lips.

I lean around him and point at Kayden. "Don't even think about saying anything right now."

Kayden lifts his hands in surrender, his lips curving, a hint of the tension between us slipping away. "I wasn't even considering it."

"Oh hell yeah, he was," Matteo says.

Kayden responds to him in Italian, and they start talking back and forth as Nathan finishes checking my vitals. "You need to learn Italian," Nathan observes.

"Yes," I agree. "I do. Are you American too?"

"Canadian," he corrects. "I came here for a woman and fell in love with the country, and out of love with her."

"Ouch," I say.

"Better to find out sooner than later," he says, returning his supplies to his bag and retrieving a bottle, which he sets on the counter. "Take one now with a full glass of water and then four times a day for five days."

"What are they?" I ask.

"The same anti-inflammatory I gave you by injection before you woke up. I use it often for patients suffering from migraines. You should be feeling pretty darn good by the time you run out. If for any reason it stops working, though, Kayden knows how to reach me. I'll stop by his place to check on you in a few days." He slips his bag on his shoulder. "And now, I am a day late for Valentine's Day and therefore have a date I can't miss."

Valentine's Day. The day for lovers, and I am pretty sure I killed the man Kayden called mine. "Thanks again," I choke out, and then realize I haven't asked about my amnesia, and he hasn't brought it up. "Wait. Sorry, but how common is memory loss with a concussion?"

"Rare to the extent you're experiencing it, but it happens. The important thing to know is that it's not life threatening or debilitating." I grimace at that, and he holds up a finger. "I saw that look. I wasn't dismissing your problem. I was simply trying to ease your mind. And you're already remembering small things. You'll remember the rest."

And I both wish for and dread that day.

His hand comes down on my shoulder, a friendly gesture that is missing all the fire of Kayden's touch. "We'll talk more about this when I stop by to check on you at Kayden's place."

I nod. "Yes. Thank you again, Nathan. I really needed help, and you were there for me."

He smiles. "And now Kayden owes me a favor." He glances at Kayden. "Or ten." He lifts a hand and heads for the door. Matteo says something to Kayden in Italian and takes off after Nathan, and just like that, I'm alone with Kayden.

Desperate to get my confession over with, I rotate and say, "Kayden," only to discover he's already standing in front of me and I've just pressed our legs together. I tilt my chin up to look at him. "I . . . You . . ."

He arches a brow. "I what?"

The words don't want to come out of my mouth. "About what happened upstairs—"

"Matteo is coming right back." He opens the bottle and pops a pill onto his hand, holding it out to me. "You need to take this now before you end up in bed again."

He's right. The last thing I need right now is to turn into a mess like I was last night. I reach for the pill, my hand going to his palm, the touch electric, and his fingers close around mine. My eyes dart to his, and I try to read his still unreadable expression. I wait for him to say whatever he intends to, but he is silent. He just looks at me, his gaze probing, and I realize he's waiting for me to say whatever I wanted to say.

"I know you're not him," I say, my voice hoarse, affected in a way that is all about this man and what I have yet to tell him.

The door opens behind me and Matteo enters, saying something in Italian to Kayden. Kayden responds and then refocuses on me. "Take the pill," he orders.

Frustrated at the interruption, I pop it into my mouth, and then accept the bottle of water and chug several long swallows. Kayden takes the bottle from me and sets it on the table. "You need to hear what Matteo has to say."

"I have to have a conversation with you first."

"It has to wait." He turns to his friend and orders, "Tell her what you found."

I want to shout at him that no, no, it does not have to

wait, but Matteo is quick to demand my attention. "Let's talk about Ella," he says as he reaches under the island and produces a file he sets in front of him.

"You mean let's talk about me," I correct.

"Okay," he says. "Let's talk about you. Only you don't exist. There is no missing 'Ella' that's traveled from the United States, or anywhere else for that matter, in the past year."

"I took your fingerprints when you were asleep," Kayden adds.

I cut him an incredulous look. "You did what?"

"Gallo is going to be at my doorstep looking for you," he says. "I had to know what we were dealing with."

He's right. I know he's right, yet somehow those prints feel more private than the clothes he stripped off me. But I want answers, and I glance between the two men. "You ran them through the database?"

"I did," Matteo confirms. "And there was no match."

"That makes no sense," I argue, convinced he's made a mistake. "I'd have to have prints on file for a passport. How can you even run my prints? Isn't it a government database?"

"The right hacker can get anywhere he or she wants to get," Matteo replies. "You have no prints on file."

My throat thickens. "Try again."

"I always double-check myself," Matteo adds. "You could be an Italian-American who lives here."

"I don't speak the language," I argue.

"You don't *remember* speaking the language," Kayden corrects.

"I don't speak the language," I assure him. "I might not

remember everything but I get strong feelings about things. I
do not speak Italian." I eye Matteo. "Do they fingerprint for
driver's licenses? Wouldn't I be on file here if I lived here?"

"No fingerprints," Kayden replies. "Just a signature."

I look between them. "This is crazy. I *have* to have a passport."

"You might have had one," Matteo responds, "but you
don't now. You might have been erased."

"What does that mean, 'erased'?"

"It means," Kayden explains, "that someone as talented as
Matteo could have been hired to wipe out your records."

"Are you telling me that even if I remember who I am, I
don't exist?"

Kayden holds up his hands. "Back up. We don't know you
were erased. We're just talking through reasons you might
think you have a passport but you don't."

"And if we find out who you are," Matteo adds, "I can re-
create your identity."

I gape at him. "Re-create my identity? Forgive me if that
isn't comforting."

Kayden rotates the bar stool around, his hands coming
down on my arms. "You aren't a stack of documents. No one
can erase who you are."

"They don't have to. I did it for them. My fingerprints
were my link to my past. My way of finding me."

"We both know you can find you, when you're ready."

"I don't have a switch the way you seem to think I do. I
can't just flip it. Why would someone wipe my identity?"

"For all any of us know, *you* had your identity wiped."

My lips part in shock. "Why would I do that?" I ask, but even as the question leaves my mouth, I picture myself opening that box and revealing that gun.

He pushes off the stool, his hands settling on his hips. "You were running when I found you," he reminds me.

"From the Italian mafia," Matteo adds. "That's a good reason to disappear."

"And you colored your hair," Kayden says. "You knew you were on the run before you lost your memory."

Again, I see a flickering image of that box and that gun. "What now?" I ask, rotating to face the table again.

"We keep working on my plan," Kayden says, motioning to Matteo.

Matteo responds by sliding the folder in my direction. "This is your new identity," he announces. "It's what Gallo will find when he pulls your fingerprints."

"New identity," I repeat, tension stiffening my spine. "I don't even know my real identity."

"That's the point," Kayden explains. "If you don't have an identity, Gallo and Niccolo will keep focusing on you. We need you to become someone distinctive that shuts down all interest in you from all directions."

It makes sense. I don't like it, but it makes sense. "Yes. Okay."

Kayden jumps on my acceptance, already moving ahead. "A few important details. Since you're sure your name is Ella—"

"It *is* Ella," I say, jumping on his hint of doubt. "My name is Ella."

"Then we can be certain that anyone looking for you will be searching by the name Ella," Matteo interjects.

"So no more Ella," I say, knowing there is no other way. Not with a mobster after me.

"Yes and no," Kayden confirms while Matteo announces, "Your new legal name is Rae Eleana Ward."

Kayden's hand comes down on my shoulder, and I look up at him as he adds, "We went with Eleana so you could use Ella as a nickname. It's a bit of a stretch to turn your middle name into a nickname, but it's still doable."

"Thank you," I whisper, my throat thick with emotion, and I'm pretty sure I just lost all objectivity with this man, who seems to have understood my need even before I did.

His eyes soften, and I watch what's left of his anger evaporate. "The hospital staff said you need stability and the familiar. Right now, that's me and your name."

My brow furrows. Is he trying to tell me I did know him before that alleyway?

He squeezes my shoulder, drawing my gaze to his. "No," he says softly, for my ears only, as if I've spoken my question. "That's not what I'm saying, and right now"—he releases me and taps the folder—"everything you need to know about your new identity is inside this. Study it and know it before you let Gallo trap you, because if you make a mistake, he will catch you."

"And when he says everything," Matteo interjects, "he means everything. I backtracked to make it look like you arrived here from the United States two weeks ago, including flight data. And since a passport allows you to be here for ninety days, no one will question you being here for quite some time."

"Does this mean I'll have an actual passport?" I ask, wondering if I can travel to the States and put distance between me and Niccolo.

"Not yet," Kayden answers. "Gallo believes you were mugged and your identification stolen. Let him run your prints, figure out who you are, and then I'll have to take you to the passport office to have identification issued."

"I have amnesia," I point out. "Won't he want me to contact my family?" And the word *family* punches me in the chest, making me wonder about my real one.

"You have no family," Matteo says, as if reading my mind. "I made sure of it. We don't need anyone looking for your relatives to confirm who you are or aren't and finding out they're fake."

"I understand the premise of your strategy," I say, "but that leaves me alone in a strange country and I can tell you right now, Gallo will use that as an excuse to stick around. He wants dirt on Kayden, and he'll use me to get it."

Kayden responds unfazed. "I'll make it clear to Gallo you're with me. End of subject, and he can kiss my ass."

I don't have time to process how I feel about the non-negotiable tone of his statement before Matteo announces, "Picture time," and starts snapping pictures on a camera he has produced from who knows where.

Glowering at him, I hold up a hand. "Can you at least warn me or something?"

"I did," he says, glancing at his watch and back at me. "And I'll make the shots I just took work. The passport system is about to do its weekly security update in an hour that, ironically, allows an easy breach. Within an hour you'll be Rae Eleana Ward, and no one will be able to say different."

A knot forms in my throat. "I have a love/hate reaction to that news."

"Make it all about love, sweetheart," Kayden encourages, "because no one is going to look for Rae Eleana Ward. And we've made sure the hospital and police report have different dates and don't include my name. Once we're done, you can hide in plain sight, and no one will connect the Jane Doe that was taken to the hospital to you. We're completely disconnecting you from that identity."

"What about the hospital staff?"

Kayden dismisses my concern. "You were registered under an alias. We're covered."

My lips press together. "I'm still worried. What about the men who followed me? Won't they keep asking around?"

"I paid a security officer to let me know if anyone is asking around at the hospital," Kayden replies, apparently having an answer to everything.

"Those men that were following me will know what I look like," I argue.

"They're dead," Kayden announces, not bothering with a preamble.

Stunned, I blanch. "What? How? When?"

"The details don't matter," he states, his words as cold as ice. "They would have killed you if they got the chance."

I give him an incredulous look. "They were human beings that probably died because of me."

"That would infer Niccolo is a human being," he replies, "and I assure you, he is not. Moving on. Your passport will have a picture. We're going to hack in and replace it as soon as it goes live."

"That includes the police report as well," Matteo interjects. "I've set up a notification ping. I'll know the minute anything changes on the police report. Basically, then you'll be a ghost."

Only there is no "then" about it. I was already a ghost before this, wiped from existence, with no connection to a past I fear I'll never remember. No one who cares about me will ever be able to find me, and if they did, they might end up as dead as I fear I will be soon.

nine

My eyes meet Kayden's and his gaze narrows, telling me he's read my reaction to the word *ghost* even before he says, "This is a good thing. You know that, right?"

I am suddenly angry at him, at me, at everything. "Like those men being dead?"

He doesn't react to my attack, his expression hard, his eyes sharp but unreadable. "Yes," he says tightly. "Like those men being dead."

I open my mouth to ask if he killed them, but a flickering memory of me on my knees, staring at that gun, rushes through my mind and shuts me up. Suddenly needing out of this tiny space, I scoot off the bar stool, facing Matteo and in profile to Kayden, my hands flattening on my hips to hide the way they stupidly shake. "Where's the bathroom?"

"There's one off the living room," Matteo offers.

"Thanks," I murmur, already moving to make my escape, but Kayden isn't about to allow it.

He shackles my arm, rotating me to face him, his touch a branding I both welcome and fear. Proof I need space to get my head on straight. "I didn't do this to you," he says, proving he's read my anger, and the blame I didn't even realize I was placing until this moment.

"That's not the answer I want," I say, afraid he's a killer. Afraid I am, too.

"You didn't ask a question."

"You know the question without me asking it."

"Did I kill those men?" he asks.

"Yes. Did you kill those men?"

"They attacked Adriel when he tried to leave the scene of your attack, and he made sure he was the last man standing. So no. I didn't kill them, but I'm also not sorry they're dead. They would have killed any of us in a heartbeat."

It's as good of an answer as I could want, considering people are dead and I'm at the root of the reason. "Can I please go to the bathroom?"

A muscle in his jaw tics, telling me he wants to push me toward acceptance, but he doesn't. He releases me, and I don't give him time to change his mind, darting for the door without daring to look behind me. Entering the living room, I make fast tracks toward the stairwell, intending to head to the bedroom, where I will be free to pace and perhaps indulge in pounding the mattress a few times. I'm already on the bottom step when I think better of being trapped in a room with a bed, with Kayden surely to follow me sooner rather than later.

Detouring, I cross to the second stairwell and boldly climb to the next level of the house. Once I'm at the top, I am beyond pleased to discover a wall of windows, and a door leading to a covered outdoor space. Somehow, watching a storm while one rages inside me is positively perfect. I reach for the gray wood door handle and open it, cringing as a buzzer goes off, alerting Kayden that I'm not in the bathroom. I don't turn back. I need every second I can get to be alone and think, without Kayden distracting me by being an overwhelming presence.

I exit onto the concrete patio that extends the length of the narrow house, the cold, wet air rushing over me, the door slamming behind me. It's shutting me outside, but then, I'm already outside every reality fathomable. Shivering, I fold my arms in front of me and walk to the waist-high concrete wall, rain and a grayish shadow draping a magnificent view of hills and rooftops. Knowing I have only a few minutes alone, I consider the situation. It seems evident that my issue is control, or rather lack thereof. I'm letting Kayden dictate everything that happens to me, and though I could give myself a pass while I was in so much pain that I was incapable of moving, I can't anymore. It's time to make decisions for myself, starting with what happens next.

Behind me the door buzzes, and already the little bit of freedom I have is being taken away. I know now that he allowed my retreat to simply relocate our conversation to a place with privacy. I face him, and while adrenaline radiates through me, the control I so want radiates from him. "I wasn't looking for a way to run, if that's what you think," I declare, backing up as he stalks toward me, tall and broad, his longish hair framing his handsome features set in hard lines.

I hit the wall as he stops a breath away from touching me, and it terrifies me how much I want him to touch me, how much I want a hero, and anger surges in me at my weakness. "If you were afraid I was running again," I lash out, "there was nowhere to go."

"Were you thinking about it?"

"You didn't give me time to think about anything."

"You didn't say you needed to think. You said you wanted to talk to me. So let's go inside where it's warm and talk."

"I like the cold," I declare, darting around him into the open space, and only when I have several safe steps between us do I turn to face him, as he does me.

"You didn't like it last night."

"I like it now," I say. "I like it a lot. It's real, when not much else is."

His eyes glint. "Why do I know that's about me?"

"It's about everything, including you. It's about you feeling familiar when you say you aren't. And me believing I'm Ella, but I'm not in the passport system. Now I'm *Rae Eleana*. She's not real, and yet she's me."

"A name doesn't define you. We talked about this."

"A name is a part of the identity I've lost. Someone just snapped their fingers and I was gone." Laughter bubbles from my lips, bitter, almost hysterical. "It might have been me. How brutal is that, when I'd do anything to have me back right now? So you see, I need the cold. The rain. I need things that are definable. That are real."

His eyes flash, and before I even know he's moved, I'm crushed against his chest, the fingers of one hand tangled in my hair, the other molding me to him. "How's this for real?" he murmurs, his mouth claiming mine, his tongue sweeping past my teeth in a deep stroke I feel in every part of me. A moan escapes my lips, and I both hate him and crave him in this moment. He knows it, too, deepening the kiss, his tongue doing a slow, seductive dance against mine. I want to fight. I want to push him away, and the more I can't, the angrier I become. He just keeps making me angry. Keeps caressing me with his seductive tongue, keeps making me want more. And when he does tear his mouth from mine, he softly declares, "That was real. I'm real. And you are not alone."

"Until I am again. Matteo just set you free."

He leans me against a beam, one hand pressed above my head, his leg nestled between mine. "And you think that means what?"

"I . . . You're out."

"I was in from the minute you opened your eyes and looked at me in that alleyway; I just didn't know it yet. So if you think I'm done with you, sweetheart, you're wrong. I've barely gotten started."

Suddenly he *is* my hero, and that means my instincts to trust him were right. It also means I have to trust my instincts about that box and that gun. "I need to go underground. If you can lend me money—"

"No. You stay with me. I'll protect you."

"And who's going to protect you?"

"Sweetheart, I have nine lives and I've only used four." He links our fingers. "Come with me." He starts to move.

I dig in my heels. "No. No. Stop. Please."

He turns back into me, his hands rubbing my arms. "You're shivering. Let's go inside."

He's right. I am. "Not because I'm cold. I can't stay here. There are things—"

"You can and you are. End of subject."

The command in his voice hits a nerve in some deep, dark

part of me, and I do not like it. "Are you protecting me or keeping me prisoner?"

His eyes narrow, yellow flecks of heat in their depths. "I'm not the man who hurt you. I'm the one who's fucking keeping you alive, and I can't do that if you aren't with me."

"You don't understand."

"'*Please* don't be him,'" he says, quoting me again. "I understand fine. You can't get past the fear that I'm him. I'm not him."

I grab handfuls of his shirt. "I know you're not him," I hiss. "That's what I've been trying to tell you and you wouldn't listen." I drop his shirt and try to scoot away again.

He's still not having it, his hands bracing my hips, his legs shackling mine. "Who is he?" he says, his tone hard.

"I still don't remember."

"Yet you suddenly know he's not me."

"I never thought he was you."

"Bullshit."

Adrenaline is buzzing through me at this point, and I don't even try to contain my anger. "Bullshit yourself, Kayden. You still aren't listening. You're attacking. So hear this. I have to leave. In case you still don't get it: I *have* to leave."

His fingers close around my wrists, grounding me in a way I don't understand, his tone a soft caress that is still stronger than I feel, as he promises, "I'm listening now. Talk to me."

His voice is silk, his eyes warm, and the contrast in this gentleness and the wolf that would kill for me undoes me. My eyes and chest start to burn and I lower my head to his shoulder. He releases my hands, his settling on my hair. "Whatever it is, you can tell me."

"It's bad," I whisper.

His hands come down on my head and he lifts it, forcing my eyes to his. "I'm no angel, just like I'm no hero."

"And yet you're trying to save me."

"No 'trying' about it. I am going to save you." His thumb strokes my cheek. *Tell me.*"

"I think I killed him. At the very least, I tried."

To his credit, he doesn't so much as blink. "The man in your flashback?"

"Yes. The man in my flashback. I had a gun, Kayden."

He takes my hand, his bigger one swallowing mine, and starts for the door, and this time I don't try to stop him. My head is spinning, and not from the pain. Because somehow speaking my fears makes them more real. I might have killed someone and I can't breathe with the idea. I try and I just can't get air into my lungs, let alone process where Kayden is leading me. I blink and we are inside a small, round room wrapped in floor-to-ceiling bookshelves, and I don't even remember how we got here.

Kayden sits me in one of two gray leather chairs, kneeling in front of me. "Easy, sweetheart," he says, his hands settling on my legs. "We'll deal with this. Tell me what you know."

I finally draw in a deep breath and let it trickle from my lips. "I was in his room and I knew he was about to return. I was pacing and giving myself a pep talk that ended in me walking to a dresser and opening a drawer. Inside was a gun."

"And then what?"

"I meant to hurt him." My words are confident, strong—the way I wish I were about everything, not just murder.

"But you don't know that you did?"

"Yes. No. *Yes.*"

He arches a brow. "Okay. Let's move to something cut and dry. Do you remember what he looks like?"

"No."

"What did you do with the gun?"

"I just remember looking at it and knowing I had to use it."

"Nothing else? You're sure?"

"That's it."

"We don't know that you even tried to kill him."

"I know what I feel."

"You also keep saying I'm familiar beyond what is the truth."

"No one else I've met feels like you do to me."

"Case in point," he says. "Your mind is sending you messages you aren't always reading right. You can't jump to conclusions until you fully recover your memory."

"What if it was Niccolo?"

"He's alive."

"What if I tried to kill him?"

He reaches in his pocket and pulls out his phone, punches a couple of buttons, and then offers it to me. "Niccolo."

I close my hand over his and take the phone, staring down at the image of a man in his thirties with curly dark hair and dark eyes, dressed in an expensive fitted suit. And I wait for the familiar feeling to follow, but it doesn't.

"Anything?" Kayden asks.

I shake my head and look up at him. "No, but you just said my memory is not working right. Maybe it's not. I mean, Niccolo *is* hunting me."

"I'm not convinced it's because you tried to kill him."

"Then why would he be chasing me?" I ask.

"That's what we need to find out."

"What if 'he' was someone close to Niccolo?"

"We'll go through pictures of everyone close to him once we're at my place."

"Go home with you?" I say. "Are you crazy? You have to see that I can't do that now. I have to go underground."

"Gallo won't leave this alone if you do. He'll chase you down and document it all."

"I can call him. I'll convince him I'm fine."

"He won't settle for a phone call that could be coerced. Even seeing you in person, he's going to check every piece of your puzzle. You need to hide in plain sight, exactly where no one will expect Ella to be. And you do it with me."

"Adriel could have died instead of those men. Anyone around me is in danger."

"They have to find you first, and obviously I don't believe that's going to happen." He stands and takes me with him. "Let's give Matteo his house back and go to mine."

"You're sure I shouldn't go underground?"

"I never say anything I'm not sure of." He reaches down and laces his fingers with mine and starts walking toward the door, and I let him for one reason and one reason only: if he's wrong, we're both dead. I can't think of any agenda he could have that makes that work for him.

∞

An hour later, Kayden and I are in the Rolls-Royce again, and he pulls us out of the garage, into a downpour. "I can't believe it's still raining like this," I say, watching the splatter hit the front window over and over.

"Be glad it is," he says, cutting onto a narrow road I assume leads to one that's more drivable. "Because I promise you, the weather made the search for you a little less aggressive and bought us some time." He motions to the file. "Test time. Full name?"

"Rae Eleana Ward," I answer as he turns onto yet another narrow road.

"Birthday?"

"July 20, 1988," I answer, and suck in a breath as he maneuvers the car around a corner and onto a path so narrow I am certain we're going to crash. "Holy crap," I say, grabbing the door handle. "Are all the streets this narrow?"

"Most of them, yes." He cuts me a sideways look. "Makes you appreciate my motorcycle a little more now, doesn't it?"

"I'd rather walk, thank you."

"Motorcycles are fast and efficient. You'll get used to riding them."

"No," I say, a thought hitting me. "I can't get used to anything. My passport is only good for ninety days."

"I have a plan," he says. "I always have a plan."

"Matteo?"

"Yes. Matteo."

We take another crazy narrow turn and I cover my eyes. "Yep. Walking for me."

"Walking's certainly popular here. In fact, you can't drive in certain neighborhoods, this one included, unless you live in the area and have approved plates."

"What neighborhood is this?"

"It's called Trastevere, and thanks to several American colleges in the area, it has a large population of English speakers."

"I'm relieved to know I'm not such an outsider here. Do people speak English near your house?"

"It's not as English-friendly as Trastevere, but it's close. And we're here." He cuts into a driveway, and I gape at the towering structure in front of me, two steps barely visible in the midst of the rapidly falling rain.

"Kayden. It's a castle."

"This area is largely medieval, but yes. It's a castle, and it has one of the few garages in the neighborhood." He hits a button and a door begins to rise.

"I can't imagine living in a castle," I say. "Is it remodeled like Matteo's place?"

He makes a disgusted sound and pulls out of the storm to drive down a ramp. "I wouldn't destroy history the way Matteo has in a place that was once a work of art. I've done some restoration work, but made an effort to keep the original architecture in place."

"How long have you lived here?" I ask. The garage is big enough to hold a mini car lot inside, and from what I can tell from the rows of sport vehicles and motorcycles, it does. He hits the button to seal us inside and kills the engine. "I inherited the castle five years ago."

Inherited. The meaning of that word is unmistakable. Someone died, and some part of me aches with a hurt that runs deeper than the moment. I cut him a look to find him resting his wrist on the steering wheel, staring ahead. "Are you alone, like me?"

"Not like you," he says, still not looking at me, his body rigid, like his voice. "No one I've lost is coming back."

My gut twists into knots, and I look away, wondering about the family I may have lost. No. I *have* lost. "Mine are gone, too," I say, my voice cracking with the admission.

"You don't know that," he says, and our heads turn at the same time, gazes colliding.

"I do. I just wish I had their memories to hold onto."

"Memories are the enemies that never die," he says, turning away and shoving open his door, leaving me with the pain carved in those words that I am fairly certain he didn't want me to hear. But I did, and they speak to me, diving deep in my soul with the blood of my own loss, and taking root. I say I want my memories back, but I'm not so sure I really do. It's an idea I reject as I shove open my door and stand.

Kayden is already at my side of the car, and I face him, the door between us. "If the memories die, so does everyone we loved. That might be okay with you, but it's not to me."

His jaw tics, but he offers me no agreement or disagreement, a wall firmly placed in between us as he says, "Let's go inside."

I step around the door, letting him shut it, my gaze scanning the four motorcycles to my right, and beyond them three cars with Jaguar logos. "Do you have a thing for Jaguars, or just cars in general?"

"Just the Jaguar F-TYPE, but I won't turn down anything else that catches my eye."

My attention shifts to a sleek, shiny blue sports car directly in front of the Rolls-Royce. And I walk toward it, stopping by the passenger's door to examine the curve of the hood. Kayden steps to my side and I glance up at him. "How rich are you?"

"I inherited a substantial amount of money and I have my own."

"Translation. You're so crazy rich it's almost dirty."

He laughs, his eyes flashing with wicked heat. "I like everything a little dirty."

I blush, having no doubt that's true, and refocus on the fancy vehicle in front of us. "This isn't a Jag, right? It's a race car?"

"It's a Pagani Zonda, and yes, it's designed for the racetrack. They only make twenty to twenty-five a year."

"Do I even want to know how much something like this costs?"

"A million dollars, give or take, but in my case, it was a gift for a job well done."

I whirl around to face him. "What do you do to earn a car like this?"

"The client wanted to pay me in cash but I wanted the car. That was my price to do the job."

I do not miss the way he's dodged my direct question and I try again. "Price for what, Kayden? What do you do?"

"I work for a group called The Underground. We call ourselves Treasure Hunters. If the price is right, and in this case the car was the right price, we find just about anything for our clients."

I remember the tattoo on Matteo's arm that matches Kayden's. "Does Matteo work for them, too?"

"Yes."

"What about Nathan?"

"No."

I dare to reach for his arm and study his tattoos, confirming that the one on his wrist is a square with a king chess piece inside. I glance up at him. "Matteo has this too."

"Everyone in the Italian division of The Underground has it."

My thumb caresses the script up his forearm. "And the writing." I glance up at him. "What does it say?"

"It's an Italian proverb. *Once the game is over, the king and the pawn go back in the same box.*"

I close my hand over the words, and it is as if they burn my palm. "In death we're all equal."

Surprise flickers in his eyes at my understanding of the meaning, but he's no more surprised than I am. "Yes," he confirms softly. "In death we are all equal."

"Why that proverb?"

"It's a reminder to us that no one, no matter how powerful, is better than The Underground."

I reach for his other arm, and trace the image of a bird with bright blue extended wings etched across his wrist. "A hawk?"

"Right again."

"Why a hawk, Kayden?" I ask, wanting, needing, to understand this man.

"It's symbolic of me being a protector. I'm the leader of this division of The Underground, thus the protector of those reporting to me."

"Like you're protecting me."

His eyes burn through me, and there is a swell of response in me that borders on longing. "Yes," he agrees, a velvety quality to his voice. "Like I'm protecting you."

I am seduced by this man, easily able to forget the questions in my mind, but I do not allow myself more oblivion to add to what is in my mind. "What kinds of things does The Underground find?"

"Whatever the client wants. It could be a car. A painting. A computer file, in Matteo's case."

"Do you break the law?"

There is a slight clench to his jaw, but his reply is instant. "Everything we do is not simple."

The absence of denial is confirmation, and I'm not sure how I feel about that. "What did you find for the man who gave you the car?"

"His ex-wife, who ran off with his money."

My throat thickens. "You found a person?"

"Yes," he confirms, his expression unreadable. "I found a person." Kayden covers my hand where it rests on his arm. "Just like I found you so no one else could. And no one else will. No amount of money will change that."

I think of the car. "A million dollars is a lot of money."

"I already have a lot of money."

"What about the other members of The Underground?"

"The only ones who know about you are my inner circle; they won't betray us. Besides, it would take a lot more than a million dollars to get the attention of any one of them."

"What if it's a lot more?"

"You're safe. You have my word." He releases me abruptly and steps back, and I can almost feel that wall slam between us again. "Let's go inside."

I frown, not sure what just happened, but then, this is my life, and what's new? I want to ask, but one look at the steely set of his jaw and I decide better. I'll figure him out inside. I walk toward the door, curious about his home, about *him*, this man who is my reluctant hero. I'm aware of him following me, and once I am at my destination, he is there too. My hand closes on the knob, but before I can turn it, he reaches around me, his hand covering mine, his warmth stealing the slight chill of the garage. "When I said you were safe," he says softly, a hint of wickedness in his voice, "I meant from everyone but me."

And somehow I know he's testing me, asking for my trust when, for whatever reason, he doesn't believe he deserves it. He doesn't know what I know. Right, wrong, or dangerous, I already trust him. He steps back from me, and I don't look back. I open the door and enter a corridor where a winding stone stairwell awaits me and start up the path that leads to both the king's and the wolf's domain. And with nothing but the clothes on my back and the purse he bought me, I am truly at his mercy.

ten

A wave of nerves settles deep in my belly and radiates lower and lower with each concrete step, and I really have no clue why. Oh yeah. I have a wolf at my back. A really sexy, rather cranky wolf, who I'm apparently about to be living with. In other words, he *really does* have me at his mercy, as he's unapologetically made clear. So why am I not afraid of him? Nervous, yes. Afraid? No. Kayden does not scare me, and unlike last night, when I ran, I don't seem to fear my lack of fear anymore. In fact, as I reach the top of the stairs and a huge dungeon-style dark wooden door greets me, my nerves are quickly replaced with the excitement of seeing the castle.

I quickly thumb down the door lever and shove it open, entering into a foyer with yet more stone beneath my feet, and I discover a giant winding staircase on the opposite side of the stunning room. In awe, I happily give Kayden space to enter behind me and cross to the center of the room, seeing towering dungeon doors to my left and right. Turning in a circle, I admire the intricate trim work around the walls with what appear to be handcrafted roses. There is a flicker of a memory in my mind that I reach for, though I do not believe it's about this place, but another. *He sent me roses. Dozens of roses.* I frown, not sure where the words came from, but nothing else follows, and I let it go to look up and inspect the conical ceiling, with more of the same design dissecting it into quarters.

Kayden joins me, stopping in front of me, his eyes half veiled, his energy dark, his expression all hard lines and shadows. "It's gorgeous," I say, when he doesn't speak. "How big is it?"

"There are three towers in total. The central tower behind us is about eight thousand square feet. The east and west towers, divided by this room, are both around six. Adriel, his sister, and the housekeeper live in the east. You'll be staying with me in the west."

I'll be staying with him. This pleases me, though I suspect he simply wants to ensure I don't lead him on another race through the rain and frigid temperatures.

"This way," he says, motioning toward one of the dungeon doors.

I nod and follow him, watching as he keys in a code and then hits a button, and the massive wooden door begins to lift. "The door is code protected," he tells me, "with an alarm if it's breached. I change the code once a week, and each wing has its own code. Right now, ours is one-nine-eight-nine."

"One-nine-eight-nine," I repeat. "Got it. Is the central tower empty?"

"Adriel runs a high-end collectibles store out of it."

"High-end collectibles?" I ask as we enter yet another foyer, with an archway directly in front of us that appears to lead to some sort of sitting room. "What do you mean by 'high-end'?"

"Anything and everything, all high-dollar items, many of which are museum-worthy."

"That can't be as profitable as treasure hunting."

"Yeah, well, his father was killed on a hunt two years ago when his sister was sixteen. She blames The Underground."

We reach the next level and enter another foyer, and before he can continue forward, I grab his arm and stop walking. "He died because of a hunt?"

"Yes."

"So what you do is dangerous."

"We each choose the jobs we take, and accept the danger that comes along with them. Generally the higher the payday, the greater the risk."

"And Adriel's father, what was he after?"

"A file that proved a certain pharmaceutical company had faked the results to clinical studies to get FDA approval. Which I damn sure found and turned the payday into a trust for Giada. She gets it at twenty-five."

"How much was it?"

"Ten million."

I gape at the astounding figure he mentions so nonchalantly. "You gave her ten million dollars?"

"Yes." Tightness forms around his mouth. "I gave her ten million dollars, but all that money doesn't bring their father back, and it damn sure didn't stop the pain." There is a hint of rasp to his voice, and he cuts his gaze to indicate the room beneath the arch and the end of the topic. "You have to enter the living area to get to the kitchen. It's well stocked, and Marabella, the housekeeper, picks up anything I need. She'll do the same for you. She has a whiteboard on the counter to leave a note." He points to the walkway forking left and right of the arch. "You're left. I'm right." He starts walking left.

I fall into step with him and enter a chilly corridor with high ceilings. We pass what looks like a library, and he motions to a set of stairs. "There's a full gym on the next level if you want to work out. And this," he says as we reach the door at the end of our path, "is your room."

This is your room. The words echo in my head, and again, I have a memory of another time and place. He opens the door, and I enter ahead of Kayden to find myself in a much warmer room that is truly made for fairy tales. The spectacular bed is the centerpiece, thick, high posts of mahogany towering ridiculously high and draped with sheers. A white wooden fireplace is alight and sits to the left of the bed and directly in front of me, with a comfy-looking brown leather chair next to it.

"Marabella turned on the fireplace for you," Kayden says, crossing the room to stand beside it. "It's gas, one of the modernizations I made to the place a few years back, to offset how cold the castle can get." He reaches for a switch and turns the fire off and then on. "Easy and effective."

"Great. Thank you. It's a wonderful room." But I'm really thinking about him. Me. And that bed.

He motions to a rectangular, narrow, floor-to-ceiling window in the corner. "It doesn't open or offer much light." Next, he indicates the flat-screen TV on the wall above a heavy wooden dresser. "The remote's in the dresser drawer, and there's a mini-fridge on this side of the bed stocked with drinks and snacks." He advances on me again, and while the man in my flashbacks moves with grace, Kayden is all loose-legged, rebellious swagger. And I like it. I like it a lot. "We can go shopping for anything you need once the rain dies down," he adds, stopping in front of me. "In the meantime, Marabella took the liberty of picking up a few things that you'll find in the closet."

"She didn't have to do that. You didn't have to do that. Thank you, Kayden." I lift my hand to touch him, and catch myself, folding my arms in front of me instead. Awareness flickers in his eyes, and I know he knows what I almost did and still want to do.

We stand there, a weighted silence ticking between us that has nothing to do with my words, and everything to do with the bed sitting behind him. He steps closer, but doesn't touch me, his gaze drifting to my mouth and back up. "You have no idea how much I want to strip you naked and throw you on that bed. But you were right about memories. They keep the past we don't want to forget alive, and they remind me of all the reasons I'm bad for you. And why I need to walk out of this room before I don't give a damn anymore."

And to my utter shock, that's exactly what he does. He steps around me and starts walking. I turn in time to watch him disappear into the hallway, the door shutting behind him. Shutting me inside. I'm not sure how long I stand there staring at the space where he was moments before, willing him to return, the way I did in the bathroom when we played out a scene almost like this one. But he doesn't return, and I finally turn to look around the room that is the closest thing to home I have. A memory surfaces, transporting me to another room. Another house. And *that* man.

He opens the huge double doors at the top of the stairs and motions me forward. I step into the glamorous room with heavy pale wooden furnishings and a floral love seat in the corner beside a window. It's amazing, and so unlike anything I have back home. I turn and face him.

"It pleases you?" he asks.

"Of course it pleases me. Thank you for letting me stay with you. I'll go to the passport office tomorrow and try to figure out how to get home."

"Don't rush on my behalf. In fact, I think I might benefit from having an angel such as yourself in the house. It will keep the devil in me in check." His eyes sweep my body and lift. "Or perhaps not." He turns and walks to the door, pausing without turning. "You should lock your door."

I smile as he exits, quite certain I will not be locking the door. In fact, I might just leave it open.

I blink back to the present, and I don't even have to ask how I ended up leaving that guest room for his. I probably did open the damn door. I rotate and face the one to this room, and while I do not feel any fear or need to lock myself inside, I hadn't then either, and this version of me does not wish to be as stupid as the one of the past. I rush toward it to turn the lock, but there isn't one. I rotate again and lean on the hard surface, irritated at the doubt rolling through my mind. That man is not Kayden, and I don't need a lock. I was naked in a bed with him and he didn't take advantage of me.

My stomach interrupts my one-on-one chat with myself with a groan of demand. I push off the door and round the bed to note the time from the clock by the bed—five o'clock—unable to remember the last time I ate. I find the fridge Kayden mentioned and go to my knees in front of it, discovering it to be quite well-stocked as promised. I grab a mini chocolate milk and an apple, and sit Indian-style to begin eating, but I'm only a few bites in when my mind flickers with the image of me tied to that damn bed.

I down the milk and put the rest of the apple back in the fridge before standing and removing my purse to set it on the marble-topped nightstand. That's when I spot the pink leather journal lying in the center of the bed, along with a pen. The bed is so high I have to go up on my toes to climb on top, and once I'm there I grab the journal and pen. Settling on my back, I open the first page, and to my surprise there's writing:

You will remember. That's an order.

-Kayden

I laugh, as I am certain is intended, surprised he has managed such a feat when he's not even here. Shutting the journal, I hug it to me, staring at the ceiling the way I did when I woke up in that hospital and rolled over to stare into his pale blue eyes. *Beautiful* eyes. And my eyes drift shut, my lips curved. I drift into a state of half awake and half asleep, but my mind will not allow me this brief time of peace, and I am no longer smiling. I am transported back to *his* room, naked and tied to the bed.

Two hours I have been like this. My hands over my head, knotted together. Cold. Angry. Scared. I am being punished for going shopping when he told me to stay home. I thought he was a Prince Charming, my Prince Charming, a man I could fall in love with. But no Prince Charming does this to a person. I just want off this bed and to go home. I should have gone weeks ago to replace my sto-

len passport. *Why didn't I replace my passport? Oh yeah. I was living a fantasy. A rich, sexy, and powerful man consumed me until I couldn't process anything else. That's time number two I've been foolish over a man. I just have to go to the passport office tomorrow and get a new one. I want to call Sara, but she'll worry and try to rescue me, and she can't. Not from San Francisco. All I will do is cause her to stress. I'll call her when I'm headed home.*

Abruptly, the doors open, and I jerk my head upward to find him standing in the doorway, tall and broad, his suit so damn expensive and perfect, like he once was to me, but not now. Not ever again. He walks toward me, personifying male elegance and grace, but radiating pure predator. Funny how that appealed to me before, even made him sexy, but all it does on this night is convince me I'm his prey, not his "angel," as he calls me.

He stops at the end of the bed, shrugging out of his jacket before walking to a chair, where he neatly folds it and lays it down. Precise. Always precise. And controlled. Everything is about control with him. Everything. He stands with his back to me, but I can see him loosening his tie, taking his time to fold it as well. Each second creeps by like years, building the anticipation, the anger. The fear. He continues with this process until he is naked, and then he walks to the chest against the wall, where he removes his watch, carefully laying it inside what I know to be a velvet-lined drawer.

Finally, he faces the bed, closing in on me, his body as perfect as his suit, his cock jutted forward. I look away, refusing to be seduced by a man who is obviously a chameleon who has only now shown his true colors. My gaze might have left the man, but it lands on the statue of a tiger in the corner, so a part of him. He says it's about power, control, and a willingness to do anything to defeat his enemies. I was wrong. He's no chameleon. He's a pure predator.

The bed shifts and his hands come down on my knees, and before I realize what is happening, he's pressing them to my chest. His fingers dig into my legs and he moves closer, leaning over me. And damn it, I am looking at him when I swore I would not. "You're angry," he says.

"Two hours," I say. "Two hours you left me here."

"I told you not to leave the house."

"You don't own me. You can't tell me—"

"I can and I will. And I left you here to make sure you think twice the next time you disobey me. A painless punishment, considering how disobeying me might have ended. I am a powerful man, angel. You know this. My enemies will lash out at anyone I care for. And that's you. So if I tell you to fucking stay in the house, I fucking mean it. Understand?"

His demand is guttural, the rasp in his tone telling me he truly feared for me. "Yes," I say, realizing now that I really was in danger today, because he isn't the only one who will do anything to win in life. So will his enemies.

He stares at me for several seconds, assessing my reply, weighing it before his voice softens. "Good girl." He lowers my legs and slides between them. "There is always a price for power, but losing you will not be mine. I protect what is mine." He leans into me, his cheek pressed to mine, his lips at my ear, to add, "And you are mine."

I jerk to a sitting position and look down to discover the journal still clasped to my chest. Scanning the bed, I locate the pen and open the journal, trying to document everything I just remembered, along with the stupid certainty that I forgave him that night. I search my mind, looking for more details, trying to see his face, or identify a clue that tells me he's

Niccolo. Five pages later, I've discovered nothing new about myself or *him*.

Frustrated at how unsuccessful this journal-writing session has been, I set the pen and journal on the nightstand, the throbbing in my scalp warning of an imminent headache. Scooting off the bed, I reach for my purse on the nightstand. I dig out my bottle of medicine and snatch another chocolate milk, downing a pill with it, and then finish off my apple. Taking my purse with me, I head to the bathroom, discovering a room of pale blue and white the size of a small bedroom and, to my delight, a massive claw-foot tub in the corner.

Walking to the tiled white counter of the double-sinked vanity, I admire the matching wooden cabinets with cute blue knobs, and I can't help but wonder what Kayden's room looks like. Dark and moody, like the man, I suspect. After setting my purse on the counter, I walk to the tub, pleased to find a small bag of toiletries on the ledge that includes razors, bubbles, and body wash. I turn the faucet and pour some of the bubbles beneath the spray of the water, the scent of sweet honeysuckle flaring in my nostrils. I ignore the razor, since I appear to be waxed, and considering how fast and horrific my first dye job was, I doubt that was to hide my hair color.

Searching for something to wear, I walk into the closet, a light automatically flickering to life to illuminate a room half the size of the giant bathroom. Clothes intended for me, I assume, hang to the left, while the right is lined with built-in drawers and shelves. A cushioned stool claims the middle, as does a variety of bags from various stores. Lots of bags, and guilt hits me hard. Kayden not only paid my hospital bills, now he's giving me a place to live and replacing all the things a woman has when she doesn't have a past. Maybe I can help in the store, or with his hunts, to do something to pay him back.

I squat down and begin digging through the bags, and guilt aside, I'm downright giddy to find a curling iron, a blow-dryer, and a flatiron, along with all kinds of makeup and products. There is also a bag of lingerie from a store called La Perla. I frown, almost certain that's the name on the label of the bra I'm already wearing. I tear away my T-shirt and remove my bra to discover I'm right. It's the same brand. I'm not sure what to make of the coincidence.

Still trying to conjure my memories, ready to evoke some magic I don't possess, I undress and select a black bra-and-panty set, a black Chanel T-shirt, and a pair of Chanel black jeans that fit surprisingly well, after several other items have failed to work out. Then I undress, pile my hair on top of my head, dig my phone from my purse, slide into the wonderful, warm bubbles of my bath, and Google *La Perla*. Aside from admiring the lingerie on their site, I find nothing seems familiar.

Frowning, I decide I need to go by the store to jar my memory and search for a location, only to discover there are stores across the world, including several in the US, including Las Vegas, New York, and San Francisco. *San Francisco.* I sit up, a memory from the dream coming back to me. Sara lives in San Francisco, which means I must, too. I reach for a towel and drop the phone. In the water. *No!* I fish it out, and have to wipe bubbles away to even see the screen and discover it's dead. Of course it is. I just gave it a bath. I grab the towel and start drying it off, when a loud pounding starts on the bedroom door. I search for another towel and can't find one, and there is more knocking, telling me something is wrong.

I set the phone on a silver tray but still have to contend with a sheet of bubbles on my skin that will leave a trail on my way to the door, brushing enough off to finally secure the towel at my chest. Grabbing the edge of the tub, I step to the small light blue rug, securing a footing at the same moment I hear the bedroom door open, followed by Kayden's voice. "Ella!"

"In here!" I call out, rushing to the door and reaching it at the same instant Kayden appears in front of me. He grabs my arms and pulls me to him, but not before my towel falls to my feet. "Why didn't you answer the door?"

"Kayden, my towel—"

"You have a damn concussion," he continues, his tone a hard reprimand. "Marabella couldn't get you to answer and she came to me, afraid for you."

It seems more like *he* was afraid for me. "I'm okay. I'm sorry. I was in the tub and—"

"I called your phone. Keep it with you."

"I dropped it in the tub."

He downright glares at me and gives a guttural "Fuck" as his response.

"Sorry," I say.

"I don't give a damn about the phone," he says, and while his gaze does not leave my face, I know from the darkening of his eyes and the straightening of his spine that he's fully aware of my state of undress, proven by how quickly he sets me away from him. "Marabella made dinner. She wants to impress you."

I grab the towel and hold it in front of me. "I'll be right there."

I've barely spoken the words and he's gone, exiting the bathroom, and he seems unaffected by me being naked. I stand there, questioning the attraction and connection I thought we shared that I can't shut out, while he doesn't seem to suffer the same affliction. But then, according to the "me" in my flash-backs, I'm pretty bad at judging men. In fact, I'd say it's a good bet that's what got me in this boat in the first place. The last thing I should want is a man, or a relationship, and yet I do want Kayden.

Several beats pass, and I realize I haven't moved, but nei-ther have I heard the door open and shut. Tentatively, I walk to the archway separating the two rooms to find Kayden still here, standing at the door, his back to me, his hand on the knob, his head on the wooden surface. I inhale and don't dare breathe, counting out several more beats before he curses and leaves the room. I lean on the doorjamb, a heavy breath es-caping my lips. He wasn't unaffected, and I am reminded of his earlier declaration about memories. *They keep the past we don't want to forget alive, and they remind me of all the reasons I'm bad for you.* A monster lurks in his past, and I wonder what torments a man as strong and dominant as Kayden Wilkens, and why do I know I'm a trigger that gives it life? I push off the wall and hurry to get dressed, determined to find out why, and ready to meet the real man behind those seductive blue eyes.

eleven

Fifteen minutes later, I'm dressed in the black jeans and tee I picked out earlier, and have paired the outfit with a pair of fur-lined lace-up boots. Opting to leave my purse behind, I exit the bathroom and head for the door, pausing long enough to stuff the phone I attacked with bubbles into my pocket. I reach for the doorknob and just happen to glance down, my gaze catching on a latch of some sort. Frowning, I squat beside it and slide it from the wall to the door. I smile, a full-blown, happy smile. The door locks. I have no idea why this pleases me so, but it really, really does.

I'm lighter on my feet as I head into the hallway, admiring the lantern-style lights along the path I missed on the first walk. I pass two closed doors, wondering if the rooms beyond them are in use, planning on a little exploration of the place later, if Kayden doesn't mind. I reach the spot where the hall unites with the archway to the living area, and I step inside the opening, the ceiling transitioning from high and flat to high and conical. The room is large, with modern brown leather furnishings that marry with the medieval architecture with unexpected elegance.

My nostrils flare with a spicy, wonderful scent, drawing my attention to yet another archway. I walk in that direction, passing a small desk on the way, and pausing as I reach the entrance of a kitchen. It's rectangular, with stunning gray cabinetry and a granite island to my right that stretches for several feet, under a stainless-steel hood. But décor and castles aren't what's on my mind. It's Kayden, standing to my left, his back to me, while he seems to stare into the darkness beyond a floor-to-ceiling window. Tension ripples off him; his broad shoulders are bunched beneath the navy T-shirt he now wears, and I'm certain that he's at war with his memories, which he's declared his enemy.

"You must be Ella!"

My gaze reluctantly leaves Kayden and lands on a fifty-something dark-haired woman, who rushes toward me. "*Ciao*, sweetie. I'm Marabella. So nice to meet you." She hugs me, her presence inviting and warm, while I sense Kayden's attention is hot and heavy.

"*Ciao*," I say, as she releases me. "Nice to meet you."

"I hear you have amnesia," she announces, "and you need stability and my good food to heal."

I laugh. "Yes. I do believe that's what the doctor ordered."

She gives me a critical inspection. "Good thing, too. You're too skinny." She eyes Kayden. "Have you been starving her?"

"Who's starving who is debatable," he answers dryly, his eyes landing on me for several beats before he lifts the cup of coffee in his hand toward Marabella. "So far this is all you've fed me."

The comment is directed at Marabella, but my stomach

flip-flops with the certainty he's talking to me, though she doesn't notice. Instead, her eyes light and fall on me, as if he's just made a suggestion she finds perfect. "Would you like a cappuccino?"

"Yes, actually," I say. "That would be delightful."

That light in her eyes brightens and she disappears around the island again, leaving me with the full impact of Kayden's attention, a thick, heavy blanket that is both inviting and suffocating at the same time. I don't know what this man does to me, but it's undeniably intense. Inhaling, I face him, my eyes meet his, and the air charges, the possibilities between us a live wire that both entices and confuses me.

I walk to the table, stopping directly in front of him, my hands resting on the back of a leather chair. "You said you don't play games."

"I don't."

"I disagree."

He arches a brow, his hands resting on the chair opposite me. "Meaning?"

"Your comment. Your look. Who's denying whom?"

"I'd say it's mutual."

"You implied it was me denying you."

His eyes sharpen, a hint of shadows in their depths, there and gone in an instant. "This is a conversation better had alone," he says, lowering his chin to indicate the file on the table. "You left it in the car," he adds, disapproval etched in his tone.

Our verbal sparring is forgotten, a burn starting in my belly. "I guess I did."

"You do know—"

"Don't say it's important. I know it is. I just . . . becoming Rae Eleana Ward feels like the end of Ella, of me, and I don't want that to happen. Which really is ridiculous since I don't even know who 'me' is." My fingers dig into the leather of the seat. "Obviously that means I don't *want* her back."

He sets his coffee on the table and moves to the high-backed leather seat to my left, and pulls it out. "Come join me."

His voice has softened to a gentle caress that manages to soothe a few of my frazzled nerves and makes me feel just a little less alone. I wet my lips and nod, claiming the seat, and allow him to scoot me forward. I wait to see which of the seven chairs he will choose, relieved as he sits next to me. "Here you go," Marabella announces, setting a cup in front of me, waiting expectantly for me to taste it.

Lifting the cup, I sip the warm beverage, a rich coffee taste exploding in my mouth. "Hmmm," I murmur. "Delicious." I take another sip. "Really delicious."

She tilts her head to study me, snickering as if she is amused by a joke I've missed. "The salads will be out in a minute," she says, glancing at Kayden and speaking to him in Italian before hurrying away.

Frowning, I set my cup down, wondering what amused her so. "Look at me," Kayden says, laughter in his voice, and the very fact that he's gone from moody to amused has me obeying.

My head turns his direction and he grasps my wrist, pulling me close and leaning into me. "What are you doing?" I ask, as he reaches up and strokes my lips with his thumb, sending my heart into a race.

"Wiping the foam off your lip, as instructed by Marabella."

Heat rushes to my cheek. "Please tell me it wasn't a mustache."

"Just a small one."

"How embarrassing."

"The part where I wiped the foam from your lips instead of kissing it away like I wanted to? Or the part where Marabella told me to?"

My eyes go wide. "She told you to kiss me?"

"Yes," he murmurs, his breath a warm fan on my lips where I want his mouth. "She told me to kiss you."

"But you didn't."

"Hmmm. I was afraid I wouldn't stop, and *that* would have been embarrassing." He smiles. "For you and Marabella." He releases me, wicked heat in his stare as he drags the folder in front of him. "Let's see what you remember. Remind me. When's your birthday?"

I blink, stunned by the sudden shift from warm to cold. "You're going to give me whiplash to go with my concussion."

His expression turns somber with his mood. "Yes, well, I don't have a choice but to give you whiplash. Gallo came by here looking for you while we were at Matteo's. He'll be back again, and we need to be ready. So I repeat. When's your birthday?"

"July twentieth."

"What year?"

"Nineteen eighty-eight."

"When did you arrive in Rome?"

"February . . . I'm not sure of the day." I reach for the folder.

He closes his hand down on it. "The first of February," he supplies. "Who are your parents?"

"Parents," I repeat, the word knifing through my heart. "I don't know."

"Carrie and Michael Ward. Killed in a car accident a year ago. You inherited a sizable amount of money from them."

"I don't mean the fictional ones. I mean *my* parents. I think they're dead, but what if they aren't and they're worried about me?"

His hand covers mine where it rests on the table, his touch vibrating through me. I stare at his hand, this man who is my self-appointed protector, and yet there is a wall between us I can't climb. "Then we'll find them," he says, drawing my gaze to his. "You have my word, but your safety has to come first, as I'm sure they would want as well. I *need* you to be ready for Gallo."

There is sincerity in his voice, and when I search his face, I find understanding that reaches beyond his claiming a role as my protector. The kind of understanding that runs deep into a person's soul, carved out in heartache and pain. I reach up and cup his cheek, letting his whiskers rasp my fingertips. "What haven't you told me?"

He curls my hand in his, and he considers me a moment, his expression unreadable. "We are not so unalike," he begins, and I hang on these words, eager for any tidbit about this man I can garner.

"Your salads have arrived," Marabella announces, stealing the moment.

Kayden's expression flashes with what I think is relief, but I cannot be sure. He releases my hand, and I face forward as Marabella sets our plates in front of us. "There's fresh pepper and Parmesan on top," she explains. "Let me know if you want more."

"Thank you, Marabella," Kayden says, and I quickly chime in by adding, "Yes. Thank you. I don't actually remember my last real meal."

"No wonder you're so skinny," she chides. "But I like a challenge. Give me a week and I'll put a few pounds on you."

"Then I won't fit all the clothes Kayden just bought me." My eyes go wide. "Oh, you picked them out, right, Marabella?"

"I did. Did I do well?"

"Very much so. I love everything, especially that bubble bath." The reminder of me naked and without my towel is out before I can stop it.

"It's honeysuckle," she says. "Such a sweet, wonderful scent. There's perfume to go with it, too. Did you find it?"

"Oh, perfume. No, I didn't, but it sounds wonderful. I can't wait to try it."

"You need familiar things, so I'll order you more to make sure you don't run out," she says, and the motherly way she's behaving stirs a funny feeling in my chest. She motions to my food. "Eat, sweetie." She glances between Kayden and me, and frowns. "You both need water. I'll be right back." She hurries away again, and my comment about my bath slides right back into the air, inspiring me to feign interest in my salad, when I'm really imagining the moment I lost my towel and his hands landed on my bare skin.

"Did the phone have as many bubbles on it as you did?" Kayden asks.

I glance at him, pleased to find the tension of minutes before gone, a hint of wicked amusement in his eyes. "I didn't think you'd noticed," I dare, because why not? I've been naked in front of him not once, but twice.

"You know I noticed."

We stare at each other for a moment, my heart racing, and somehow I actually remember the original question. "I think I won that battle of the bubbles," I admit, "but just barely. Speaking of which." I dig the phone from my pocket and set it beside him. "Does it come with bubble coverage?"

He smiles, and it's a stunning smile that I get the impression he doesn't show often enough. At least not to me. "I don't remember taking out bubble coverage," he says, "but it doesn't matter. I'll get you another one tomorrow."

Like he promised to get me another five-thousand-dollar purse. "You're spending way too much money on me, Kayden. I need to pay my own way. Can I help you with one of your hunts or work in the store, or—"

His mood goes from playful to nonnegotiable and hard in a split second. "No. I have money to blow and you need to get well."

"I *am* getting well," I argue, not about to let him shut down the topic as he obviously intends. "But I want to do my part and you don't have to get me another phone. I have no one to call."

For a beat, maybe two, his jaw is set hard, his eyes harder, but then he surprises me. "What if I get separation anxiety and want to call you?"

I laugh, pleased his good humor has returned. "That's what they make teddy bears for."

Now he laughs too, low and sexy, and motions to our plates. "We had better eat before Marabella scolds us."

I pick up my fork, unable to contain the curve of my lips at the exchange. I'm not just attracted to Kayden. I like him. I like Marabella. And with the thrumming of rain on the glass beside us, good food, and good company, I have this sense of being cocooned in warmth and safety. I also know without question it is not a feeling I have often enjoyed in my life, and yet these two virtual strangers have given that to me. It matters to me in a deep way I might not fully understand, but value. And for the next little bit, we finish our salads, while Kayden shares details about the neighborhood, encouraging me to try a bakery nearby and visit the little shops he's described.

Too soon, our plates are removed, and Kayden taps the file. "Time to study. Let's start with, why did you come to Italy?"

"After my parents passed away, I resigned my secretarial position in Dallas, Texas, at Reynolds Electronics to travel. What if Gallo looks up the company? Does it exist?"

"Yes. They're a major corporation, which means human resources won't know you personally, and they will handle any inquires if anyone tries to find you. And yes. You have a record."

"I can't believe how far Matteo took this."

"I told you. I'm confident we've hidden you in plain sight. Next question, and you can bet Gallo will check this one: What's your home address?"

I blink and sit up straighter. "San Francisco. I can't believe

I didn't tell you this already. I had a flashback, and I'm certain I'm from San Francisco. The man, whoever he is, was letting me stay with him after my passport was stolen."

"The man?"

"I still can't remember his name or face. Just that he's powerful and rich. I don't think he's Niccolo. I saw his picture and still didn't place him in my memory."

"We'll look through pictures tomorrow. Anything else you can tell me before I call Matteo?"

"I have a friend named Sara, no H, in San Francisco. I know I'm close to her, but aside from her being a pretty brunette, I really don't remember anything else. It's not much to go on, I know."

"Matteo doesn't need much," he assures me, already punching the button on his cell to dial him.

I sip my cappuccino, anxiously waiting for the call to go through, eager for answers. Kayden announces into the phone, "Ella thinks she's from San Francisco." He listens a moment. "Right. And she has a friend named Sara—S-A-R-A. That's all I have." Another pause, and he scrubs his jaw and adds, "You pull this off, and we're even, as far as I'm concerned." He ends the call and sets his phone down. "The ball's in his court now."

"Did he think he could find out anything?" I ask.

"He didn't say, but if anyone can, he can. He's that damn good."

"Dinnertime," Marabella announces, returning to the table with two huge bowls of spaghetti. "This is my grandmother's recipe, passed down to my mother and now me." She kisses her fingertips. "*Perfetto!*"

Kayden and I dig in, both of us raving about how *perfetto* it truly is, and I go so far as to add, "Even without my memory, I believe it's the best pasta of my life."

My admission has her glowing and humming her way back to the stove.

"You've made her very happy," Kayden assures me. "And for the record, everyone who needs to eat her food is too skinny for her."

"How do you not get fat with her cooking for you?"

He pokes a meatball with his fork and holds it up. "That's why there's a full gym upstairs."

I laugh. "I will definitely be visiting it, and soon."

We eat for a few minutes in comfortable silence, and I think it's a sign of how well we get along. It stirs a million questions about what had him staring into the darkness tonight, what haunts him, but I'm afraid if I ask, he'll withdraw. I am almost certain that he will. Marabella is quick to join us, chatting a little and taking our plates.

"Dessert?" she asks. "I have cheesecake."

I pat my belly. "I'm stuffed. I'd better not."

"I'm with Ella," Kayden agrees. "Maybe later."

"Then I've achieved my goal," Marabella approves, setting fresh espressos in front of us and casting her attention on me. "Before I head to bed, there's a whiteboard on the counter. Leave me a list of anything you like and I'll pick it up tomorrow."

It's a pleasant revelation to realize I know what I like. Chocolate. Coffee. Cheese. Pasta. "I'm allergic to shellfish," I say, glancing at Kayden.

"That's a good thing to remember," he says.

"And before you have a reaction," Marabella adds.

"I might not want to remember who I am," I comment, "but apparently my mind still wants me to survive."

"We'll protect you and be your family," Marabella promises. "And now I'll leave you two alone. I'll be in early to take care of the dishes."

"Thank you for the wonderful meal," I say. "And for all you have already done for me."

"Taking care of this castle and the family inside is my life, as it was my husband's. Eduardo was with Kevin before he knew me, and before Kevin adopted Kayden. And like him, I'll be here until the day I die, if Kayden allows it." She blows him a kiss and rushes away.

Kayden's energy shifts, thickening the air. "Kevin adopted me when I was ten and brought me here. He and my father were both Hunters and best friends, so when my family was killed, he took me in. And because I know you're going to want to ask, but will be afraid to, they were murdered while I hid in the closet my father stuffed me into. The case was never solved."

He stands and takes his cup with him, and it's all I can do to contain a gasp, the pure horror of a young boy hiding while his parents were slaughtered inconceivable. Suddenly everything I'm going through seems like nothing. Kayden walks to the sink and places his cup there, his hands settling on the counter in front of him, and I can almost feel the past cut through him.

I don't even think about staying in my seat. I cross to stand beside him, my hand settling on his back. The instant I touch him, he drags me in front of him, caging me between him and the counter, his hands setting back on either side of me, but nowhere is he touching me. "Every time you've asked me why, it came back to one thing. You were alone in a strange country with no family or friends. Things I know all too well. And the moment you opened your eyes and knew nothing but me, I had to protect you."

My eyes burn, and not with my pain. With his. "That's why you feel familiar. It's a bond of shared experience you knew we had, but I didn't." I reach for his cheek, but he grabs my hand, holding it between us.

"Every time you touch me," he says, his voice laden with some unidentifiable emotion, "I forget you don't know who you are or what you want."

"You said yourself that a name doesn't define me. I know who I am. And I know what I want, and that's you and whatever this is between us."

"I'm not a hero, Ella. But I'm not the asshole who is going to take advantage of you, either."

"Whiplash again, Kayden. One minute it's 'I'll fuck you until you don't know your name.' The next, it's this."

"You know damn well what that was about. You thought I was him, and it pissed me off."

He pushes off the counter and takes a step back, running a rough hand through his hair and leaving it a tousled, sexy mess. "I'm going out for a while." He doesn't wait for a response. I blink and he's gone. And I am suddenly cold and painfully alone.

twelve

I linger in the kitchen for a long while, finishing off my coffee and inspecting the contents of cabinets and the refrigerator, and in general killing time while hoping Kayden will return, but he doesn't. Of course he doesn't. I'm here and he's wherever he is, forgetting I'm here, and I have no right to care. He's helping me. He's not obligated to me.

Finally, I accept that I'm going to bed alone, and do so with *foolish* stamped all over my heart that shouldn't even be involved. I dim the lights in the kitchen to a glow, and then do the same in the living area before walking the chilly hallway. It's a path that comes with plenty of creaks and moans of the castle, and who knows, maybe a ghost or two is watching, considering this place has to be three centuries or more old, but I have far more to fear in my own head right now to worry about such things.

I open the door to my room, finding it colder than I remember despite leaving the fireplace running. Bigger and emptier, too. Shutting myself inside, I don't lock the door when there's no one to keep out anyway. I go straight to the tub and run another bath, eager to sink into the warmth.

Soon, bubbles surround me as I replay my encounter with Kayden. It doesn't take me long to decide his pain is too raw to be about the death of his family when he was ten. There's more.

Leaning into the bath pillow, I close my eyes and intend to keep my thoughts on Kayden, looking for answers. Instead, I keep seeing myself naked and tied up on that damn bed, and then sitting in front of that drawer, staring at that gun. Frustrated, I stand up, grabbing a towel, not sure why my mind keeps showing me the same thing over and over instead of the complete picture. I hate it. I hate it so much.

I dry off and pat on honeysuckle lotion before slipping on a silk button-up sleep shirt in a soft pink, and brushing my hair. Walking into the bedroom, I stare at the journal on the nightstand, and I want to throw it out the one window in the corner. I don't want all of these pieces of the puzzle. I want the completed story. My story. And I want Kayden's, too, neither of which appears willing to be explored.

Grimacing, I stop resisting and grab the stupid journal, sinking down on the floor and opening it. I have no idea why, but I start drawing a butterfly. A butterfly, of all things! It's just odd and I have no real thought to drive the action. I finish an elementary image and give it a disapproving eye. "You are definitely not going to make your fame and fortune as an artist, Ella." I shut the journal and leave it on the floor, pushing to my feet to glance at the clock. How did it get to be midnight?

Feeling claustrophobic, I need out of this room and my own head. Deciding to go make a shopping list for Marabella, I hunt for a robe I don't find, and settle for slippers and a zip-up hoodie I wear over the top of my silk night-shirt. Opening the door, I listen, and I'm not really sure for what, but all I hear are more creaks and moans, disappoint-ment filling me when there are no lights or any other sign of Kayden's return.

I enter the hall and hurry toward the archway to the liv-ing area and kitchen, and when I reach it I end up staring to-ward Kayden's room. I bite my lip, telling myself to go the other direction, but I think of him standing at that window, at the torment rolling off him, and I'm not sure if it's me who needs him or him who needs me. Somehow my feet are mov-ing toward his door. He's not even here, so it won't matter anyway. Still, my heart races, thundering in my chest, and it's pure adrenaline that pushes me to his door. I stop and look at it, but I can't seem to get myself to knock. I shouldn't knock. Or maybe I should. No. I shouldn't.

"Ella."

At the sound of Kayden's voice I whirl around to find him standing only a few feet away, his light brown hair tousled, his dark jeans and T-shirt paired with black boots and a sleek black leather jacket that confirms he's been gone, somewhere, perhaps with someone.

"Is there something wrong?" he asks, an air of the rebel about him, of danger, that I perhaps find far too sexy.

My fingers twist together in front of me and I drop them, afraid I look as nervous as I feel. "Nothing is wrong. Or not really. I just wanted to talk to you."

His eyes narrow sharply, his displeasure with my answer slicing through the air, and I don't know why. What is wrong with talking? He advances on me, a predator closing in on his prey, his anger a live wire that has me backing up until I hit the door. He stops in front of me, towering above me, his big body a wall between me and the rest of the world.

"You wanted to talk?" he demands, his voice low, fierce. "In your nightgown?"

My defenses bristle. "I wasn't thinking about what I was wearing."

"In your *nightgown*, Ella."

"Yes. I'm in my nightgown because I couldn't sleep. I meant to go to the kitchen and then I ended up here because I wanted . . ." His reaction cuts like his anger. "Just never mind." I try to move around him but his hands press to the wall beside me, caging me, and now I'm angry. "Are we doing this again? Don't bully me. My stupid flashbacks are doing a fine job of that on their own. I said I'm sorry. Just let me go back to my room."

"You wanted what?"

"I wanted you to do what you swore you could," I blurt, having nothing to lose when everything is already gone. "Only I don't want you to fuck me until I can't remember my name. I want you to fuck me until I stop thinking about that man and the gun. Because you were right. Memories are the enemies that never die. But I know you don't want—"

His hand slides under my hair and he drags me to him, my hand flattening on the hard wall of his chest. "I do *want*. So fucking bad it's killing me."

My palm is directly over his heart, and I can feel it racing, the air around us crackling with barely contained passion. "I don't need a hero to save my virtue tonight. I need *you*. So please. Fuck me and then fuck with my head so no one else can. Let me choose my own sins."

He is stone, unmoving, his body steel, his expression unreadable, the sexual tension crackling between us. "You want sin, sweetheart," he says. "I'll give you sin." His mouth closes down on mine, his tongue licking into my mouth, wicked with demand, and I can taste his hunger, his need. A deep, aching need I want to fill. This is what I've sensed in him, a pain that runs deeper than that of a ten-year-old boy, raw and open, carving him inside out. This is what brought me to his door. I wrap my arms around him, sinking into the kiss, the hard lines of his body absorbing my softer ones, a shelter and escape from the storm raging inside me.

But just as I am lost in the kiss, in the man, he tears his mouth from mine, jolting me back to reality and staring down at me, shadows etching those blue eyes. I don't know what he searches for but I do not blink, holding his stare, letting him see that I have no hesitation in me. And he must get the message, because he turns me to face the door, his big body hot and hard against my backside as he reaches around me and opens it.

"Go inside," he orders softly, and a shiver of pure feminine arousal runs through me. It's an order, but also a choice, and that choice is to be taken, controlled, and possessed. And beyond reason, and in defiance of anything I know of my past, that is exactly what I want and need.

I step forward, entering the dimly lit room that is identical to mine but for the darker, heavier furnishings, and it is warm and luxurious, decorated in brown and cream, while I am already burning hot. So very hot. But it's the centerpiece of the room, the massive four-poster bed, *his* bed, that stays my footsteps and sends an eruption of nerves to my belly. Kayden's boots scrape the floor behind me, the door shutting with a heavy, final thud. I glance over my shoulder to find him shrugging out of his jacket, readying himself to come for me, and I dart forward, rounding the bed. I don't stop until I'm at the edge of the thick brown rug in front of the fireplace, kicking off my slippers to step onto the soft tread.

Music starts to play, "The Story" by 30 Seconds to Mars, and I close my eyes, letting the words roll through me. *I've been thinking of everything, of me, of you and me.* The words rip through me, speaking to the darkness inside me. But I don't like the story of my life, and his. His hurts him.

I feel Kayden's approach rather than hear it, certain he's removed his boots, and then he is behind me, his hands on my shoulders, his touch somehow leaving me a little less lost than moments before. He leans into me, his big body cradling mine, and I think he inhales my scent, his breath a warm whisper on my neck that sends a shiver down my spine. He affects me. He speaks to me in ways that are far beyond sex or my understanding of where I've been or where I'm going. I relax into him, and his fingers flex where they hold me and for long moments there is just us and the song, two people lost in the stories of our lives, of our pasts. *And I swear to God I'll find myself in the end.*

He inches back, his hands caressing my jacket down my arms, dragging it away and tossing it who knows where, his fingers teasing my skin and leaving goose bumps in their wake. I face him, this man who has come into my life and taken it by storm, yet still sheltered me from the storm of my past. My self-appointed protector with motivations I do not understand any more than my need to be here with him, but I do not fear these things or him. His hand slides under my hair, warm and strong, wrapping the back of my neck, dragging my mouth to his, where I want it to be. "I fully intended to find another woman tonight, to bury every thought of you I had in her. One who didn't give a shit that I was using her."

His words ripple through me, and deliver an unexpected slice of pain I shouldn't feel but I do. "If you're telling me this is just sex—"

"I don't know what the hell this is. I just know that *she*, whoever she might have been, wasn't you, and that made her not good enough. No one else was good enough. Nor would I have tasted her without tasting you." He kisses me then, his mouth closing down on mine, and it's a punishing kiss, hot and hard, as if he isn't pleased that I have such control over him, and it's unforgiving in its demand. And when I moan with the effect, it's as if I set off a trigger.

He rotates me to press my back to the wide span of a bedpost, tearing his mouth from mine, and the mix of dark passion and haunting shadows in the depths of his eyes steals my breath. He doesn't speak. I don't speak. But there are things unspoken between us, an understanding that we are alike in ways few others ever will be. His eyes darken, filling with intent I do not understand, until he reaches up and closes his hands around the two sides of my silk shirt at my collarbones. A challenge flickers in his eyes that runs deeper than his quest to undress me, to a place not yet realized, but I want to know it and him. He waits a beat, then two, and he yanks the shirt open, buttons popping and flying here and there. I am panting, aroused in ways I am not sure I have ever felt before, a feeling that defies my absent memory, as does my understanding that I want to touch him, but I shouldn't. Not yet.

His gaze drops to my breasts for a sizzling inspection that has my nipples puckering and my sex clenching, and I ache for the touch that he doesn't give me. Instead, he tears his shirt over his head and tosses it on the bed, muscles rippling with the action. I reach for him, my hands finding his chest, the light brown, almost blond hair teasing my fingers. He reaches up and under the silk of my shirt, caressing it away, silk pooling at my feet, the chill of the room touching my skin, while the heat of this man warms me inside and out.

He surprises me then, pressing my hands to the post behind me. "Move them and I stop touching you," he orders, his fingers splaying on my back, and as if delivering motivation for me to comply, he cradles my naked body, molding it to his, his eyes probing mine, his expression hard, intense. "Understand?"

And as he had when we entered the castle, I have this sense of him asking for my trust, but also demanding control. "Yes," I whisper, amazingly unafraid and willing to give him what he wants, needing him to prove he deserves it. "I understand."

He is pleased with my answer, his eyes darkening, his gaze sweeping low again, lingering, and heating my skin before he looks at me and declares, "*You* are the one who is beautiful, and I promise you, I fully intend to show you just how beautiful." He lowers his head, his teeth scraping my shoulder, his fingers giving a gentle flick to my nipple. I bite my lip at the sensations rolling through me and his palm flattens tantalizingly on my belly, caressing lower, one finger traveling the line above my panties.

"Kayden," I pant, pleading for some unknown something I'm desperate for him to give me.

"The minute you stepped into my room," he murmurs, nibbling at my neck, "you became mine tonight. Mine to tease. Mine to please. Mine to fuck how I want." His breath teases my ear. "Say it."

"Yes."

"Mine to fuck how I want," he states, the boldness of his words, of the words he wants me to speak, shivering through me.

I wait for fear to replace shock, for the past to attack me, but there is only desire, and the clenching of my sex. "Yours to fuck how you want," I say, sounding breathless. *Feeling* breathless.

He leans back, letting me see the satisfaction light his eyes, and his reply is not words, or a kiss, but ripping the silk between my legs from my body. I've barely recovered from a gasp when he's exploring the slick, wet heat of my sex, stroking, teasing, two fingers sliding inside me. Filling me, stretching me, and promising soon he will be there, inside me, fucking me the way he promised.

I moan with the sensations spiraling through me, clinging to the post when I want to hold onto him, but I know he meant what he said. He'll stop touching me if I let go and I cannot bear the idea. My lashes lower, fingers digging into the unmovable wood, breasts thrust in the air, and I want him to touch them and me. One of his hands flattens in the crevice between them, teasing me with how close he is to giving me what I want, the other intimately caressing the ache swelling in my sex, and he leans in, his breath warm on my ear as he murmurs, "I'm not going to let you come yet."

My eyes pop open. "What?"

"You heard me." His fingers leave my sex, and before I can recover, he turns me to face the post, forcing me to catch myself on the wooden surface. He pins me between it and him, his powerful hips bracing mine, and his hands slide around me, cupping my breasts, caressing my waist, my back-side. Everywhere but that sweet spot between my thighs where he left me burning, and not for his fingers anymore, but for him.

"Don't move," he orders. "Not until I tell you to."

But I do. I try to turn and he flattens his hand on my back. "*Wait* for me, sweetheart. *Trust me.*"

Trust me. Those are the words that undo me and slam me with realization. I need someone to trust and he needs to be trusted. I know why this is true for me but I do not know why it is true for him. "I do," I whisper, meaning it. Right or wrong, I've gone too far with him to question what comes next.

He doesn't immediately move away, and I can almost feel him riding a stormy wave of emotions, each one crashing against the walls he tries to erect to protect himself. Seconds tick by and his hand slowly glides down my back and disappears, leaving my skin tingling in its wake. The air shifts and he is no longer behind me, but I feel him everywhere, inside and out. His body. His lust. His *heartache.* I want to turn, but not because I do not trust him. Because pain cuts him deeply, and he bleeds, and bleeds some more. Suddenly, I am far less worried about what haunts me and more about what haunts him, and I want desperately, if only for tonight, to drive away his memories, *his* enemies.

There is a shuffle of clothing, and a promise of him undressing, followed by a tear of paper, a condom wrapper, and unbidden, no matter what I desire, what haunts me will not let go, thrusting into the past. I am stepping out of a giant sunken tub in a bathroom of cream and blue tiles. The bath was an escape, a way of comforting myself, and I don't know why. I try to pull myself out of the memory, trying to just be with Kayden, but I go deeper instead.

The door opens and he bursts inside, stalking angrily toward me. He grabs my arm, the towel falling to my feet as he yanks my wet body against his perfect suit-clad body. "You disobeyed me again."

Fear shoots through me. He knows. How does he know? "No. I—"

He turns me to face the tub and grabs my hands, wrapping them with some kind of rope. "What are you doing?"

I whirl around to face Kayden at the same moment he returns, naked, beautiful, everything about him power and sex. And safety. He is safe. My hands flatten on his chest. "I . . . trust you. I do. I just . . . waiting made my mind crazy and—"

His hands cover mine, concern darkening his stare. "A flashback?"

"Yes. I'm sorry, and I don't want you to think I'm some sort of wilting flower you have to be careful with. I'm not, but—"

His fingers tangle in my hair, roughly, erotically. "You are the furthest thing from a wilting flower," he declares, his mouth closing down on mine, and his kiss is not gentle. He does not treat me like that wilting flower. He is demanding. He is the wolf. And this is the part of him I want to know, the part he tames, but I want set free. And I am free with him.

I touch him, everywhere, anywhere, indulging in the best of the sins I can wish to commit tonight, his thick erection at my hip. And I do not hold back. I reach down and wrap it with my hand, feeling the pulse against my palm. He presses me against the post again, cupping my backside and lifting me. "I need to be inside you," he rasps against my lips.

"Yes. Please."

He balances me, pressing the thick head of his erection into my slick heat, and I feel the sweet stretch of my body as he enters me and pulls me down on top of him. And with him buried inside me, we are steady, unmoving, savoring the moment as our gazes connect in a collision of raw, dark emotions, one part mine and one part his. His arm wraps around me, hand flattening on my back, and he lifts me off the post, holding my weight, holding *me*. He molds me close, breathing with me, long seconds passing before we start to move. Slowly at first and then faster, he is pumping into me and I am grasping his shoulders, driving against him. Driving everything away but the feeling of him inside me. And he answers every need I have. Pumping harder. Faster. Giving me more when I want more. More of this. More of him. More of the escape.

And *oh God*, I can feel the ache in my sex, the promise of release. I do not want to come. Not yet. But Kayden feels so good, and I bury my face in his shoulder, holding on, barely aware of the moment he presses my back onto the mattress, the sweet weight of him settling over me. His hands cup my head and the pause comes, the moment when we don't move, and just breathe together. And I can breathe again. Because of him.

"Kayden," I whisper, asking for some indescribable something only he can give me.

His lips brush mine, the soft, sensual caress touching every nerve ending I own. He cups my breast, squeezing it, a rough, erotic sensation that has me arching into him, a moan slipping from my lips. He swallows it, kissing me, a deep stroke of his tongue and we start to move again, and this time it's a slow, sensual dance. The music I'd forgotten invades the moment, the same song on replay. *And I swear to God I'll find myself in the end.* But here, now, with him, I lose myself. *He* is the burn in my belly that moves lower and lower, and I stiffen with the tight ball of pressure in my sex, unable to move.

Kayden pumps into me, deeper, harder, and I explode, spasming around him, clinging to him, as he drives once, twice, and on three his body shudders and shakes. Time swirls in and out, and the muscles in my body ease, in his too. "What are you doing to me, woman?" he whispers near my ear, nipping my earlobe. "Don't go away." He pulls out of me and rolls to his side, and, I think, takes care of the condom. Before I can figure it out, he's returned and he's pulling me against him, my back to his front, the warmth of the fire and his body sending me into a deep, drugged state of satisfaction. "You tried to take my gun when you felt trapped. You aren't a wilting flower."

My chest tightens. "I might be a little too comfortable with guns."

He rolls me onto my back and pulls me around to face him, grabbing a blanket and draping it over us, his hand settling possessively on my hip. "Any idea how you know how to shoot?"

My mind flickers to that image of myself at a gun range. "I remember going to a gun range. I was younger, so I think I learned young."

"So maybe your parents were in law enforcement?"

My mind produces an image of a man in a uniform. "Military," I say. "I think my father was, or is, military. I'm not sure if he's alive or dead." There's an image of a woman in my mind with red hair like mine, and the idea of her hurts my heart. "My mother's dead."

"You're sure?"

My eyes pinch. "Yes. Thinking of her makes me sad. And my father feels distant. Out of my life or dead." I swallow hard. "I'm alone. That's why no one came looking for me."

His hands settle on my face. "You're not alone. Not anymore."

"I might be a killer. You sure you want to keep me around?"

"You *are not* a killer."

"I know what I remember."

"Which isn't killing someone, unless you've remembered something you haven't told me."

"No. No, I haven't, but Kayden—"

"You aren't a killer, but that doesn't mean you didn't kill him. Surviving is human nature."

I squeeze my eyes shut, and an image of me naked and tied to that bed flickers in my mind. "I *was* trying to survive."

His finger slides under my chin and I look at him. "Can you talk about it?" he prods softly.

My chest tightens again and I roll to my back, facing the ceiling. "I know I lost my passport and money. I met him and I have no idea where or how. I just remember he let me stay with him. He gave me my own room and I ended up in his."

"I do not like how familiar that sounds."

I roll to face him again, curling my fingers at his jaw. "It's not. I mean, it is, but different. *You're* different. What is between us, whatever it is, isn't like what I had with him. I'm not infatuated with you and you don't treat me like you're on a pedestal looking down on me or that I'm your subject who should be so very pleased to have your good graces. You're real in a way he never was, and I know that I'm real with you in a way I couldn't be with him. Maybe . . . I'm able to be real because I don't know what to hide."

"We all hide from things."

"Including you?"

"Yes. Including me." I want him to go on, to explain the torment I sense in him, but he doesn't. He draws my hand in his and asks, "When I turned your back to me, you had a flashback. What was it?"

I press my hand to my face, the demons of my past clawing at my mind.

"If you don't want to tell me—"

"I do," I say, dropping my hand to look at him. "He wins if I hide from this. And he *can't* win." I draw in a breath for courage. "He started out like a Prince Charming, until he wasn't. You know he offered me a place to stay. I thought it was a fairy tale. But I remember the day it changed. I went out when he told me not to. When he returned home he was displeased. He stripped me naked and tied me to the bed and just left me there for hours. When we were . . . when you turned me around, I remembered another time when he turned me around and tied my hands behind my back."

He drags me closer, his leg twining with mine. "I'm sorry," he says, his hand slipping under my hair, at my neck. "I won't—"

"Don't say you won't. Please. He wins again if you treat me like a delicate flower. And you'll make me feel like I can't tell you what I remember. You have to be you with me. That's what I respond to. That's what feels right. I mean, assuming you want—"

"I do. Very much, Ella. I think you know that, and I won't coddle you, but you have to promise me you'll tell me if I hit a trigger."

"I did tonight. I will. I promise. Kayden, when he tied me up, he said it was punishment for not listening to him, but also said that he is very powerful and that his enemies would kill me because I was his. He sounds like Niccolo, doesn't he?"

"There are many men who have money and power. Just know this. Whoever he is, he's not ever going to touch you again. You have my word."

For just a moment I'm back in that alleyway, and he's leaning over me, the only good thing in the midst of the pain, with his spicy raw scent and those blue eyes. *Don't leave me*, I'd whispered.

"I remember you that night in the alleyway," I whisper.

"What about that night?"

"I begged you not to leave me. You promised you wouldn't."

"Yes. You did, and I did." He brushes hair from my eyes, the touch tender. "And won't. We'll figure this all out together."

"I may never get to be Ella again."

"You *are* Ella."

"Ella lived in San Francisco, and I fear I will never fully remember her unless I return. But more so, I fear returning and putting others, like my friend Sara, in danger."

"If we need to go back for answers, we can do it without anyone knowing you're there."

"We?"

"I told you. We'll figure this out together."

You are not alone, he'd said, and I think . . . I think he's been alone a long time and I want to know why. "Where were you from before you moved here?"

"Houston."

"Do you remember it?"

"I remember it. I've been back. But mostly I remember my father. He is Houston to me."

"Your dad was a Hunter, you said?"

"Yes. That's how I started." He gives a sad laugh. "And a regular cowboy. Boots. Jeans and pickup trucks. I still listen to country music."

"What country music?"

"Jason Aldean. Luke Bryan. Keith Urban."

"Those people are fairly new on the scene. Well, not Keith Urban, but Jason Aldean and Luke Bryan."

"You know your country music."

My brow furrows. "I guess I do. Hmmm." An image of my father working on a pickup truck, with music playing in the background, comes to me. "My father liked it, I think." I shake off the thought that for some illogical reason makes me uncomfortable. It's just music. I happily, eagerly refocus on Kayden. "We were talking about you. You're more biker than cowboy."

"Biker." His lips quirk sexily at the corners. "A few motorcycles does not make me a 'biker.'"

"Okay, maybe that was the wrong choice of words. Rebel is more like it. Or wild card. Very dangerous."

"Dangerous? Is that what you still think of me?"

"Your own words."

"Yes," he agrees, his voice tight. "My own words."

I wait for him to explain. He doesn't, but nor do I sense the wall between us as I have in the past, so I cautiously push for more. "And your mother. What did she do?"

"Music teacher."

"Music teacher?" I whisper, a shadow of a memory stirring in my mind.

"Memory?"

I shake my head. "No."

"You don't sound certain."

"I get feelings sometimes but I don't know what they mean." I refocus on him. "I don't know why, but I'm afraid to ask the next question."

"You want to know about my sister?"

"Yes."

"She was eight. We'd had a fight right before they were murdered."

"All siblings fight, and you were kids."

"But most of them don't have to remember that as the last

moment the other was alive." He shuts his eyes a moment, the lines of his face harder now, tighter, and when he looks at me again, he's done talking. "Let's go to sleep."

"Did I upset you?"

"No."

No means yes. I feel it. "I'm sorry."

He rolls me to my back, leaning over me. "You're the one who's dangerous. You make me—"

A loud buzzing sounds from the corner of the room and Kayden stiffens, cursing under his breath and throwing off the blanket. He is off the bed and pulling on his jeans by the time I sit up, clutching the blanket to me and noting the sound seems to be confined to a corner of the room. "What is that?"

He shoves his legs in his pants. "Security system. Some-one breached the castle perimeter."

I glance at the clock, realizing it's three a.m., and I'm suddenly afraid that I've brought trouble to Kayden's doorstep. Maybe he's right. Maybe *I am* dangerous.

thirteen

The alarm continues to sound, a constant buzzing contained to this room. "Does that mean someone's breaking into the castle?" I ask as Kayden yanks his shirt over his head and I scramble to the ground to snatch up my own and slip it on, reminded I have no buttons or panties.

"They aren't inside yet," he says, grabbing his black lace-up boots and walking to the fireplace, where he punches a button by the mantel. To my shock, a panel beside it opens. He disappears inside and the alarm stops, assumedly by his hand. I quickly follow, entering what appears to be a surveillance room, to find him sitting at a long, built-in desk in front of a row of monitors showing various parts of the castle.

He curses and scrubs his jaw, his urgency turning to agitation.

"What is it?" I ask. "What's happening?"

He indicates a monitor showing a woman hunched over by the front door. "It's Adriel's sister, Giada. She appears to be at the front door of the west tower, throwing up, when her passcode is for the east tower." Relief washes over me that it's nothing more serious. "Adriel's off with some woman tonight,

so she clearly didn't want to call him. I told you. She's a mess."
He stands. "I need to go get her."

"Should I come? Maybe a woman can help?"

"She doesn't know you and she's prone to outbursts, so stay put." He grabs me and pulls me to him. "And be naked when I get back." He kisses me, hard and fast. "Understand?"

I smile, pleased that he wants me to stay. "Yes. Understood."

His lips curve. "Good." He releases me and exits the security room, and I claim the seat in front of the panel to discover Giada sitting with her knees at her chest, rocking back and forth. My heart aches for this young woman so obviously heartbroken; she really is "messed up," as Kayden had called her. The bedroom door opens and shuts, signaling Kayden's departure. I glance at the various views of the castle and back to Giada, and immediately get to my feet at the sight of a man rushing toward her.

"Gallo," I whisper in shock. I yank my shirt together and dart across the bedroom. I pull open the door and start yelling, "Kayden! Kayden!" I'm at the top of the stairs, looking down over the railing, as he starts running back in my direction.

"Gallo is with Giada."

He stops in place. "Holy fuck. What the hell is he doing here?" He points up at me. "Stay where you are." He turns and takes off down the stairs and I stand there a minute in stunned disbelief. What the hell *is* Gallo doing here? And why am I standing here when I could be watching the action on the monitors? I take off running again, my feet brutalized by the cold, hard stone floor, but I don't slow. Finally, I'm in the bedroom and back at the monitors, letting the shirt gape as I watch what is happening.

Giada is still on the ground, on her knees, and I watch Kayden reach the porch. She starts screaming at him, but Kayden doesn't react, focusing solely on Gallo, the two men stepping toe-to-toe, looking like they are about to come to blows. I reach for the keypad to the MacBook connected to the cameras and try to figure out if I can get volume, with zero success. Gallo waves a hand at Giada and then points at Kayden, and I've heard enough of the war between these two men to know Gallo is blaming Kayden for the mess that Giada is in. I hold my breath, fearful of how this will end. While I am certain Kayden is a man of control, not easily rattled, I am equally certain this trait will infuriate Gallo and drive his actions to who knows where.

As if proving I am right, Gallo throws his hands in the air and starts walking away. Kayden watches him until he is long gone, only then focusing his attention on Giada, who either starts screaming at him again or never stopped. Thank goodness the place is too big for next-door neighbors to hear. Not even Marabella has surfaced with the disturbance, though I'm fairly certain that will change once they enter Giada's tower. Kayden reaches for her and she starts kicking and punching him. Lord help that man, she is testing him, and still he doesn't become rough with her. He patiently snags her arm, I'm guessing to wait for the effects of the alcohol to deplete her surprising supply of energy.

I stand up, wanting to go to him and help, but I know better. He's right. She's a mess and I very well might make it worse. Still, she is kicking the crap out of him and my fist goes to my mouth as I watch the hellish struggle he's having with her, until finally, he's had enough. He picks her up and throws her over his shoulder and enters the house. I switch to another screen to watch as she continues to punch at his back, brutalizing him as he punches in a code for the east tower, and the dungeon door seems to take forever to open. Apparently impatient—and who can blame him?—he ducks under it and I sit back down and wait, and wait some more, but he doesn't exit. Activity appears on one of the monitors as Adriel's Rolls-Royce pulls into the drive, and I'm wondering if Kayden called him on the way downstairs or if Adriel's in for a fun surprise. Either way, I have a feeling Kayden isn't going to be back anytime soon.

My mind goes to Gallo, who was surely watching the house, and I'm not sure if he's protecting me or stalking me. I'm not even sure this is about me at all, but rather about hurting Kayden. His hyper-focus on either one or both of us scares me and, while I know he's whatever Italy's version of a detective is, something feels off. Very, very off. Kayden was worried about insiders working for Niccolo in the police department. Could Gallo be an insider? Surely not, or Kayden would be more worried about him. Still . . . maybe Kayden doesn't want to freak me out, so he hasn't expressed that concern.

I grab the pad and paper sitting on the desk and write *Gallo* on it. Then I underline it. I'm not sure why. I just need to make my mind work. Then I write *Niccolo*. I underline it as well and wait for either name to really mean anything to me, but they just don't. Niccolo can't be *him*. I don't know his name or his image. I start writing again and the name I end up with on the page is *David*.

"David?" I whisper. "Who the heck is David?" Images start to flicker in my mind and I see myself standing in a hotel. I write down *Hotel* and underline it. It feels important. I'm in a hotel, and this David person is there. He's tall, blond, refined, and good looking, but he's not *him*. I write that down: *Not Him*. I shut my eyes. I see him and his face clearly. I'm yelling at him. *"We were supposed to elope and we can't even legally get married here."*

My eyes pop open. *Elope?* My hand goes to my throat. How many men were in my life? I didn't even *love* that man. I force myself to think, closing my eyes again. We keep fighting, but this time I can't hear the words we're speaking. I just see and feel the anger between us, my hands swiping in the air, his jabbing at his hips. He takes a call, as though it's more important than our conversation, and he ends the call and leaves. Just . . . leaves. My mind tracks forward in time, and I have a sense of hours having passed. I'm pacing the room and he hasn't returned. *Something isn't right. He's not who he says he is.*

I open my eyes and write that down. *Not who he says he is.* I stare at the paper. "He wasn't who he said he was," I whisper, and one certainty comes to me. David is how I ended up turning to *him* for help. I went from one evil to another. David left me. He betrayed me, but I don't know how or why. I blink, and I'm drawing another butterfly. Why am I drawing another butterfly? It's ridiculous. No wonder my head is starting to hurt, an unwelcome reminder that I need to go to my room and get my pills.

I push to my feet, closing my shirt around me, and exit the security hideaway to enter the bedroom. Pausing in the archway, I stare at the room that is as masculine as the man who owns it, replaying the way he'd touched me. The way he'd kissed me. The way he is somehow demanding and controlling, and yet gentle, even tender. What he makes me feel is the polar opposite of what the man in my flashbacks does, to the point where I don't know how I could have ever considered them to be the same. I'm not sure I really did. The two of them create intense feelings in me. But David? No. I don't understand how I let him into my life.

My eyes catch on my hoodie and I pull it on, zipping it up to hold my shirt shut. Next come my slippers, and I hurry to the door, eager to take my medicine before I end up in troubled waters again. I hurry to the door and crack it open, listening for any activity, disappointed to find only the same old moans and creaks, now becoming as familiar to me as Kayden has always been.

I step into the hallway, the chill of the castle touching my bare legs, urging me to double-step toward my room. Once I'm inside, I rush to the bathroom and grab my purse, opening it and staring at that damn gun again. "Glock 41 Gen4," I whisper. "My father's favorite handgun." My hand presses to my forehead. He loves guns. Or he *loved* guns. I don't know which for sure. He was—is?—a gun enthusiast, of that I know, and he expected me to be as well. He made me go to the gun range. I have a momentary flashback of myself at a target range, and him yelling at me for my horrible shooting. He got angry when I couldn't hit the targets. *Very* angry, and so I got very, very good with a gun. A wave of nausea rushes over me and I double over, grabbing the edge of the sink. I start breathing hard, sucking in air with effort.

Angry at my weakness, and for other reasons I don't understand, I straighten and open a drawer, shoving the gun inside, sealing it away, out of sight and I hope out of mind. I
grab the bottle of pills and open it, popping one in my mouth
and cupping water in my hand from the sink to swallow it.
Then I shove the bottle into my pocket and enter the bedroom, where I grab my journal from the nightstand. I open it
and stare down at the butterfly. I shut it again and set it back
on the nightstand, frustrated by the games my mind is playing
with me. That's when it hits me that I've left the folder I'm
supposed to study in the kitchen. That's what I can use to
consume my mind while I await Kayden's return.

I'm at the archway to the living room before I remember
making the decision to even leave the bedroom, which is
pretty darn scary, but I am here now, and I cross to the
kitchen, not bothering to brighten the lights, actually wel-
coming the shadows that fit my mood. I head for the table
where the folder should be and stop dead in my tracks at the
outline of someone sitting at the opposite end.

"Ella," Kayden says, and this time I swear my name on his
lips is blood bleeding from those wounds I'd felt in him early
tonight.

My fingers dig into the chair I'd held onto before dinner
and it hits me that he might be here because I was in his room
and he couldn't go there. "I can go to my room."

"Come here."

It's an order, not a question, his tone low and rough, and
I'm not sure if that's good or bad. I don't ask. I don't care. I
want to go to him and I do, rounding the table to join him.
He pushes his chair back just enough to pull me in front of

him, his hands branding my hips through the thin silk of my gown, my backside pressed to the table. He doesn't look at me at first, but I feel him. *Oh God*, how I feel him. I am tingling all over, aware of this man in every part of me, in a way that reaches far beyond the physical. Finally, his head lifts and our gazes collide, cutting through the darkness and the connection we share, shaking me to the core, leaving me vulnerable and exposed, but not afraid as I am in my flashbacks.

I'm not sure who moves first, but our foreheads come together and we stay like that, just breathing together, every second driving the anticipation of what will come next. I cup his face and I know whatever was said to him downstairs affects him. "I don't know what happened between you and Gallo, but you aren't to blame for what's happening to Giada."

He leans back to look at me, and there are no shadows, no matter how deep or dark, that could hide the shame in his eyes. "This is *my* chapter of The Underground. I run it, as Kevin did before me. I am responsible for every person beneath me. I let her father take that job."

"Did you believe he was in danger when you did, any more than you do with any other job?"

"No. I didn't."

"Then you are *not* to blame."

He sets me on top of the table, scooting his chair closer to me, and his head drops in front of me, blocking his emotions from my sight. "There are things you don't know or understand."

My fingers slide into his hair. "Make me understand."

He looks at me. "I don't want you to understand. Not

now. Not ever." He drags me onto his lap, my legs on either side of his hips, his hand cupping my head, his breath warm on my lips.

"Kayden—"

"No," he says, his tone nonnegotiable, dragging my mouth to his, his tongue stroking against mine, ending the chance for words, but he lets me taste the answers he will not give me. The hate. His hate for himself in the here and now that I do not understand. I want to understand. But I am still new to him and he to me, and I can tell that questions are not what he needs from me now. I wrap my arms around his neck, and telling him I am his with my kiss, I hold on to him and refuse to let go, my actions echoing his earlier words to me.

He unzips my hoodie, his hands traveling up my waist, over the curve of my breasts, and my nipples tighten and ache with a soft brush of his fingers. He twirls them, his touch rough, arousing. Then his lips leave mine and he looks at me, letting me see what I have tasted, but he refuses to speak. In a blink, his expression has become guarded, the emotion banked deep in some part of him I know I will touch again tonight.

His hand slides to my back and he leans me toward the table, forcing me to catch myself on my elbows. He holds me there, his body cradling mine, his lips a breath from a touch. "I won't let you fall."

"I know," I say, and I do now. Beyond time and reason, I trust this man.

His mouth brushes mine and then trails down my jaw, slowly teasing a path to my ear, where he whispers, "I'm not going to claim to own you the way he did." He flattens his hands on my belly, possessiveness in the touch. "I'm just going to make you wish I did."

My lips part with the erotic promise, and he is already kissing me, licking into my mouth, his tongue a sultry, seductive promise that he can make good on his vow. And while I do not wish anyone to own me again, I want what he offers in a way that defies reason.

He nips my lips and licks away the sweet ache, and somehow I feel that lick between my thighs where I am already wet and aching. His whiskers rasp on my cheek, down my neck to my shoulder, a wicked burn that is torment and pleasure at the same time. Like he is. His hands settle on my waist, lingering there, teasing me with all the places they could go, until finally he is caressing my body, up and down, a slow, sexy, torturous exploration.

He pinches my nipples again and he is not gentle, but I do not seem to want gentle. My sex clenches and my knees crush his hips. His lips curve to a small, satisfied smile that is wickedly sexy, and rawly male. He leans in and licks one of my throbbing nipples, sending a shiver down my spine, and I arch upward, the table biting into my elbows, but I do not care. He is sucking me, dragging deep on the knotted peak, and pleasure tingles through my nerve endings, my sex, forcing my legs to squeeze his hips again.

My arms tremble with my weight and he responds without me asking, moving closer and laying me on top of the table. My spine flattens on the hard surface and he lingers above me. "I want more."

"More what?"

"Everything," he says, his lips nuzzling my ear as he repeats, "*Everything, Ella*. Can I have it?"

The question affects me, but not as much as the way he waits, genuinely seeking my approval. He takes power but somehow gives it to me as well, and this is freedom to me, safety. Things I do not think I have often felt in my life. "Yes," I whisper. "Yes."

He inhales as if my approval surprises and pleases him, as if it is a gift he relishes, not a property he owns. And it is then that I give myself the freedom to just let go, the muscles in my body easing in ways they hadn't before. I do give him everything. His mouth caresses mine and he whispers, "That's what I wanted," as if he knows I've made that decision.

And already his lips are traveling down my neck, tongue flicking here and there, his hand caressing, squeezing my breast. He assaults my senses with pleasure, touching me, kissing me, driving away my memories and enemies. His whiskers rasp my belly, his lips pressing to the center, his tongue flickering into my navel, and I tremble with the silent promise it will soon be where I want it to be. His hand flattens over my sex, inches lower until he is flicking my clit, back and forth, back and forth.

He lifts my legs to his shoulders, spreading me wide, and I am vulnerably his, and aroused beyond belief. He lowers his head, his breath a warm tease on my sensitive places, and I grip the edge of the table, bracing myself for what is to come. He laps at my nub, the barely there touch, and I am breathing hard, wishing I could touch him, incapable of moving, and the muscles of my sex clench so tightly it hurts.

He licks my clit and I am both relieved and on edge in the

same moment, ready for more, for that everything he has promised me. Another lick follows. *Yes, please, more,* I think, and as if he's heard my silent plea, he gives it to me. His hands slide beneath my backside and he lifts me to his mouth, and it is nothing shy of sweet bliss when his mouth closes down around me. He sucks, drawing deeply on my sensitive flesh, lapping at me, licking me again in all the right ways and right places. I am panting and moaning, and I barely recognize the sounds as my own. Sensations ripple through me and when his fingers slide inside me, I am undone, tumbling into orgasm. The intensity jerks my body and I lose all time and space. It's escape, sweet, blissful escape, and he keeps me there, slowly bringing me down, the licks of his tongue growing softer, slower. Until I am sated, limp, and he pulls me back onto his lap, my head resting on his shoulder, his hand flattening between my shoulder blades.

"Everything or nothing," he whispers, and this time, I do not believe he is talking about orgasms and pleasure.

I lean back to look at him, and the idea of what we are becoming is a sweet seduction, threatened by the emptiness of my past. "What if everything is too much?"

He drags two fingers down my cheek. "Sweetheart, I don't have a ceiling. We're going to find out if you do."

He ends the conversation there, standing and lowering my legs to the ground, my feet settling there and my pill bottle tumbling from my pocket. Kayden reaches down and grabs it. "Maintenance, or are you hurting?"

"Just a little pain."

He does not look pleased. "I pushed you too hard tonight."

"No, I—"

He scoops me up and starts walking, the movement forcing my shirt and hoodie open, leaving me all but naked. I don't
fight it or him, though. There's a message in the way he picks
me up all the time, a part of him being the protector he has
vowed to be so many times, *to me*. But I get it now. I've hit a
nerve with Kayden. He doesn't just want to protect me. He *has*
to protect me. I'm not sure how to feel about that. What does
that make me to him? What do I want to be to him?

We reach the hallway and I hold my breath to discover
whether he goes left or right, and relief comes hard and fast
as he turns toward his room. That is how much this man has
slid under my skin. But knowing I could be some moral obligation terrifies me. He enters his room and goes straight to
the bed, pulling back the blanket and setting me on the mattress. I climb underneath the covers, expecting him to undress
and follow me. Instead, he stands above me and stares at me,
and that wall he's evoked between us in the past is here in the
present. I can't read him. I find myself holding my breath
again, waiting, but for what I do not know. I'm blown away
when he turns and walks away, leaving the room and shutting
the door behind him.

I stare at the door. I seem to do a lot of that where
Kayden's concerned, and I'm more confused than I've ever
been in my life.

fourteen

He doesn't come back. It's nearly five in the morning when the physical and emotional toll of the past few days wins, and with nothing but Kayden's unique spicy scent clinging to the blankets and surrounding me, I fall asleep. I wake to sunlight and an empty bed. As I sit up, disappointment fills me as I scan the room for any sign he's been back, but find none. I glance at the clock and it's nine in the morning, not exactly the definition of a good night's rest. A sound comes from the bathroom and, certain it has to be Kayden, I throw off the blanket to climb out of the bed, tugging my shirt closed and rushing in his direction.

Reaching the open doorway, I scan the solid white room, disappointment filling me at the absence of the man whose presence I crave. That is, until he walks out of the closet, stopping in the archway, his hair lying in damp tendrils around his face, while black jeans and a snug black sweater, tugged up to display his powerful forearms, hug every inch of what I know to be his perfect, hard body.

He doesn't speak, his expression impassive, his gaze never leaving my face, and the silence that follows is not as comfortable as it was at last night's dinner. In fact, I'd call it excruciatingly awkward, and I can't take it. "Hi," I say, offering a ridiculous little hand wave that couldn't make my nerves any more obvious.

His reaction is to close the distance between us, and there is no mistaking the predatory gleam in his eyes, matched by his long strides. When he stops in front of me, there is no question that he is pure sex and intimidation. "Ella," he says softly, and my name does not bleed from him this time, nor is it a greeting. It's . . . I don't know what it is.

"When did you come back?" I ask.

"An hour ago."

"Where did you sleep?"

"I didn't."

"Because I was here?"

"No. Because I needed to think."

"About me?"

"About a lot of things." A muscle in his jaw tics. "Who's David?"

I swallow hard at the reference that tells me he read my notes in the security room, wondering how I'd managed to sleep through his return, and his obvious shower. "I came to Italy with him."

"Who is he to you?"

I'm embarrassed that there was yet another man in my life, and my gaze lowers to his chest. "Ella," he repeats, and this time my name is a command.

I press my lips together and look at him. "We were eloping, but things went very wrong."

A beat of silence throbs between us. "Did you love him?"

"I feel nothing but anger when I think of him. I don't understand why I was eloping with him. It makes no sense. Nothing adds up."

"Did you *love* him?"

"No," I say. "I did *not* love him."

"But you thought you did."

"No, I don't think so. No. No, I didn't love him. I'm telling you, there's more to the story. I just can't remember it."

"What was his last name?"

"I know nothing else."

His one reaction is a slight narrowing of his eyes, and I now have confirmation that he chose to let me see his emotions last night. He doesn't choose to do so today. I might still be in his room, but I fear he's already shut the door with me on the other side.

"There is more to the story," I insist.

"I'm going out," he says, obviously done talking. "Until we deal with Gallo, you're stuck in the castle. Study the file and when I get back, we'll figure out what comes next." He's already walking away.

I rotate and follow him, and he's almost at the door, and I don't want him to go. "Kayden," I call out, and he stops but doesn't turn, stirring dread in me over what I'm about to ask. "You brought me here and then left. Do you want me here?"

"Too much. That's the problem."

He exits the room, shutting the door with a finality that tells me he won't be back any time soon. *Too much*, he'd said. I decipher that as confirmation of what I'd thought before, and the reason he'd been angry when I'd shown up at his door. While he drives away my demons, I'm the trigger that awakens his. I shouldn't be here.

✕

Everything or nothing. Kayden's words replay in my mind as I walk to my room. I then proceed to take a long, hot shower, and the only flashbacks I have are of last night, every single kiss and touch we shared. The idea that he might have chosen "nothing" twists me in knots. I know that he and I are new to each other, but we seem to know each other in ways no one else can. I'm also fairly certain that our bond tears down a wall Kayden doesn't want destroyed.

Once I've dried off, a clawing need for stability has me organizing the items in all of the bags on the counters and in drawers. I avoid the one with the gun, though, as I'm really not in a mental place this morning to deal with the memories it creates. I just need a little peace and quiet today. With the bags unpacked and folded, I dress in a light blue V-neck sweater and faded jeans, and pair the outfit with ankle boots. I open my new blow-dryer and flatiron and put them to use before moving on to my makeup. The selection of products in the bags is impressive but I keep it simple, satisfied with the pale pink shadow and gloss I use. My hair is another story, though. The honeysuckle shampoo and conditioner paired with a pass with the flatiron have rid me of frizz and turned my dark hair impressively soft and silky, but I still don't look like me. This color is just wrong, like David. I shake off the thought, afraid it will trigger one of the flashbacks I'm avoiding this morning.

"Coward," I whisper, and I force myself to grab the journal before heading to the kitchen, promising myself I'll write in it while attending to my growling stomach.

As I make my way down the hall and into the living area, my thrill at the architecture I can't wait to explore in more detail is detoured by the smell of fresh-baked bread that lures me straight to the kitchen.

"Smells yummy," I say, stopping in the entryway as Marabella hums while preparing sandwiches.

Her head lifts, eyes lighting at the sight of me. "Good morning! How are you feeling?"

"Hungry," I say, not about to explain my lack of sleep. "Is that homemade bread?"

"Is there any other kind? And fresh mozzarella as well. Sit down and I'll bring you a plate."

"Sounds terrific," I murmur, my eyes landing on the table, a memory of lying naked on top of it, while Kayden's mouth was in the most intimate of places, heating my cheeks. Eager to direct my thoughts elsewhere, I sit down, sliding the folder closer and opening the journal to stare at my not so masterful butterfly. The image takes me back to that hotel room I'd shared with David. *"We can't even get married here!"* I yell. *"They don't allow US citizens to get married here."*

"An oversight."

"You don't make *oversights."*

His cell phone rings and he answers it. "I'll be right there." He ends the call. "I'll be back."

"Where are you going?"

"Out."

I grab him and he slaps me so hard I fall to the floor, my hand going to my burning cheek. The door slams, and I push through the pain and to my feet. I rush to the hallway just as the elevator shuts and go back into the room, leaning on the door and yanking off the necklace he'd given me. It lands at my feet and I stare down at it. A butterfly with blue stones and a ruby in the center.

I grab the journal and write: *Deceit. Danger. A secret.*

"Here you go," Marabella announces, setting a plate in front of me.

Mentally shaking myself back into the present, I shut the journal. "Thank you. I can't wait to try it."

She sits down and studies me. "You look tired, sweetie. Did the commotion wake you up last night?"

I hesitate, pretty sure she knows I wouldn't have known about the alarm if I wasn't with Kayden. "I heard something about it. It was Giada, right?"

"Yes. She's a troubled girl. She's horribly angry at Kayden, when he's done nothing but help her. She's missing a female role model and I'm just too old to connect with her. I was hoping you might try?"

I'm shocked at this request, since I am as new to the castle as I am to their lives, and will easily be gone before I've ever become settled—which tells me she must be desperate to help Giada. "Of course I will. How is she today?"

Disapproval etches her brow. "Hungover. She was throwing up at the doorstep last night. She couldn't remember the passcode to our tower, but she's known it for years. Or rather, she claimed it didn't work. When she finally stopped throwing a fit, she was embarrassed and crying. Poor child is just lost."

"I guess she's in bed today?"

"Adriel made her get up and work in the store. Maybe you could stop by and visit with her."

"Of course. I'll be happy to. I can stop by the store after I eat and meet her."

"Well, today might be bad. She's pretty foul."

I laugh. "You should see me when I have PMS."

She chuckles. "Warning noted."

"You'll be glad I remember that about myself."

We share a laugh and she glances at a square, black-rimmed clock on the wall. "Oh, goodness. I'm sorry, but I have to head out to an appointment. I'll check on you this afternoon. But before I leave, Kayden left something for you."

A mix of curiosity and more than a little anxiety rushes through me. What could he have left me? She pushes to her feet and walks to the cabinet by the sink, returning with a box she sets on the table. "Here you go." She glances at my plate. "I'm keeping you from eating."

"No. You're the reason I get to eat such great food."

"My pleasure." She hesitates. "I think it will be good for Giada to have you here, but it's even better for Kayden. I've been worried about him since . . ." She waves it off. "It's been a long time since any one woman has held his attention."

This news both pleases me and confirms my worries: I've torn down walls he simply doesn't want down. I downplay her observation. "I was mugged and left with no resources. He kind of inherited me."

Her lips curve. "Oh now, missy. Don't discount what's happening between you two. Kayden would have found another way of helping you if he didn't want you here, and I see how he looks at you. I'll see you soon." She breezes out of the room, and I am left thinking of my exchange with Kayden. *Do you want me here?* I'd asked, and his reply had been, *Too much.*

I shove aside my plate and grab the brown box Kayden has left for me. Flipping open the lid, I find a separate white box with an Apple logo on top, plus a note:

I asked for bubble proof but they tell me that feature is still in development.

I laugh and keep reading.

You'll find the following numbers programmed into the phone:

> *Me*
>
> *Matteo*
>
> *Nathan*
>
> *Marabella*
>
> *Adriel*

These people are my people, so now they're yours.

—Kayden

My chest tightens on that last phrase, which implies I'm staying in his life. Considering I'm running for my life, which makes a person think about her end of days, he's given me all the encouragement I need. I open the box and remove the phone, quickly finding Kayden's number and punching the "call" button. He answers on the second ring.

"Ella?"

His voice does funny things to my stomach. "Hi," I say, sounding a bit breathless.

"Is something wrong?"

I feel like we're replaying the conversation from outside his bedroom last night. "No. I just . . . When are you coming back?"

"Why?"

"Because . . . the David thing. He didn't mean anything to me. I don't know why I was with him, but I think . . . I was lost, and I feel found with you. I know that's crazy, because we just met—but you said 'everything or nothing,' and we are not nothing. But we can't get to everything if you shut me out."

Silence crackles on the line. I wait. And wait. And I'm going crazy when he finally says, "There are things about me you don't know."

"You said that already, and there are things about me we both don't know. What I do know, though, is that I need you, and I'm not alone in this feeling. I know I'm not."

"Ella—"

"*Please* don't shut me out."

"I'll be back in a couple of hours."

I do not miss the way he phrases this sentence to avoid the word *home*, when he's lived here since he was ten. "Okay," I whisper, feeling defeated.

His voice softens. "We'll talk when I get there."

"Okay," I say again.

"*Ella*. Sweetheart."

"Just come back." I end the call before he can say something else I don't want to hear.

Everything or nothing. I don't think I can do in between. I need to get my memory back. That's all there is to it. I reach for the journal and my hand shakes, partly from hunger, and partly from the emotional toll that is Kayden Wilkens. I pull my sandwich forward and start eating, opening the folder and studying the new me who has replaced the old me. An hour later, I've eaten every bite of my wonderful sandwich, Kayden hasn't returned, and I've spent way too much time drawing butterflies. And I've read my file at least ten times and just can't do it again. I place my plate in the sink and leave the folder, box, and journal on the table, and decide to do as promised and try to make friends with Giada.

I stick the phone in my back pocket and make my way to the stairwell, eager to see this store filled with collectibles. A little history that's not my own will be welcome right about now. I take the winding staircase to the main foyer, peeking into the room to the left, thrilled to discover a giant library with overstuffed chairs, a desk, a fireplace, and walls and walls of books. *This* will be my next stop.

I punch the button to open the dungeon door to the main room, reminding myself there is a code to reenter that I thankfully remember. Once I'm in the main foyer, I glance up at the ceilings, the trim wrapped in roses, and again, there is a stirring of something familiar that I can't quite remember. I let it go and face the fact that I'm stalling, not exactly eager to face Adriel, admitting to myself that I am afraid he will stir some memory I don't want to exist.

Frustrated at the idea, I hurry up the center stairs, a red-

and-cream-colored rug beneath my feet and thick, shiny wooden railings at my sides, greeting the next level by another tower dungeon door. I glance left and right to find a stairwell on either side. Had Kayden said the store was street level? That's the logical place, so I decide the door is the right choice. Noting a button to the left, I press it. The heavy wooden surface lifts rather quickly and I enter what resembles the corner of a museum, complete with two huge white pillars on either side of the room, shelves filled with books on the walls, and glass cases here and there. It's an intriguing place that begs to be explored.

I walk forward, noting rooms to the left and right framed by beautiful arches, etched in more roses, and I don't know why roses stand out to me, even call to me, but never fully evolve into a memory. Shaking off the thought, I continue, reaching the front of the store to find an inviting sitting area with high-backed brown chairs facing the public entrance, framed by bookshelves and decorated with stone tables a shade darker than the floors. To my right is a glass counter containing statues, and behind it is a doorway, voices lifting from inside. A male and a female are arguing in Italian, and I feel more than a tad awkward. I can't speak Italian, but they might not know that and it feels like I'm eavesdropping. Part of me wants to leave. Another just wants this first meeting with Adriel to be over.

I inhale and make my decision. I'm here. I'm doing this. I call out, "Hello!"

Their conversation stops abruptly. I wait. And wait, worried about the first moment Adriel appears until finally it happens. He appears in the archway of the door, his features hard, even sharp, his black hair thick and curly, his deep green eyes fixed on me. He also has a long scar down his cheek that I have a bad feeling came from treasure hunting, and a picture is forming. People die and get hurt when they work for The Underground. *Kayden* could die or get hurt, and this realization is not a good one. I'm falling for him, and I fear that is a dangerous proposition in ways I have yet to fully understand.

"Ella," he says in greeting, his jaw clenched hard, his navy collared shirt and dark jeans framing a large and muscular body. "Does Kayden know you're here?"

I wait a moment to reply, and this time the blank space in my mind is pure bliss. I don't know him, and I bite back a joyful smile he won't understand. "Of course Kayden knows I'm here," I reply, only to receive a skeptical arched brow, and I quickly amend with, "I mean, not exactly. I'm in the castle, so it's logical I'd end up here."

"I doubt he'd agree," he says, his tone downright cynical.

Puzzled, I open my mouth to dig for more information when a brunette with olive skin appears beside him, managing to look quite pretty in an emerald silk top and jeans despite the dark circles under her eyes. "Kayden hates this tower," she informs me.

"Giada," Adriel snaps in warning.

She grimaces. "Right. Keep my mouth shut. Anything else you want, 'master'?" She glances at me. "You must be Ella. What was it like being mugged?"

The random, out-of-the-blue question has me blanching. Adriel gives me a warning look that I read as "step cautiously," though I'm not quite sure why. She's his family. "Scary," I reply, "and it came with a bonus headache."

"I bet it's not as bad as mine."

"A different kind of headache. Neither is fun. Hopefully yours came with some fun in advance."

"Don't encourage her," Adriel snaps. "She could have ended up mugged like you did." He cuts her a warning look. "Or raped."

She glowers at him. "Shut up, Adriel. I'm not doing anything you didn't do." She rounds the counter and walks away.

I close the distance between myself and Adriel, stopping at the opposite side of the glass from him. "Sorry," I say softly. "I think I made that worse."

"Most things do." He lowers his voice. "She has a big mouth and we all want to stay alive. Your story to her is the same as your story to Gallo, which means amnesia right now. Understand?"

"Yes. Of course. And Marabella? Is it okay to speak honestly around her?"

"Yes. You can tell her anything. Same thing applies to Nathan and Matteo. Just not Giada." He gives me a probing stare. "Any improvement in your memory?"

There is no concern in his voice or his eyes, just an obvious disapproval that hits like a slap. He doesn't want me here. I don't know why, but considering the death of his father, I would guess he thinks I'm dangerous. Like I thought last night, when that alarm went off. I *am* dangerous. And selfish for being here. "I should go," I say, and when I would move away, he shocks me by covering my hand and holding it on the counter.

"What just happened?" he demands softly.

"You don't want me here. I don't blame you."

"Did we have a conversation I wasn't a part of?"

"You didn't require words to get your point across. So *I repeat*. You don't want me here."

"I don't want you dead, either. And without us, you would be."

Either. That's the word I latch onto. "But I bring Niccolo to your doorstep. I get it." I glance at my hand, then back at him. "Please let me go."

"Don't tell Kayden I made you feel unwelcome."

Not *don't go*, but *don't tell*. "If you hide it from him as well as you did from me, I'm certain he already knows."

The door to my left chimes and opens. Adriel releases my hand and curses under his breath. I rotate quickly and my heart falls at my feet.

Detective Gallo is standing inside the shop.

fifteen

He's dressed in a gray suit with a blue tie, both a bit rumpled like his dark brown hair. While I'm certain his gritty, rough-edged good looks appeal to many women, I'm not one of them. All I see is anger, and too much trouble to feel safe.

"There you are, *bella*," he says, his gray eyes lighting on me. "I was surprised you left the hospital without telling me, but I'm even more surprised to find you here, after Kayden told me you took off on your own."

Though I wasn't prepared for this meeting, I somehow pull a rabbit from a hat for an answer. "I saw the hospital bill, and I didn't want to add a heart attack to my concussion. I was going to call you Monday."

"Today *is* Monday."

I laugh, hoping it doesn't sound as fake as it feels. "I still have a concussion. I thought it was Sunday—but I've slept the past two days away."

"I got the impression you left in a hurry and were worried about something."

I stick to my story, hoping it matches what Kayden has told him. "As I said, it was the bill. I thought if I tricked Kayden into thinking I left, he'd leave. It was a silly, concussion-induced idea, and that's really quite embarrassing."

He arches a cynical brow, and who can blame him? It's a ridiculous story. "You must be feeling better to be up and about."

Adriel steps to my side. "She remembered part of her name," he interjects, clearly not wanting me to say more. "We're hoping the rest comes soon."

Gallo arches a brow my direction. "Really?"

"Yes," I agree, following the lead Adriel has given me. "My name is Eleana. Actually Rae, but I go by my middle name, Eleana."

"Eleana," Gallo repeats. "Beautiful name." He couldn't be less sincere. He glances at Adriel. "Eleana and I would like a few minutes to chat alone." He cuts me another look. "If that's okay with you?"

The many ways this could go wrong has me regretting my trip to the center tower. "Of course."

Gallo eyes Adriel. "Is there a private place we can chat?"

Adriel motions to the sitting area. "It's all yours," he offers, but he doesn't move.

Gallo doesn't look pleased but waves me toward the sofa. I head in that direction when I hear Giada say, "Detective Gallo," and I turn to find her standing in front of him, looking rather smitten as they have an exchange in Italian. I glance at Adriel. My stomach sinks to the floor with the certainty there is trouble brewing, and I quickly attempt to avert it.

"Detective," I interrupt, thankful to easily draw his attention my way, "Kayden and I have dinner plans tonight, and I need to rest beforehand. So if we could chat now?"

He glances in my direction, his expression impassive. "Of course." He eyes Giada and wraps up their conversation with softly spoken Italian, his tone bordering on intimate.

Adriel gives Giada no time to respond, snapping out an angry-sounding reply. Giada visibly pales and whirls on her brother, glaring at him before rushing away, while Adriel fixes Gallo in a cutting look. "Make this meeting with Eleana fast," he clips, giving us his back as he rounds the counter and disappears into his office, leaving the door open.

Gallo sighs and scrubs the one-day stubble on his jaw. "I'm not making any friends here, but I care about protecting people, not becoming buddies with people." He motions toward the couch. "Shall we?"

Remembering how shredded Kayden was last night, I'm reminded that this man's motives are not wholly pure. I nod, and claim a chair by the sofa. "Why were you here at three in the morning?" I ask as he sits down on the stone table in front of me, rather than on the sofa. Too close for comfort, considering I can see the blue flecks in his gray eyes.

"I was worried about you. And I couldn't miss Giada at the doorstep in need of help."

In other words, he's watching the castle, and probably chose this time to visit because he knows Kayden's not here. He reaches in his pocket and produces a small plastic box. "Fingerprint kit. Let's get these done, and then we'll chat."

His push to go right to the prints has me thinking again that he's either suspicious of me, or working for Niccolo and trying to prove I'm Ella. Whatever the case, it hits me that by denying my returned memory, I've given him the ticket to set me free, thanks to Matteo's handiwork.

"Thank you," I say as he opens the box and removes an ink pad. "I'm eager to have my identity back."

"Exactly why I can't quite get my head around you leaving the hospital like you did."

"Concussions don't make for logical thinking," I say. "I felt claustrophobic and embarrassed about the bills that were piling up. Thankfully, Kayden found me and I slept off the insanity."

"Let's get this done and we'll delve into the many shades of Kayden Wilkens." He holds the ink pad out to me. "Press your fingers on top."

I do as he instructs and then push down on a hard card he holds out to me. "That's it," he says, offering me a tissue, which I accept. "We'll have the results later today."

"That fast? Wonderful."

He sticks the kit back in his pocket and gives me a steady inspection. "Look, Eleana. I know this castle and Kayden's money are alluring, even a fantasy, but you don't know him. Jumping into a relationship with a stranger, while you have amnesia, in a strange country, could be dangerous."

Gallo stirs thoughts of *him* that I shove aside. Kayden is nothing like that man. "Before you go on, Detective Gallo," I say, "you've made it evident that you have a personal bone to pick with Kayden, and it's hard to feel protected when that's your motivation. You can't tell me you'd be sitting outside a house at three in the morning if Kayden wasn't involved."

He leans his elbows on his knees, even closer now than before. "People who become intimately involved in his life die. I get chills just being in this place."

"What are you talking about?"

"He didn't tell you what happened here?"

Dread fills me. "What happened?"

"Five years ago, the prior owner of the castle—"

"Kevin."

"Yes. Kevin, and Kayden's fiancée, Elizabeth, who was living here, were both slaughtered. Kayden was conveniently gone."

I am gutted by the news, understanding Kayden better now than ever, and I'm also angered on his behalf, lashing out in response. "Convenient? Are you accusing him of actually hurting the people he loved?"

"People *die* when he's around. That is a fact. Two years ago—"

"I know what happened two years ago. You act like he was the cause."

"The Underground. Do you know them?"

"He told me about them."

"Tell me what you know."

"They find things for people for a price."

"And do you think what they do is legal?"

I shrug. "He did work for the police."

"Kayden is the kingpin of a massive, dangerous organization. He makes the decisions. He leads them to hell, and if you think he doesn't do what he has to do to keep his slate clean, you're going to end up dead like the rest of them. I'm trying to protect you." He softens his voice. "Please listen to me, Eleana. I am truly trying to protect you."

"No, you're trying to turn me against him." I stand. "I think you need to leave."

"Yes. You need to leave," Kayden says.

At the sound of Kayden's voice Gallo grimaces, and I'm relieved this meeting is over. Gallo turns and Kayden's stare is pure contempt. Gallo doesn't cower. "I am helping Eleana find her way back to *her* life—not yours."

"Leave, Gallo."

Gallo's lips twist sardonically. "I'm not quite done here."

"Leave," Kayden bites out. "*Now.*"

Gallo glances at me. "How should I reach you to give you the fingerprint results?"

"Kayden," I say, making it quite clear which side of the line drawn between these two I stand on. "Call Kayden."

He smirks. "I'll just come back by." He turns and rounds the table to stand face-to-face with Kayden.

"Move along," Kayden instructs. "You're on private property and I'm fully within my rights to throw you out. Actually, make my day and give me a reason to toss you out the door myself."

I hold my breath, aware Gallo would like to push Kayden, and the heavy seconds that follow are eternal. Finally the detective saunters toward the door, pausing with his hand on the knob. "You know where to find me, Eleana," he states firmly, and leaves.

Adriel moves in behind him, locking the door while Kayden closes the distance between us, his fingers clasping my wrist. Without a word, he begins leading me toward the back exit. I hurry to keep up as we pass Giada; I don't look at her and neither does Kayden. He's angry. So very angry, and not just at Gallo. We reach the door and he punches in a code to exit, and it's barely lifted before he's ducking under and taking me with him. He doesn't wait for it to close, leading me several feet, and out of hearing range of Adriel or Giada, before turning me to face him, his hands settling on his hips.

"What part of 'I don't want you in the store' did you not understand?"

My defenses prickle. "You didn't say not to come to the store. You said you didn't want me to work here."

"Semantics."

"No. You specifically said you didn't want me to work here. That's a different thing than telling me you don't want me here. This is your house, and you've taken care of me. I would have respected your request if you had made it. And I only came because Marabella asked me to try and bond with Giada."

"Marabella," he repeats flatly.

"Yes, and please don't be mad at her. She cares for you and Giada deeply. It would hurt her to feel she caused this today."

"What did you tell Gallo?"

"I told him I only remembered my first name, and made sure he fingerprinted me. That's what you wanted, right?"

"What did he say to you?"

"He told me The Underground is dangerous and so are you."

"We are. What else?"

I know he has the right to know the rest, but I can't seem to speak the words.

"Ella—"

"He stole your right to tell me something in your own time."

He stares at me, silent. Intense. His hand runs through his

hair, and that hawk that establishes him as a protector flashes. "He told you about five years ago."

"Yes. About Kevin and . . ."

"Elizabeth." Her name is sandpaper on his throat, pain ripped straight from his heart.

"Yes."

His jaw clenches. Seconds tick by. "It's time Gallo and I have a heart-to-heart." He turns and is through the door to the store before I know he's moved.

"Kayden!" I shout, running after him. "Kayden!" I enter the store and he's already at the front door, exiting to the street, with no coat and no explanation.

"Adriel!" I shout. He rushes out of his office. "He went after Gallo for telling me about Elizabeth."

"Fuck!" Adriel is already rounding the counter. "Stay here and lock the door." He grabs a coat from a rack and disappears out the door.

I hurry forward and lock it. Sinking against the wooden surface door, I suck in air, my heart hammering against my chest. This is bad. I grab my phone from my pocket and dial Kayden, willing him to answer, but it rings and rings and then goes to voice mail. I walk to the sofa and sit down, trying again. And again. I press the phone to my forehead and shut my eyes. Maybe I shouldn't have told him. *No.* I had to tell him.

"You okay?" Giada's standing in front of me with two steaming cups in her hand. "Hot chocolate. I thought you could use some."

I set the phone on the table to accept the mug. "Thank you."

"Of course." She sits down next to me. "So. *Are* you okay?"

I turn to face her. "Kind of. Thank you. What about you? You had a rough night."

"I broke up with my boyfriend a few days ago, over Adriel harassing him. I tried to drink away my heartache. It didn't work."

"It usually doesn't," I say, sipping the hot beverage.

"You sound like you speak from experience."

I smile. "Well, I do have amnesia, so I'm not really an authority on my past right now."

"Oh, that's right. I'm sorry. That must really suck."

I shrug. "My memories are slowly coming back, and I also seem to just *know* some things. Like I've tried to drink away a man before, and failed."

She curls her legs to her side to face me, and I do the same with her. "What's up with you and Kayden?"

"Still up for debate. I saw you last night on the monitor screaming at him."

Her eyes drop sharply to her cup. "Yes. I guess I did."

"What did you scream at him?"

Her gaze shoots to mine. "Mean things. Horrible things, Ella. My father was working for him when he died."

"I know."

"Kayden told you."

"Yes."

She hesitates. "What did he say?"

"Not a lot, but he hurts, too. Badly."

Her throat bobs with a hard swallow. "My father worked for Kevin before Kayden. They were all close, but I didn't meet Kayden until after it happened."

"You moved here after your father died?"

"Yes. Kayden wanted us here where we'd be safe. I guess he had new security installed after . . ."

"Five years ago," I say. "I know." And I suddenly have a renewed need to hear Kayden's voice. I set my cup down and pick up the phone, and dial his number. Ring. Ring. Ring. Voice mail. "Damn it," I whisper.

Giada sets her cup down as well. "What's up with him and Gallo?"

"Gallo blames him for something in his past, like you do."

"I don't blame Kayden." She purses her lips. "Okay, maybe last night I did. I was drinking and hurting."

"I meant what I said. He's hurting too. You have to know that—right?"

"He's hard to know."

"Because he carries the burden of so much loss that he can't let anyone in." I face her, hesitating to share Kayden's past, but gamble that dropping a tidbit of his past is okay. "Do you know about his family?"

"He never talks about them."

"He lost them when he was ten. That's when Kevin adopted him."

"Oh, my God. What happened to them?"

"It's not my place to share that story, and please don't mention that I told you at all. But I'll try to get Kayden to tell you." An image forms in my mind of a pretty redheaded woman who is smiling at me, and my chest expands painfully. *My mother*. She's gone, and it hurts so much. I will away the tears threatening to form, my voice hoarse as I continue. "I think Kayden can relate to your loss more than you realize."

And me, I add silently, swallowing hard and forcing myself to look at her. "Instead of blaming him, I think he might be a good person to talk to."

"He's kind of scary." Her lips curve. "And sexy, which is intimidating."

I laugh. "Hmmm. Yes. I can relate." We both end up smiling and there's a connection between us. "Where's your mother?"

"She died of cancer when I was ten."

Cancer. The word slides inside me, and finds an open wound that has my mother's memory all over it. I know it as familiar and horrible, just like I know sympathy can be painful. So I don't offer it. "Tell me about her."

She starts talking and we both end up lying down on the couch, while I clutch the phone and will it to ring. Better yet, I just want Kayden to walk through the door.

∽∾∾

Loud knocking on the street door wakes us up, both of us jolting to a sitting position where we've fallen asleep on the couch. The throb in my head is instant. "Oh God," I murmur, pushing through the dull ache to grab my phone and check it to find no calls.

"Good grief," Giada mumbles. "Some customers don't take no for an answer."

I stare at the time on my phone in disbelief. "It's six o'clock. We've been asleep for hours!"

"I feel better," she says. "I needed the rest Adriel wouldn't allow me."

"And I needed to take pain medication a good hour ago."

"You're hurting?" she asks.

"Yeah."

My phone rings and I see *Nathan* on the caller ID. "Nathan," I answer, hoping he can tell me where Kayden and Adriel are. "Is something wrong? Where's Kayden?"

"I'll tell you in a minute. I'm at the door knocking."

"I'm at the store."

"Right. Adriel said you might be, so that's where I am. Are you going to let me in?"

"Yes. Coming now." I end the call and stand, only to have a dizzy spell hit me that forces me to call on Giada for help. "Get the door, please. It's my doctor."

Giada's eyes go wide. "Yes. Of course." She crosses to the door while I'm pathetically forced to sit. When she opens it I'm able to stand again, steadier now.

Nathan speaks to her in Italian, and I'm fairly certain they know each other. Then he walks in my direction, looking exceedingly handsome and preppy in khakis and a white buttondown, along with a tan leather jacket.

"What's happening with Kayden and Adriel?" I ask.

"They're fine," he says, shrugging a brown leather bag off his shoulder and motioning for me to sit. I comply and he perches on the edge of the stone table across from me.

"What does 'they're fine' mean?"

"Yes," Giada chimes in, sitting next to me. "What does that mean?"

"Gallo arrested them."

"*What?*" Giada and I say at the same time.

"Why?" I ask.

"Yes, why?" Giada echoes.

Nathan sets his bag on the table. "He says they threatened him. Kayden says that's bullshit and I believe him. He's too smart for that."

"We have to go get them," I say, trying to stand.

His hand clamps down on my arm, holding me in place, the look in his eyes sharp, hard, unlike anything I've seen from him before. "I'm sure I don't have to tell you the many reasons why that's a wrong decision. Besides, Kayden is a very rich, powerful man, and his attorney is a beast when he has to be."

My stomach knots. "I feel like I brought this on them."

"The Underground brought this on them," Giada says, bitterness lacing her tone. "It's dangerous, and Kayden is the ringleader."

Nathan releases me and cuts a stern look at Giada. "Gallo's bitterness over something personal brought this on. And ever since your father died, Kayden has been allowing his people to take fewer jobs and doing all the dangerous ones himself. Why do you think you have this store?"

"Adriel wanted it," she says. "He didn't want to work for The Underground anymore."

"Right," Nathan says, clearly meaning "wrong." Then he focuses a probing look on me. "You're hurting."

"I fell asleep and missed my pill."

"Take it now."

"I left it in the other tower."

His look is pure reprimand. "The medicine has a cumulative effect. I didn't say four times a day for no reason." He reaches for his bag. "Good thing I brought some with me." He digs out a prescription bottle and glances at Giada. "Do you have some water?"

She nods and hurries away, and Nathan lowers his voice. "It kills me not to tell her that Kayden fired Adriel so he wouldn't end up dead, but it's not my place. He wants her to believe Adriel left on his own, to protect her."

"So Kayden remains the monster."

"Yes. He believes he deserves that title—but I'm hoping like hell you're the one who'll ground him. No one else has."

"In five years," I supply.

He arches a brow. "You know. I'm surprised he told you this soon."

"Gallo told me. That's why Kayden went after him."

"That doesn't surprise me. But neither would Kayden taunting Gallo into an arrest in order to be there when he ran your prints."

He offers me a pill I take from his hand, and I give him a curious look. "You sure know a lot for someone who isn't with The Underground."

"I've become the doctor to The Underground, and a friend to Kayden. I was with him when he found Elizabeth and Kevin." His expression tightens. "I couldn't help them. They were already dead."

My stomach churns with the certainty that although he and Kayden might have barely known each other before that night, the unlikely pair were deeply bonded from that point forward.

"Here you go," Giada says, offering me a bottle of water.

"Thanks," I murmur, opening it and sucking down my pill and half of the water. Afterward, Nathan checks all my vitals while Giada hovers. "How's your memory coming along?" he asks.

"Improving, but it's coming back in confusing pieces."

"I predict that will continue until a trigger brings it all back."

A trigger. Like I am to Kayden. Like he was afraid he'd be to me. I'm not sure if that's good or bad for either of us.

Once he's repacked his bag, Nathan stands. "You need to rest: that's the key to everything. Call me if you need anything. Kayden and Adriel should be back before bedtime."

I walk him to the door, and he gives my chin a brotherly nudge. "It's all going to work out."

I shut the door and lock it, then Giada sets the alarm. "It's going to be a long few hours waiting for their return, and I really don't want Marabella watching over me like a child tonight," she says. "Can I hang out in your tower with you?"

"Yes. Sure." We go out the back entrance, and when we're in the main foyer and I need to punch in the code, I have the oddest sense of unease. I actually find myself blocking her view as I press the numbers to ensure she can't see them.

We enter the tower foyer, and she surprises me by saying, "I've never been in this tower," as we walk up the stairs. Does Kayden not want her here? "Kayden's a bit of a hermit," she adds.

"Interesting. I haven't thought of him that way."

We reach the main floor, and when that odd sense of unease expands in my chest, this time I know I'm not taking her to my room. I motion her to the living area. "The kitchen is this way. We can eat. I'd say we could watch TV, but I won't understand it."

She snorts. "Are you kidding me? Kayden has the place set up with Netflix."

We enter the kitchen and I grab a couple of sandwiches from the fridge. "I didn't know you could get Netflix in Italy."

"This is Kayden we're talking about," she reminds me. "He's got a way around everything."

Translation: Matteo has Netflix magic in his fingers. Giada gets us bottles of water and we settle at the table to eat, planning a shopping trip together. Later we move to the living room, where she turns on the TV.

"I'm obsessed with *Breaking Bad* right now. Do you like it?" she asks.

"I don't know it. What's it about?"

"Good guy who gets cancer, and starts dealing drugs to take care of his family."

The word *cancer*, along with Gallo's warnings about Kayden being a "kingpin," axe that idea for me. "Not my thing. Any chance they have *Friends* reruns?"

"Oh, I love *Friends*! And they do have it."

She flips to the show and we alternate talking, watching TV, and playing tic-tac-toe for hours, and still there's no word from Kayden and Adriel. By ten, Giada's fallen asleep on the couch, and I'm in a chair next to her scribbling butterflies in my journal when my phone finally rings. Giada jerks to a sitting position as I check the ID.

"Hi, Adriel," I say, disappointed it's not Kayden.

"Come to the front door."

"Why? What's wrong?"

"Nothing is wrong. Just come downstairs. And bring your coat."

"Where's Kayden?"

"Just come downstairs," he repeats irritably.

"What about Giada? She's with me."

"Just you."

He ends the call and I frown.

"Well?" Giada prods.

I stand. "He wants me downstairs. Just me. Not you."

"Nothing surprising there," she quips. "That's all he said?"

"Yes. That's it."

"That's curious."

"Yes, it is. I need to grab my coat."

"I'm going down to talk to my brother." She rushes away.

Uneasy, I walk to the bedroom and put on a black trench coat that is once again Chanel, which tells me there must be a Chanel store nearby. I pop another pain pill, grab my purse and cross it over my shoulder, and stop in front of the drawer I swore I wouldn't open. For reasons I can't explain, I'm nervous with Adriel again.

Where's Kayden? His absence makes no sense. I'm worried about him. And I'm worried about me, too. I open the drawer and grab the gun, placing it in my purse and heading for the door.

sixteen

Nervous energy shoots adrenaline through me, and I all but run down the stairs to jab at the button to the dungeon door separating me from the main foyer. It opens and I cut under it before it fully rises, to find Adriel waiting for me by the door and Giada nowhere in sight. "What's going on?"

"Let's walk and talk."

I wet my suddenly dry lips, noting he now has on a black jacket, when he'd left without one. He also killed two men less than a week ago. "Walk?" I ask.

"Yes. Walk. Cars are hell to drive in this neighborhood." He opens the door, motioning for me to exit, and while he seems more agitated than dangerous, at least for the moment, my hand settles on top of my purse for easy access to my gun.

Moving toward him, I cross the length of the foyer and step onto the porch and into a chilly night, uncomfortably aware of Adriel at my back. I scan my surroundings for potential trouble, finding the castle grounds draped in inky blackness, thunder rumbling from a deep hollow in the sky, promising yet another storm. The door shuts and I face Adriel. "Where's Kayden? Is he still in jail?"

"He's been out for a couple of hours."

The news is a blow, since he hasn't called or taken my calls. "Where is he?"

"Getting wasted in a bar a few blocks from here." He lifts his chin. "Let's walk."

Kayden doesn't strike me as the "getting wasted" type. "Where?"

"To go get his ass."

"I don't think he wants me there."

"Bullshit. You're exactly what he wants and needs. Let's go before he finishes off the bottle of tequila he's working on."

He starts down the stairs and I hesitate to follow, but the truth is, he's baited me with his comments about Kayden needing and wanting me. Praying it's a good choice, I dart down the steps to catch up to him in the center of the circular driveway. "You don't even want me here and now I'm suddenly what he needs?"

"What I want and what Kayden wants often don't align. But he's The Hawk, and we need him to be strong and focused."

I'm not sure how I feel about that answer. I'm not sure how Kayden would feel about it, either. "How far away is Kayden?"

"A few blocks," he says, ending this stretch of our walk at the edge of a stone gate with heavy metal spikes and lights glowing at various spots. He punches in a security code to unseal the entry and faces me. "As for me not wanting you here, I did some thinking about you this afternoon. You're making him face the demons eating him alive, and in my book, that's a good thing for us all."

He doesn't invite a reply that I don't plan to offer anyway, motioning me forward. I gladly move outside the property line and away from him, wondering why every action and word from this man's mouth seems to be framing an agenda that might not be in Kayden's favor. Is he as angry at Kayden as Giada? Is Kayden too blinded by guilt to see it?

Adriel joins me, shutting the gate behind us, and we begin walking through what appears to be some sort of town square with a giant, stunning church opposite the castle, and a few people milling around here and there. "This way," he says, and we cut left and onto a lively, extremely narrow cobblestone street, with restaurants framed by cute umbrellas and various shops marked with signs. "It's busy for a Monday night," I comment, relieved to be in a public area.

"This area draws the college crowd and tourists. You should see it on the weekend."

Tourists. Weekends. Small talk. I don't have it in me. "What happened with Gallo?"

"He accused us of threatening him. Our attorney accused him of harassment, and his excuse for the extra attention was worry for you."

"So the harassment you mentioned is because of me."

"You're just one of many tools in his revenge chest. He'll use anything against Kayden. He hates him."

I want to ask for a reason, but I stop myself. Already, Gallo has stolen Kayden's ability to tell me about what happened five years ago when he was ready. It's Kayden's right to tell me this when, and if, he's ready. Adriel glances at me. "You aren't going to ask why?"

"No. I'm not. Did Gallo run my prints?"

"He wouldn't say."

"That makes me nervous."

"Matteo handled things. You know that."

"You sound confident, but Nathan alluded to you two getting arrested to be there when he ran my prints."

His jaw clenches. "Nathan needs to keep his mouth shut."

"Is it true? Did you and Kayden get arrested on purpose?"

"Why or how we were arrested doesn't matter at this point. What does is the end result. We didn't get charged."

"That's good, at least."

"And Gallo didn't show his hand."

"Oh. That's not good. That sucks."

"Everything about Gallo sucks," he replies, drawing us to a halt in front of a door with a huge sign over the top that reads BAR, the sound of muffled music vibrating the walls. "He's sitting in the back corner at the bar."

"At a bar in a bar," I say. "Check. Got it again."

He waves across the street. "I'll hang out over there somewhere in case you need an escort back, though I find that doubtful."

He walks away, crossing the narrow street. I watch him for a few beats, and my unease with him just isn't going away. Shaking off the thought, I turn to the door and enter the bar, to find a dimly lit room wrapped in brick. On a mission to find Kayden before I chicken out, I weave my way through clusters of tall tables with stools as seats and find him sitting at the bar as expected, with his back to me. I pause and inhale for courage, not sure how he'll react to me showing up here. I take a step forward but halt as I have the uncomfortable realization that the gorgeous, big-breasted brunette bartender is not only in deep conversation with Kayden, she's leaning over the counter, and giving him a healthy view of her cleavage.

My stomach knots with the certainty that *she* is his distraction from me, not a bottle of tequila, and it hurts, when it shouldn't. We had sex. *Just* sex. That does not spell exclusivity or commitment. I'm about to turn away when the big-breasted bartender looks up, and for some reason her gaze lands on me. Adrenaline surges through me and I turn to flee, only to have a man step in front of me, momentarily delaying my departure. I cut around him, and manage all of two steps before Kayden grips my arm and whirls me around to face him.

"Let go," I hiss, shoving against him, my chest burning with emotions, my palm burning where it's landed on his chest. "I shouldn't have come here."

He grabs my other arm and pulls me to him. "Ella. Stop."

"I didn't mean to interrupt your . . . whatever that was."

"It wasn't what you thought. You're hugely overreacting."

"You're right, and that only makes me angrier."

"I don't even know what that means."

"It means I shouldn't let you get to me, but you're here with some big-breasted bartender, avoiding me, and I'll just state the obvious. It upsets me." I jerk against him. "Let go."

"I'm not letting go. I told you that."

"You don't get to make that decision. I do. *I* do, Kayden."

His arm circles my waist, bringing my hip to his, and he starts walking, forcing me to follow or make a scene we both know I don't dare. My mind is plotting an escape, but there isn't one. Far too quickly, we've traveled a short hallway, and he's already opening a door and entering some room while taking me with him. "Rosa owns the bar," he announces, pressing me against the desk and pinning me with his big body, his hips aligned with mine, his hands on the surface behind me.

"And you want to fuck her," I say, oh so aware of his hard thighs against mine.

"She's Adriel's on-again, off-again girlfriend."

"And you want to fuck her."

"Holy hell. No, Ella, I do *not want* to fuck her."

"You're here, staring at her cleavage rather than being with me, and you smell like tequila. I guess that's better than smelling like her."

"That woman always has cleavage. I don't even see it anymore."

"You were here and not—"

"I know. *I know.*" His hands come down on my arms. "I wanted to be with you."

"Then why weren't you?"

"Because 'this'—us—wasn't supposed to happen." Now he sounds angry.

"I can leave. Just let me borrow some money."

He scrubs his jaw, looking tormented as he settles his hand back on the desk. "I don't want you to leave any more than I want to be in this shitty bar right now."

"But you are."

"Because I don't know how to protect you and be with you, but I also don't know how to let go of you and trust you'll be safe. And the honest fucking truth is I don't *want* to let you go."

My anger evaporates, my throat thick with the crazy emotions he stirs in me. "Then don't."

"It's not that simple."

"Make it simple."

"I *can't* just make it simple. If you're with me, you're with The Underground, and it comes with risks that I can't, and won't, walk away from. Kevin maintained the values of the organization. I promised him I'd do the same when, and if, that time came, and it came."

I reach down and turn his hand over, revealing the tattoo on his wrist. "Protector."

"Yes. And that is the way I honor Kevin."

"I admire you for that commitment, and it doesn't scare me. I can handle it."

"You *think* you can handle it."

"I have a mobster chasing me. I'm not exactly living a life of roses and chocolate, with or without you."

He studies me for several heavy seconds. "We're going to fight."

"Yes. We are."

"We're going to fight about my insane need to protect you."

"I'm a redhead. I'm good at giving what I get."

His jaw sets hard. "You say that, but after what you told me about that man—"

He hits a nerve, and my response is instant. "I told you. I don't even know the person I must have been to let him treat me that way, and you're nothing like him."

"That's not completely true. In his fucked-up way, he

claimed he was protecting you. And I *will* protect you at all costs."

"Just don't tie me up and leave me and I won't shoot you with the gun you gave me, like I most likely did him."

"Sweetheart, if I tie you up, it's about pleasure, and I'll be right there giving it to you, but to be clear: I want you, just you, but you need to know that women and sex have been vices that have served me well, and now I'm focusing all of that on you. I need to know if you can handle it." He leads me to the door, opening it and placing me in front of him, his cheek near mine as he whispers, "Let's go find out."

I swallow hard at the erotic challenge, and his hand settles at my back, branding me and guiding me forward. We enter the bar again, and I swear I feel Kayden's powerful presence in every nerve ending of my body, anticipation burning through me. We pass tables, and random people, and I do not miss the way heads turn as he passes, the way he claims the attention of those around us as he does me. I cannot be alone with him soon enough—a desire sidetracked as two dark-haired men, one tall enough to be eye level with Kayden, the other slightly shorter, step in our path.

The taller one speaks to Kayden in Italian, and the only pieces of information I pick up are the names *Enzo* and *Matteo*. From there, the three of them have an exchange, and it's clear to me the dark-haired men are Hunters looking to Kayden for guidance. The two men leave without so much as a glance in my direction, and I'm not sure if that's because I'm considered just another one of his women or because they don't think it will please Kayden. Whatever the case, he urges me forward and outside, and it hits me that he still doesn't have on a coat, but is seemingly immune to the cold. I suspect there is far too much Kayden has been immune to these past five years.

"Adriel was waiting for me across the street," I say as Kayden drapes his arm over my shoulder and we begin walking.

"Fuck Adriel."

It's a harsh, guttural statement that speaks of tension between the two men, and a shift in Kayden's mood from sexy to troubled, even bordering on angry. "Are you okay?"

He stops walking and faces me, hands on my arms as those pale blue eyes of his fix me in an unreadable stare. "Do you know how long it's been since I let anyone close enough to know or care to ask that question?"

I am not sure what reaction he's looking for from me, if any, and I'm not blind to the honesty and vulnerability he's dared to expose. "Do you want to talk about it?" I ask, my gut telling me he does.

"Enzo," he says without hesitation, confirming I was right. "He's a French kid that works for me. I let him take a job against my better judgment. He didn't show up for the chartered flight from Milan back here tonight, and no one can reach him."

This is his life. Danger. Torment. And it should scare me. It does scare me, but there is no denying that part of me is already too connected to this man to care. "What kind of job?"

His cell beeps with a text and he digs it from his pocket, grimacing at the message, his gaze lifting to scan the area we've just traveled, his jaw setting hard. "We have company."

I frown and follow his gaze, my lips parting at the sight of Gallo fast approaching. "What is he doing here?"

"According to Adriel's text message," he says, returning his phone to his pocket, "he followed us from the bar. I hope you memorized that file, because now is the time to get your memory back and shut him down."

"I did. I'm ready. I hope."

"You'll do fine. Just follow my lead."

"It's almost midnight, Kayden. Why would he be here? What if he found the real me? What if I—"

"Easy, sweetheart. *We* couldn't find the real you. He didn't. And he's here now for the same reason he was at the house at three a.m. last night. He's on a mission to rattle me, and you because of me, it appears. Let's show him he can't win."

"Yes. Okay."

"Good. We're going to turn together and face him."

I nod, inhaling as we move, his arm casually draped over my shoulder again as Gallo stops in front of us, his hands in his trench coat. "Twice in one day," Kayden greets him dryly. "Proof there is a God."

Gallo smirks and focuses on me. "I thought you'd like to know the results of your fingerprint search."

Nerves attack me from all directions, and I can't seem to form words. Fortunately, Kayden has no such problem. "So you tracked her down on our date at nearly midnight. Ever heard of a phone?"

"A date after being arrested," he gibes. "At least you have something to talk about." He glances between us. "Why don't we find someplace to sit down and talk? Unless you'd both rather invite me to the castle. Or I can pick up *Eleana* in the morning and we can chat at the station."

Eleana. Is that sarcasm, or confirmation of Matteo's success? My heart jackhammers with fear, but Kayden is oh so cool. "*We* aren't going to the station, and I ran out of invitations to the castle. Lucky for you we're standing next to a twenty-four-hour coffee shop. And since you were obviously following either me or Eleana, or both, and know we just came from a bar, let me preface your disappointment. I don't do drunk and stupid, so don't count on this going anywhere."

It's then that I realize I might have smelled tequila on Kayden, but he's so far from drunk, I'd be surprised if he had more than one shot. Adriel just used that to get me here, and I have the weirdest idea that he's the one who told Gallo where to find us. Which is just me being crazy paranoid again, considering he warned us of his approach. Isn't it?

Gallo gives us a deadpan look. "Let's go inside."

"Is that an order?" Kayden challenges. "Do you want to make this official? Should we call our attorney? Or perhaps your boss?"

Gallo bristles and fixes Kayden in a hateful stare. "We're going to do this one way or another."

"Yes," Kayden agrees. "We are, but with two different agendas."

I have no idea what that means, but Kayden urges me in front of him, placing himself between me and Gallo, and I have the sense that's what he intends to do this entire encounter. I hurry to the door, feeling like I have two predators at my back about to go for each other's throats. Kayden quickly joins me at the door, holding it open to allow me to enter the quaint little coffee shop, with a pair of large black chairs in one corner and a cluster of tables here and there. He indicates the largest of the quaint tables to our left, his hand on the small of my back as we travel in that direction.

Once there, I sit down facing the large window, the lights of the active street, where I'd rather be right about now, twinkling beyond the glass. Kayden claims the seat next to me, his arm resting protectively on the back of my chair. For extra measure, I pull my coat around myself, huddling into it rather than making an effort to remove it, which might suggest I'm willing to stay a while. Gallo isn't about to make this easy on me, placing me in the spotlight of those brutal gray eyes as he sits directly across from me, but the fact that he keeps his coat on as well gives me hope this will be short, if not sweet.

"Good news," Gallo announces, focusing solely on me. "We got a hit on your prints. As you know, your name is Rae Eleana, but I have the last name as well. It's—"

"Ward," Kayden supplies. "We were actually out celebrating her returned memory."

He stares at Kayden, his look a blade of ice. "Funny. I thought you were celebrating getting out of jail," he says, sharply shifting his attention back to me. "Just this morning you didn't remember more than your first name."

"I had a dream that was a trigger. My doctor said that's normally how it happens. And some of the swelling in my brain may have gone down." I press my lips together, having no idea where that came from, before I say something wrong.

"Interesting timing," he says dryly. "What doctor?"

I bristle at the nosy question laced with accusation. "That's rather personal, detective."

He grimaces and leans closer. "What do you remember?"

"My name and that I'm from Texas. I know who my employer was, or rather ex-employer. I quit my job to travel."

"And your parents?"

My shock and offense over his bringing up a topic that would upset me, if my file weren't fictional, is not feigned. I hope. "Why would you go there? You have to know their loss is raw. In truth, that's probably what I was trying to shut out with my amnesia."

His lips press together. "I'm sorry." He's not convincing, but rather responding to being put in his place. "Why don't I take you to the passport office tomorrow to get your passport replaced? I can help cut through the red tape."

"I can handle it," Kayden assures him. "I'm good at cutting through red tape, as you saw today. We both know I didn't threaten you." His arm lifts from around me and he leans forward, his powerful forearms resting on the table. "By the way. While you were trying to trump up ridiculous charges against me this afternoon, your boss begged me to work for him again."

Gallo stands, his hands pressed to the table, his stance a threat, his glower a promise. Kayden's lips quirk in feigned amusement. "Problem, detective?"

"You are not above the law."

"Neither are you. Don't let bitterness turn you into something you don't recognize as you anymore."

"Speaking from experience, are you?"

"Damn straight, man. Let this go."

Gallo glares at Kayden and I hold my breath until he says, "No." Nothing more. Just . . . no, and then he pushes off the table and heads for the door. And while he might be leaving, and my identity has been protected, dread and certainty fill my gut. He's coming for Kayden and he won't stop until someone ends up dead. I am left with one question. What did Kayden do to create this kind of hatred in this man?

The silence between Kayden and me is absolute as Gallo disappears into the night, my unasked question in the air, a pin about to drop. Kayden doesn't let it fall, but neither does he face me as he speaks. "Just before Callisto—Adriel and Giada's father—died, I aligned The Underground with the police department, trying to take us to as ethical a place as I could get us. Not an easy task when the money wasn't what my people expected to get paid. My contact for our first job was Gallo and a woman named Cira." He hesitates. "I fucked her. She was just a nameless escape that would be gone when the job was over. I had no idea she and Gallo were in a relationship. She didn't tell me and there were no signs."

"So this is all because you were with his woman?"

He looks at me, his expression taut with the promise of more to the story. Something bad. Really bad. "Gallo walked in on us. He and I fought. She left in a fit of tears and proceeded to have a car accident."

"Oh God," I murmur, feeling the blood run from my face. "Please tell me this doesn't end how I think it does."

"I wish I could. She died, and he blames me."

"But you didn't kill her. It was just one of those horrific things that happen in life. His anger is illogical."

"A need for revenge is rarely logical, but too often it feels like the salve that will heal the wound." There is deep under-standing in those words that make them more a confession than a statement. "He thinks he needs it to survive."

"Does he?" I ask, and I'm not talking about Gallo any more than he is.

"Yes. He does."

I don't know what to say to that, so I leave it alone. "You aren't going to take the job you mentioned, are you?"

He laughs without humor. "No. My people would de-throne me if I went down that path again. No matter how any of us frame our hunts as honorable, it's always about money."

"Is it to you?"

"I have more money than I know what to do with as it is."

"It's about Kevin."

"It's about a lot of things, none of them money."

Revenge. I think he's just told me it's about revenge, and I want to ask for more, but he stands and faces me, offering me his hand, and I have this sense of the gesture being *his* silent question. Am I still with him? Has he scared me away? Per-haps that's why he told me the story, but it hasn't worked. His honesty, his willingness to share what is not easy to speak about, let alone live with, has done nothing but draw me closer to the flame that is the fire in this man. I slide my palm against his and he helps me to my feet, and when our gazes meet, I see in his eyes what I know myself. My decision to stay with him is a choice, and good, bad, or ugly, I'm staying with Kayden Wilkens. We're both destined to live with the conse-quences that may follow.

seventeen

Kayden answers my silent reply by cupping the back of my head and kissing me hard and fast before wrapping my hand in his and leading me to the exit. We step outside and I shiver with the night that has turned colder, and Kayden responds, cocooning me in the warmth and shelter of his body, but I think that it's him who needs shelter.

We fall into easy steps together, silence settling between us in that comfortable way it had over dinner last night. Blocks pass, and even with the absence of conversation, I can feel the heaviness of his thoughts, but I also believe he just needs me to be with him. I know this, and I don't know why but I have this sense of togetherness with him that, beyond the emptiness of my past, I do not believe I have had before in my life. Even if I have, what matters is this man, and having it with him.

His cell phone rings, and for some reason, the sound fills me with dread. Without his pace faltering or his arm moving from my shoulders, he digs it from his pocket, answering the call and listening a moment before replying in Italian. It's a quick, terse exchange that ends when we reach the entrance to the castle, his expression unreadable as he releases me to slide the phone back into his pocket and punch in a code to open the gate.

"Two-seven-two-seven," he says, giving me the gate code, and I remove my phone from my purse and type it into the notes.

"Got it," I say, as we cross to the private grounds of the castle. "I'll delete it once I get all these numbers straight in my head."

He hits a button to close the gate and wraps his arm around mine as we begin the walk toward the front door.

"I'm not trying to be nosy, but please just tell me that call wasn't bad news."

"You aren't being nosy. You're being concerned about one of my men, and that will never upset me. Matteo pinged Enzo's phone and hacked his email. There's been no activity in twelve hours."

"That doesn't sound good."

"If you don't want to be found, you go radio silent. It could be a choice, but it still means he's in trouble."

"You didn't get to tell me what the job was. Can you? Will you?"

He hesitates. "Recovering a stolen piece of art."

"You didn't seem to want to tell me that, but it sounds like a reasonable job. Why didn't you want him to take it?"

"Because the man who stole it has connections to a drug cartel. I finally agreed that he could commission the hunt, on the condition that he do nothing but find the painting and report the location to the client, without recovering it."

"You think he tried to recover it."

"He's young, and as most young men do, he thinks he's immortal. So yes. That's what I think."

A drop of rain hits my nose, and I stupidly look up to be splattered in the face. "Come on," he says, grabbing my hand as we launch into a run and rush up the castle steps, reaching the overhang just in time to avoid a downpour.

"This is a crazy amount of rain," I say, wiping off my coat. "You'd think it was rainy season in Paris." I go still, and Kayden arches a brow. "Paris," I whisper. "Kayden, I know Paris."

"During rainy season," he adds. "Matteo did a broad sweep for the name Ella, but I'll have him hyper-focus on Paris. Do you remember anything else?"

"Of course not. Why would I make this easy on us? I don't even know where that comment came from."

"It's a seed that might grow, and that's better than no seed at all." He snags my fingers. "Come here. I want to teach you how to get in the door."

"I need a lesson?" I ask, letting him put me between him and the door. "Is it that complicated?"

"Not complicated, but there is a specific process or you'll set off the alarms." He taps the panel by the door. "First the code." He keys it in. "Two-seven-one-one." He holds up a key. "Then the lock. If you do it the opposite way, it won't work."

"And the alarm sounds."

"Exactly." He unlocks the door and flattens the key into my hand, curling my fingers around it. "That's yours. You and I are the only two people who have access to enter through this door. Don't tell anyone the codes and don't let anyone use your key."

"Not even the people who live in the castle?"

"That's right. This way, if one tower is breached, the others aren't."

"You don't trust Adriel or Giada."

"Trust isn't high on my list, and I don't like people in my private space."

The significance of that statement being his bringing me to his tower immediately, and my oversight earlier today. "Then I should tell you that I let Giada hang out with me in our tower. I didn't let her go anywhere but the living room."

His eyes glint steel. "I don't want her there."

"Why, Kayden? She's just a young girl."

"I don't always have a reason, just a gut feeling, and they never fail me." He changes the subject, making it clear he doesn't want to talk about Giada. "Let's go to bed." He pauses and softens his voice. "Together."

Together. It is a word I do not believe he knows well, but he offers it to me, the certainty warming me in places beyond my skin. "Together," I repeat, sealing what feels like a deal.

The flecks of deeper blue in his eyes tell me that he is pleased with my reply, and as he had in the bar, he reaches around me and opens the door. Nervous energy spikes through me and I enter the castle; my feet carry me to the center of the foyer, where my gaze lands on the center tower steps. I swallow a knot in my throat at the knowledge that death occupies the rooms above. I wonder if Elizabeth felt safe here. I wonder if Kayden thought he could protect her. I wonder if he even knew that at that stage of his career, with Kevin still alive, he needed to protect her. And I wonder if this place is haunted by ghosts, or just the heartache of loss.

Kayden steps to my side, his gaze following mine. "We lived in that tower together for all of three months before they were slaughtered there like animals, which is why I hate every inch of it. I kept it sealed for three years."

I shiver at the words "slaughtered like animals" and I turn to him. "You have no idea who did it?"

"No," he says, scrubbing a hand through his hair. "But if it had been about me, they would have come for me, too, and believe me, I wish they had."

"If not about you, then Kevin?"

"It had to have been about something he was involved with, and Elizabeth just happened to be here when they came to kill him. She wasn't a Hunter. She was a fashion designer by trade, who made me feel like my life was a little more normal. I met her at a retail store, looking for a gift for Marabella."

"She gave you an escape from this world."

"She hated The Underground and I pulled back from it because of that." He hardens his voice to pure steel. "You need to know that won't happen again. Had I been more involved with what Kevin was doing, I might have stopped it from happening. And so we're clear: not only do I hate that fucking tower, I hate your being in it. Let's go upstairs." He walks to the door dividing the main foyer from our tower and punches in the code.

I hesitate, unmoving in the aftermath of his obvious anger. But it is not at me, though I have obviously stirred to life demons he hasn't fully restrained. And while I am not sure what that means for us long term, I do know he needs someone to anchor him to the present and drive away the past, if only for tonight.

Crossing to stand next to him, I dare to link my elbow with his and say, "I hate that tower, too."

He disengages our arms and wraps his around my neck and brings my chest to his, his breath a warm tease on my lips. "That was the right thing to say," he declares, his mouth slanting over mine for a quick, deep kiss, the taste of his lingering anger spiking my taste buds and then fading as he releases me and leads me across the threshold to our tower. We pause just on the other side, and when he hits a button to close our door I have this sense of us being sealed in our own private world, at least for the rest of this night.

Side by side, we start up the stairs, barely touching when I want us to be touching everywhere. But the higher we climb, the more uncertain I become of what comes next, the memory of him leaving me alone in his bed sharply etched in my mind. Even more so, the certainty that no matter where we lie tonight, he is not a man to be held on to. He will leave. Or I will leave, and I can't fall for him. But I am, I so am, and I can't seem to care what kind of danger lies in the path to fully realizing all I can be, and feel, with this man. He halts at the main level, his hand sliding away from mine, a question in his action. Am I coming with him or not? But there is more. Am I afraid? Can I handle who, and what, he is? He is asking me to make the decision. There really is no real question in my mind about where I'm going, and where I want to be this night, and the way he can demand, command, and still offer me freedom seals my desire for this man.

I start walking toward his room and he falls into step with me, my pulse quickening with each inch we travel, until he opens the door and I step inside. He follows, flipping a lock into place and punching a button on the wall beside us. The fireplace across the room flames into life in response, and while the room is cold, my skin heats as he touches me again, leaning me against the door, towering over me.

But, much to my distress, his hands fall away, flattening on the wall on either side of me, signaling that a mindless escape isn't as close as I'd hoped. "Before we go any further," he says, "you need to understand exactly what you're getting yourself into."

"I told you at the bar. I'm not afraid of The Underground."

"I'm talking about what I am and what motivates me. I wasn't ready to tell you what happened five years ago, but you know now, which means you need to understand what it was and what it means to me. What happened to Kevin and Elizabeth was no car accident. It wasn't an accident at all. It was murder. And make no mistake, if I find out who did it, I *will* kill them, and it will be with zero remorse. Just like I'll kill anyone who threatens you with *zero* remorse. Make sure you can live with that, because I damn sure can." He pushes off the wall and leaves me standing there as he disappears into the bathroom.

I inhale, barely able to breathe for the intensity of his emotions slamming into me. Yes, he has given me honesty, but I am certain this is driven by the same kind of doubt in him I'd felt walking up the stairs. He is trying to scare me, to push me away. But he has failed. No matter how brutal those words are, they are real. He is real, the wolf who doesn't bother with the sheep's clothing I'd first seen at the hospital, and his realness is part of his appeal. I need that. I think he does too, but maybe he needs to know that I come with no demands or expectations for a Happily Ever After I know he can't give me and I'm not sure I even believe exists anyway. At least not for people like him and me.

The shower comes on and I allow myself no hesitation, crossing to the bathroom where his clothes are piled on the floor and he is hidden behind the stone walls of the stall. I take a deep breath for courage and undress, walking to the glass door. His back is to me and I have a full view of the tattoo between his shoulder blades, counting five skulls, and their meaning shakes me to the core. His mother, father, sister, Kevin, and Elizabeth.

I open the door and his shoulders bunch slightly, telling me he is aware of me, but he doesn't turn. I step to him and press my hand to the center of those tattoos. "Everyone you've lost."

He reaches around and pulls me in front of him, out of reach of the spray of water, walking me backward until I hit the wall. "Yes. Everyone I've lost, and I do not intend to let you become part of that circle. But if you want out, if you want to leave—"

"I thought you said you wouldn't let me go."

"Do you want to go?"

The question catches me off guard, but I don't falter. "No. I don't."

"After all you've learned today, are you sure about that?"

"If you're afraid I want more than you can give—"

"I'm afraid I want more than I can, or should, ask of you. But I seem to be incapable of stopping myself." His gaze sweeps low, a hot caress over my naked body that I feel in all the places I wish he were touching me.

I reach for him and he captures my hand. "When I said I like things a little dirty, that was wrong. I like things a lot dirty."

My pulse leaps wildly with the promise of dark, sexy things I want to know with this man. "Show me," I say.

"I need to know I'm not going to scare you."

I blink up at him, a cold spot in my chest expanding, the realization a blow I did not expect. "You think because he tied me up that I am afraid of your version of *dirty*? Damn it, Kayden, I told you. If you hold back and treat me like a wilting flower, he wins."

"Sweetheart, that's when we're talking and not fucking. I'm warning that I'm not going to hold back. I *won't* hold back. If you say yes to what I ask for, I will take full advantage of what that means."

"Yes," I say, sounding breathless, my knees weak and my nipples tight. "My answer is yes."

His eyes darken, a muscle in his jaw flexing, and I can almost feel him restraining himself, holding back, and I hate it. I hate it so much. I flatten my hand on his chest, damp tendrils of light brown hair teasing my fingers. "I am not his captive. I will not be that and you will not make me that. So let me repeat my answer. *Yes.*"

His eyes glint hard and he turns me to the face the wall, the way he turned me to face that bedpost last night, and I know he's testing me, pushing me. "Are you sure about that?" he demands, his erection at my hip, his hand cupping my breast and squeezing it roughly, erotically.

"Yes," I pant out. "Yes."

"Let's define the meaning of *yes*." His hand flattens on one of my butt cheeks. "*Yes* means I won't just make you want me to own you. While we're fucking, I *will* own you." He steps to my side, at my hip, his shaft resting at the back of my thigh, his hand squeezing my backside. "Own you," he repeats, his head resting against mine.

"What part of 'yes' do you not understand?"

He cups my sex. "And *I will* tie you up."

"You said that," I remind him, frustrated that he feels the need to go there again. "Stop warning me and just do this."

"Do I get to define what 'this' is?"

"As long as you do it now."

His teeth nip my ear, and I swear I feel it in my sex right where his fingers are pumping and moving. "Let's see. Should I lick you? Bite you? *Spank* you?"

Shock rips through me and I try to turn, but his hand flattens on my back, holding me in place. "I thought you wanted it dirty?"

"Spank me? I—"

"Is this where you say no? Because you can always say no."

"I've never—"

"Are you sure?"

"Oh yes," I say quickly. "Yes, I am quite sure."

"Good. Then I'll be the *only one* you trust that much." He turns me around again, nestling me in the corner, my wrists shackled over my head where he grips them. "The word *yes*," he says, dragging his free hand over my breast, down my body, until it cups my sex again, "has a consequence. You know that, right?"

"What consequence?" I pant out, his fingers pressing inside me, thumb stroking over my clit and sending darts of pleasure straight to my nipples.

"Trust. Complete, absolute trust, and I will demand it in ways you can't begin to fathom." He brushes his lips over mine, fingers stroking deeper into my sex, moving back and forth.

"How is that a consequence?"

"It gives me control. It lets me own you, and when I do, I'm going to make sure you want more. Do you want more now?"

"Yes. Oh yes."

"Close your eyes and don't move your hands when I let go. If you do—"

"You won't let me come."

"Exactly. Now, do it."

My lashes lower and his hands leave my wrists, and it is all I can do not to satisfy my need to touch him, my breath panting from my parted lips. But I am motivated to comply by the way he is touching me. Everywhere, all over, and sensations roll through me, pleasure lighting up every nerve ending in my body. I can barely take it, and yet it's not enough, and I moan with the need for something else. For that "more" he wishes me to crave, that I wish to be *him* inside of *me*.

"Kayden," I plead, and he answers by sinking to one knee, his tongue lapping my swollen nub; then he suckles deeply, while his fingers, his amazing fingers, slide in and out of me. And my hands are too heavy over my head, my fingers knotting in my hair, the only way I can stop them from lowering to his, and I cannot control the sounds of pleasure escaping my lips.

There is a swell of arousal in my belly, low, lower, and I both want to quell it and want to drive it to the next blissful place, and it does go there. To that sweet spot from where there is no return. I lose control, my fingers twining into his hair, but he does not punish me or deny my release, as I feared. He lets me touch him, his tongue and his fingers slowly easing, becoming gentler, and then slipping away as my knees all but collapse.

Kayden stands and turns off the water, then returns to me to twine fingers in my hair, pulling my head back and forcing my gaze to his. "You have to learn to follow orders. Action equals consequence. Remember that."

"I tried, but you—"

"There is no *try*. There is only *do*, but I'll show you. I'll teach you."

I'll teach you. The words speak to the woman in me in ways perhaps they should not, but I don't care. They just do, and he does, and when he kisses me, licking into my mouth, the sweet, salty taste of me on his lips, he does own me. I tangle fingers in his hair, and he tears his mouth from mine, giving me one of those wolfish stares as he cups my backside and lifts me.

We exit the shower, and he sits me on the counter, wrapping me in a towel before he secures one at his waist, tendrils of water that beg for my tongue sliding down his arm. He steps into me again, his hands settling on my legs, branding me as if he hasn't already, but the wolf is gone; warm tenderness is in his eyes as he asks, "You okay?"

It's what I'd asked him, and my lips curve with that reference and with the idea that, while he's pushed me, he's still protecting me, even from himself. "Yeah," I say, "I'm okay."

He smiles his approval and gives me a low, sexy command of "stay here" that leaves me curiously tracking his every step as he disappears into the closet.

Grinning at just about everything that just happened in that shower, I cannot contain my desire to see what the sexy "king of the castle's" closet looks like. I slide off the counter and quickly dart in that direction, only to have him appear in the archway before I enter, now wearing a pair of pajama bottoms, with a shirt in his hand. "I told you to wait."

I grimace at his attempt at a reprimand. "I take orders better when naked than not."

He arches a brow. "Is that right? You're almost naked now."

"I have a towel."

"I can fix that."

I clutch it to my chest. "I want to see your closet."

"See it when you move your things in tomorrow."

I blink, certain I've misheard. "What?"

He slides the shirt over my head and I slip my arms inside, my towel falling to the ground. "That's so I can concentrate and give you a chance to make a decision."

"Decision?"

"Either you're in my bed or you're not. I want you in it."

I am pleased. I am confused. I am so many things with this man that I can't even begin to define. "But you left last night."

"Fucking some random woman and wanting you in my bed are two different things. I had to come to terms with what that meant for me. I have. Now it's your turn."

"What it means for you? If the answer is that I open raw

wounds, I'll choose nothing. If the answer is it lets you protect me and that is all you want and need, I'll choose nothing."

"I want you in my bed, Ella. I've said that to no one in a very long time. Why do I want you there? I just do. That's the only answer I have for either of us. It's back to you. Choose, Ella. Now."

I just do. It's my answer exactly, and perhaps the only one either of us can give this early in our time together. My decision made, I turn and walk into the bedroom and don't stop moving until I'm in his bed, under the covers. By the time I am, he is joining me, making it clear he's not leaving tonight. He lowers the lights, casting us in the dim glow of the fireplace, and moves close to me.

"Right here," he says, wrapping me in his arms, my back to his front, and I am suddenly warm and sheltered, and he feels right in ways that make my lost memory second to this and him. But I do not miss the way he holds me a little too tight, as if he's certain someone, or something, will soon rip me from his arms. And the truth is, I fear the same.

eighteen

I wake to the dull thrumming of more rain, not sure where it's coming from, and I don't care. Kayden is wrapped around me and I have zero desire to wake up. My lashes lower and I will myself back to sleep, the thrum of the rain a song lulling me into slumber, and suddenly I am back in that hotel room moments after David left. It is the moment after he'd gone and I'd ripped the butterfly from my neck.

Appalled at what I have done, I stare at the necklace on the floor, stumbling forward and falling to my knees. I grab the butterfly, and frown as I find a piece of paper sticking out of the back. I tug on it and stare at the handwritten words.

I blink drowsily, my gaze catching on the fireplace, and Kayden shifts behind me, his hand slipping under my shirt to flatten on my belly. I cover it with mine and hold on tight, squeezing my eyes shut and trying to force my mind back into that hotel room where I can read the words on that piece of paper. Instead, I am transported back to a moment with *him.*

He is angry. He is always angry. He is also at my back, stalking me as we walk down a hallway in a club he says I will soon enjoy as he does. There was a time when he would have said such a thing to me and I'd have believed him. That time has passed. The path ends and he punches a code into the door panel, an odd thing in a club, but of course, he wouldn't frequent any place that isn't exclusive in every possible way. The door buzzes open and I enter what looks like a small, round coliseum, stepping past two huge pillars to find a naked woman with long, dark hair, on her knees, with her arms tied to some sort of posts. I gasp and turn to leave, but he *steps in front of me. "Where do you think you're going?"*

"I don't want to be here."

"You need to see what happens if you disobey me again."

"I already promised I'd listen from now on."

He caresses my cheek and I cringe. He notices and is not pleased, his fingers digging into my arm as he turns me to face forward. "You watch. You learn. If you move right now, you will become her." He shoves me to my knees, his legs at my spine, and my gaze meets the woman waiting for whatever punishment is soon to be hers, but she is not afraid as I am. She welcomes it. She wants it. A door opens to the left, and a beautiful blond woman in leather holding a whip enters the room.

"No!" I stand and face him. "No. No. No."

He grabs my hair and drags me toward the two women, glancing over my shoulder to say, "She goes first."

"Ella. Sweetheart. Wake up."

I roll over to stare into Kayden's blue eyes, blinking several times to make sure he's real. "Oh God." I cup his cheek. "I'm so happy you're here."

He covers my hand with his. "Flashback?"

"Nightmare. Flashback. Whatever you want to call it."

"Him again?"

"Yes. Kayden, he's . . ." My throat thickens. "It doesn't matter. It's over."

"It does matter. Talk to me, sweetheart."

"No. I can't talk about this and it doesn't change anything. It doesn't help us figure out who he is."

"How do you know?"

"It *doesn't* help," I insist. "Please. Just let it go."

He strokes hair from my face. "I won't push, but I want you to be able to talk to me. Everything or nothing, remember? That doesn't change when your memories come back. Remember that."

His cell phone rings, and he kisses my forehead and then rolls over to grab it from his nightstand, sitting up to take the call. I sit as well, curling my knees to my chest, and while the beating isn't important, the necklace is, and that means talking about David, a subject not easily broached with Kayden. I listen as he speaks quickly in Italian, deciding it's time I learn the language. He ends the call, scrubbing a hand through his hair and exhaling.

"What is it?" I ask.

"Matteo picked up some internet chatter early this morning that he thought was a lead on Enzo, but it went cold on him."

"You have a bad feeling about this, don't you?"

"Yeah. I do. Really fucking bad, and my feelings aren't wrong."

His phone rings again while he's still holding it and he grimaces and glances at the number. "Adriel," he says. "He's looking for Enzo too." He answers, looking both irritated and confused. "Giada? How do you have my number?"

She doesn't have his number? That's odd.

"Hold on," he says, and offers me the phone, looking exceedingly grumpy as he announces, "For you."

I accept it, thinking her timing has not played in her favor with Kayden. "Hi, Giada."

"Hi, Ella. I was wondering if you want to go shopping?"

I glance at the one window in the corner opposite the fireplace, watching rain hitting the glass. "It's a pretty wet day."

"We have indoor shopping centers. It will be fun and we can talk."

Talk. That is her real goal. She needs another woman to bond with, just as Marabella had thought. "Hold on," I say, covering the phone to run the idea by Kayden. "She wants me to go shopping with her."

He scowls and takes the phone. "She'll call you back." He hangs up.

"Oh my God. Kayden. That was horrible. I know we have to go to the consulate for my passport, but I could have worked around that with her. And I could have handled it nicely."

"Gallo will be waiting on us if we go today. We'll go when his boss can make sure he isn't around."

I forget about Giada. "You have that much pull with his boss?"

"Yes, I do. And before you ask, Gallo has no idea just how much."

"How is that possible, if you don't work for the police department?"

"I do a few things on the side for them when necessary.

This will cost me one of those jobs, but so be it to keep the relationship and get what we need." He rolls me onto my back, his arm bracketing my body. "Today we stay here. Just you and me."

"Don't expect me to complain about hiding out with you on a rainy day, but you were still mean to Giada."

"I don't want her negativity influencing you."

"I'm my own person, and she needs a positive influence. Actually, Kayden, you lost your family as a minor as well. You could help her. Maybe we could take her to lunch."

"No," he says, his tone flat and absolute.

"Kayden—"

"No. End of topic." He rolls off me and the bed, and is crossing the room and entering the bathroom before I've sat up.

I gape in disbelief, but I am not dissuaded from the topic or finding out what the heck is up with him and Giada. I scramble off the bed, quickly crossing to the bathroom, where I find him slathering on shaving cream at the sink. "No?" I demand. "You sound like Gallo. I only take orders in bed. I am not one of your Hunters."

He sets the brush down and turns to face me. "Is that right?"

"Oh yes. That's right."

"You really *are* a redhead, aren't you?"

I have a flickering memory of my mother, and my temper deflates. "Yes. I am."

He drags me to him. "Then you leave me only one option," he declares, his tone flat.

"And that would be what?"

He kisses me, and I gasp into his mouth as shaving cream

smudges all over me. I shove on his chest to free my mouth. "No, you didn't."

He grins, and it's truly sexy and hot in every possible way. "That's what you get for messing with me, sweetheart."

I laugh and push to my toes and kiss him again. He cups my head and gives me a long, drugging kiss, and then turns me to the mirror, and I have as much shaving cream on me as he does him. I grab the towel he has sitting on the sink and pat my cheeks.

"Now you know what happens when you argue with me," he teases, reaching for the brush again.

"I'll do it," I say, stepping in front of him and taking the brush from his hand, our laughter in the middle of what could have been a fight feeling right in the same way our comfortable silences are.

He lifts me and sets me on the counter. "Are you as dangerous with a razor as you are with a gun?"

I grin. "Of course, but at least I'm accurate with the gun."

"You aren't making me confident about putting a blade in your hand, and how do you know you're accurate with a gun?"

"My father made me practice. I resented him then, but it's actually really comforting to know I can handle myself."

"You will get no argument from me on that. What else do you remember?"

"My mother was redheaded and beautiful."

"No surprise there."

I blush with the compliment. "Thank you, Kayden."

He drags a finger down my cheek. "Just speaking the truth, beautiful. Anything else?"

"I was close to her, and I think she died of cancer." I shake my head. "I said that so matter-of-factly, but it didn't feel that way when I remembered it. You know, Giada lost her mother to cancer too."

"That doesn't make you like her."

"She's alone. She has no one."

"She has her brother and Marabella."

"Not you?"

"I look out for her, and she knows it even if she doesn't like it." He gives me a heavy-lidded stare, his hands flattening on my bare legs beneath his shirt. "You aren't alone. You have me now. You know that, right?" A firestorm of emotions attacks me, jumping around in my belly, and I cut my gaze. His finger slides under my chin and he gently brings my eyes back to his. "You have me."

"For now."

"Not for now. You don't know that yet, but you will." He reaches for the razor. "This is what you call trust."

I close my hand around the razor, heat sliding up my arm and over my chest as our fingers touch. "Trust," I whisper.

"Yes. Trust."

We stare at each other and the air shifts and almost burns, the connection between us expanding, deepening, and he is safe and right in ways that matter more than ever after my flashback this morning. "Last night . . ."

The blue in his eyes darkens. "What about last night, Ella?"

"I just . . ." I wet my lips.

"We can go slow."

"That's not the point. I just wanted you to know that I . . . slept pretty good with you."

He gives me a curious look, those sexy lips curving into a smile. "I slept pretty good with you too. Now. Shave me, woman."

I laugh and am about to go to work, but I'm not ready to let go of his grumpiness from minutes before. "You know—"

"Don't bring up Giada again."

I pause mid-swipe. "How did you know I was going to talk about her?"

"Because I'm figuring out quickly that you don't give up easily."

"You can be a big brother to her."

"See what I mean?"

"I'm serious, Kayden."

"She has Adriel."

"Who she resents."

"She resents me."

"Please—"

"No."

I glower openly. "We're back to 'no'?"

"We never left it."

"You're being stubborn."

"Yes. I am."

I set down the razor I haven't even used and scoot off the counter. "You need to shave yourself."

"Because of Giada?"

"Because if I stay this is going to become our second fight," I say, inching away from him.

"Second?"

I pause at the doorway. "The bar last night was number one. If I stay right now, we'll be two for two, so I'm not staying right now. I'm going to shower. Alone." I accent that statement by leaving, making a beeline for the door and exiting into the hallway, where cold stone meets my bare feet. I pass the stairwell and realize that Marabella could be here, and I start running. I enter my room and shut the door. I wait, half expecting Kayden to follow, but half not, his desire to avoid a Giada conversation powerfully evident.

Inhaling, I'm trying to figure out what sore spot she hits in him, and failing. After flipping on the fireplace switch I cross to the bathroom, undress, and turn on the shower, taking my new products with me when I enter. I step under the warm stream of water and quickly wash my hair and drench it in conditioner, returning to my prior dilemma. What is it with Kayden and Giada? And why do I feel so weird with Adriel? Actually, I felt kind of weird with Giada when we were here yesterday, so maybe being stalked by cops and gangsters has me feeling paranoid.

I'm deep in thought when the shower door opens and I turn to find a very naked, very sexy, clean-shaven Kayden stepping inside. "I said alone."

He ignores my reprimand, advancing on me and wrapping me in his arms. "I'm not the influence I want her to have."

"You are the exact influence she needs."

"No. I'm not, and I have often regretted bringing her here."

"You brought her here to protect her."

"And that brought her into the fold of The Underground. I say it's time for her to start a new life somewhere far away, like the States. But Adriel won't send her away. He feels he can't protect her from a distance."

"Like you do me."

"Yes. It's a damned-if-we-do, damned-if-we-don't situation you're in, Ella. It's not easy to get out."

"I don't want out."

"Neither does Giada, and yet she now hates me, Adriel, and everyone in her life. There's no win to that."

"She hates The Underground."

"She's just plain angry."

"If she could deal with her pain, maybe she wouldn't be angry. Don't make yourself someone for her to hate. Make yourself someone she can relate to."

"What's right for me is not right for her."

"Let her decide what's right for her, but give her the emotional tools to do it."

"I'm pretty sure her emotional tools are exhausted."

"I'm not giving up on her and I'm not letting you, either."

His hands slide down my conditioner-slicked hair and he tilts my head back. "You don't take no for an answer, do you?"

"That's not true. I wouldn't have gone to the tower if I'd known you didn't want me there."

"I believe you." He kisses me. "Let's finish this shower and go eat. Someone worked up my appetite."

I laugh and we shower, really shower, together, and once

we're done he exits first, and we both dry off and bundle up in towels—well, I do. His is slung low and sexy at his hips as he disappears inside my closet.

"I don't think anything in there will fit," I call out.

He reappears with the clothes I'd had hanging up draped over one arm, and bags in the other. "That's why we're going to my room."

"Now? We have no clothes on."

"We'll fix that when we get there. Grab some stuff." He takes off walking.

"*Who* doesn't take no for an answer?" I shout after him, gathering up bags and tossing toiletries in them before dashing for the hallway to find Kayden heading back in my direction to help me, his towel barely hanging on.

I laugh and hurry forward. "You're about to lose your—"

Marabella appears at the top of the steps and I cringe, cheeks heating and all words lost. She starts laughing, and I hurry past her to call out, "I can't explain this, so I'm not going to try."

Her giggles follow me, and Kayden grabs my bags, barely containing a smile, far too amused by this turn of events. "I'm making pancakes, you two," Marabella calls out, and Kayden outright laughs, disappearing inside the room.

I follow him and he heads to the bathroom, where I enter as he disappears in the closet. I charge after him. "She's making pancakes. She told me while I was in a towel running after you."

"I heard," he says. "And let me tell you. She makes a hell of a pancake."

"I'm mortified."

He runs his thumb over my cheek. "I'll talk to her about calling before she enters."

"We could just not run around in towels."

"What fun would that be?" he asks, emphasizing that statement by tugging mine away.

I yelp and find myself lying on top of some sort of wide leather stool, with Kayden leaning over me. "What are you doing?"

"I haven't been inside you for far too long."

"That's because we never have a condom."

"We do this time." He reaches down and opens a drawer, producing one packaged condom. "I bought a box yesterday, but we really need to get you to a doctor for birth control."

"Not Nathan. He's your friend. That would just be weird."

"Agreed. We'll ask him who to go to." He leans in to kiss me.

I cover his mouth and grab the condom. "We can't do this now. We're expected for pancakes. If we don't show up she'll think—"

"That I'm inside you, enjoying the hell out of myself."

My eyes go wide. "Kayden!"

He laughs and presses his cheek to mine, whispering something oh so sexy and Italian in my ear.

My lips curve with what I am certain fits his definition of *dirty*. "What did you say?"

He nips my ear. "Learn Italian and you'll know."

"That's not fair."

He inches back, those blue eyes gleaming with wicked heat. "I never claimed to be fair."

"Just dirty," I tease.

"That's right, sweetheart. Let me show you how it tastes."

I laugh and he kisses me, his tongue licking seductively against mine, and it's official. I forget all about pancakes.

∞∞

An hour later, it is a surreal feeling to be lost and yet found in Kayden's world, having claimed one of the two sinks in his bathroom—*our* bathroom, as he's called it quite freely—where I've arranged various toiletries for my use. I blow-dry my hair while Kayden lets his dry on its own and dresses in faded jeans and a black tee. He looks absolutely yummy when he exits into the bedroom to answer a call. I dig around in my bags and choose a pair of comfy black leggings that I pair with a long-sleeved, light blue sweater, and I slip on a pair of UGG boots for warmth, since we aren't going out today.

I head into the bedroom, and, finding the security door open, continue in that direction to find Kayden sitting at the desk and instant messaging with someone. "Hi," I say.

"*Ciao*, beautiful," he says, turning to me. "Did you take your medicine?"

"I did," I say, charmed that he's running The Underground and still manages to be concerned about me. "Thank you for reminding me, though."

His eyes gleam with wicked heat. "It's self-serving, sweetheart. I have plans for you when you've fully recovered." He grabs my hips and drags me to him. "When you trust me."

"I do trust you, Kayden. I've told you that."

"There's a whole lot more to trust than words."

I curl my fingers around his jaw. "You'll teach me, right?"

His eyes light with approval. "Yes, I'll teach you, but I'm starting to think I have some things to learn from you, too." He cups my hand and kisses it. "Are you ready for breakfast?"

"Isn't it close to lunch?"

He glances at his watch, and *damn it*, it stirs that odd, familiar feeling I don't understand. "Eleven thirty," he informs me. "We'll call it brunch. Give me a second." He releases me and I lean on the desk while he returns his attention to his keyboard, typing in a reply to whomever he's chatting with, and stands. "Done. Now we eat."

"Any news on Enzo?"

"Nothing yet, but that was one of my men in Milan, where Enzo was last known to be. He's digging around."

"How many Hunters do you have reporting to you?"

"Fifty across Rome and France."

"I thought you only ran Rome."

"I recently took over France as well."

"Please tell me it's not because the prior Hawk, or whatever you call the leaders, is dead."

"We do call them Hawks, and no. He's not dead. He moved to another country, like my father did when Kevin took over Rome years before I was born."

"Has any Hawk from any country died?"

"Sweetheart." He wraps me in his arms. "Don't do this."

"I can't start needing you and then you go and die on me."

"The feeling is mutual. Neither of us is going anywhere but to the kitchen to get pancakes. Okay?"

"I'd make you promise, but I know it's not a promise you can keep."

He strokes the hair from my face and tilts my head back. "I promise," he says, his words absolute steel, as if his sheer will can make it so when we both know that isn't true. "And I don't make a promise I don't intend to keep."

His computer buzzes with a different sound than before and he gives me a quick kiss. "We're going to be okay," he assures me, sitting back down at the desk to check his screen. I step closer, and the very fact that we fear for his Hunter's life tells me any version of "okay" with Kayden is still dangerous, and yet he's somehow, illogically, safe. I don't know what to do with that piece of information.

"News?" I ask, as he keys in a message and stands once more.

"Unfortunately, no. It's just someone wanting to talk to me about a job. They can wait."

"A Hunter or a client?"

"A client." He picks up a large notebook from the desk. "This contains pictures of every person we know who works for Niccolo."

"Why do you have that?"

"Money is a common denominator between Hunters and mobsters, and I try to steer our paths in different directions. That requires knowledge and effort."

And there it is. The answer I realize I'd still desperately wanted. Or at least part of it. "Have you met Niccolo?"

"Unfortunately, yes." When I would ask more, he changes the subject. "I figured you can look over the photos while we eat, and then we can try and forget all of this for the rest of the day."

I draw in a heavy breath and exhale on an admission: "I

really hate the idea of those photos when I should be embracing them for the answer they could hold."

He caresses a lock of hair behind my ear. "We can wait until morning, if you prefer."

The touch is tender, and I wonder what it says about me that the combination of the gentleness in this man and the dirty, dark danger that is also him is so very alluring. But what isn't alluring is running, hiding, and dying. I take the notebook from him.

"I want to get this over with," I say, unsure of why I am so certain this book holds a secret I'm not ready to reveal.

nineteen

Kayden and I leave his room to head to breakfast, and the memory of me running down the hall in a towel manages to take precedence over the photos in my hand. "Marabella is going to embarrass me, isn't she?" I ask as we reach the entryway to the living area.

"Oh yeah," he confirms, amusement in his voice, his lips quirking in a near smile.

We cross to the kitchen and I glower fiercely at him. "You think it's funny."

He grins. "Guilty as charged."

"It's not funny," I chide. "It's embarrassing. I'm not hungry anymore."

I try to turn away but he snags my waist, kisses my temple, and before I can steel myself for the impact, walks me in front of him and through the kitchen entry. "*Ciao*, you two," Marabella greets us from behind the island, her ear-to-ear grin instant. "Have you worked up an appetite?"

I groan and cover my face and Kayden chuckles, sounding way too sexy for how infuriating his amusement is becoming.

It's made worse as he says, "Why yes, we have. In fact, make my pancakes a double stack, please."

I sink into a chair at the table and set down the notebook, dragging my journal and the file I'd left behind last night to join it. "Can you put booze in my coffee, please?" I plead, while Kayden sits down next to me and taps the notebook, obviously eager for me to take a look. I grimace and add, "Make that a double shot, not stack, for me."

Marabella giggles like a schoolgirl and delivers two cappuccinos to the table, a cute apron decorated with patches of strawberries covering her knee-length dress. "No booze for you," she tells me. "Kayden doesn't keep any in the castle."

She hurries away and I ignore the notebook to pick up my cup. "You're more of a control freak than I realized."

"I'm hopeful that comment comes with a good memory of last night."

My cheeks heat with the replay of his words in that shower. *I will lick you. Bite you. Pinch you. Spank you.*

He leans closer. "What are you thinking, Ella?"

"I was just thinking—"

"Right now. What are you thinking right now?"

I swallow hard. "I plead the Fifth."

His lips quirk and he leans back in his chair. "That's no fun."

He's playful and funny, and enjoys teasing me way too much, but I like this part of him too much to mind. "You don't drink because it creates a lack of control you don't like."

He lifts the cup, his eyes lighting with wicked heat. "Control is much more alluring than the other options. Don't you think?"

"Hmmm. I don't think I'd know, but maybe I'll give it a go."

"You can try."

I set my cup down, the delicious scent of pancakes cooking filling the air. "I will."

"Looking forward to that battle of wills," he assures me, tapping the notebook. "Let's get this over with and go get naked again."

I inhale a sharp breath, ready to do anything other than look at those photos, including broach the awkward subject of David. "I need to talk about something else first."

"I'm listening."

"David."

"David," he repeats, the name a blade sliding through the air. "The infamous fiancé."

"Kayden—"

"Tell me."

"He gave me a necklace. It was a large butterfly, and I found a handwritten note inside it."

He goes very still, the lines of his face sharpening with his tone. "What did that note say, Ella?"

Unease flits through me. "I don't remember. It could have been a silly love note."

"You claim to just 'know' things. Is that what you think it was?"

"No. No, I do not." He studies me with hooded eyes, his lashes hiding his gaze from my prying eyes, and I can't take his silence. "Why aren't you saying anything?"

"Because I don't like what I have to say."

My fingers curl into my palms. "Just say it, please."

"I think you were what is called a 'carrier.'"

"I don't like how that sounds."

"For good reason. A carrier is an innocent person who's targeted to transport items from one country to the next."

"How do you know this?"

"The Underground has encountered just about everything over the hundred years it's been around, and we have databases to store the history of those experiences. And I've personally encountered this kind of situation."

"And you think David chose me to be a carrier."

"It fits. Usually someone is directed to get close to the potential carrier and ensure they meet certain requirements."

"What requirements?"

"You really want to hear this?"

"I have to hear this." He still hesitates. "Kayden, please."

"The targets have no family and very few people in their lives to miss them."

Okay. I'm officially twisted in knots. "Confirmation my family's dead."

"I'm speculating, Ella, but Matteo found no missing Ella who traveled from San Francisco and no one in the DMV that fits your profile."

"They wiped me out completely. But there have to be people who know me. Jobs? Sara?"

"Of course there are, but they aren't going to make it easy for you to be found."

"That's a lot of effort."

"Not for someone like Matteo."

"What about a police report in the States? A missing persons report."

"Nothing. Not there or in Europe, but that doesn't mean it wasn't filed. It could mean it was erased from the computer databases and if it's reentered, a flag will ensure it's erased again."

I can see where this is headed. "What happens to carriers when the job is done?"

"Ella—"

"What happens to carriers when the job is done, Kayden?"

"They end up dead."

I am remarkably calm considering the harshness of that explanation. "That would explain so much."

"There's good news in this."

"There is not good news, Kayden."

"Hunting you because you're a carrier will not remain a priority."

"Unless I'm a carrier gone rogue who did kill someone."

His cell phone rings, and he ignores it. "We don't know you killed anyone."

"I know, Kayden. But I need to be realistic here and so do you. Please get your phone. It could be about Enzo." He hesitates. "I'm good. I'm fine." And it's amazingly true. "Please take the call."

His lips press together and he digs it from his pocket. "Gallo's boss." He answers and says something in Italian before covering the phone and eyeing Marabella, telling me he doesn't want her to hear the conversation. I guess Adriel was wrong. Marabella doesn't know quite everything. "I'll be right back," he murmurs.

I nod and sip my coffee in an effort to dislodge the cotton

in my throat but fail, my gaze landing on the notebook I don't want to open. "Where'd he go?" Marabella asks, rounding the counter with plates in her hands, as well as a small pitcher of syrup she's juggling between her arm and breast.

"He had to take a call."

"Always on that phone of his," she says, setting her load down on the table, a sweet maple scent teasing my nostrils as she claims the seat across from me. "Thank you for what you did with Giada. She really took to you."

"We had a good time talking and watching TV."

"She says you might go shopping?"

I inwardly cringe at the realization that I haven't called her back. "We're going to plan it soon."

"Excellent. She's a good girl with a hole in her heart."

My understanding of that statement becomes more complete by the moment. "I can see that in her."

"You're going to be good for her."

"*You're* good for her. Maybe all three of us can go shopping."

"I'd love to, but I'd never catch up with you ladies. It wore me out doing your shopping." She presses a finger to her lips. "Don't tell Kayden, but Giada helped me. She's closer to your age, and I wasn't sure what you would like."

"Oh. I'm surprised she didn't tell me."

"I asked her not to tell anyone. Kayden's a very private person. He wouldn't like her being involved."

He is private and he doesn't want Giada involved in much of anything, which I aspire to change, but right now, the idea of shopping reminds me of my lingerie. "The store where one of you bought my lingerie. Is that nearby?"

"It's right next to Piazza di Spagna, which is the shopping area where we bought the majority of your items. It's a drive, not a walk. I think that's where Kayden got all of your Chanel items."

I smile. "It's hard to imagine him in a women's department store."

She laughs. "I'm sure all the women wished he was shopping for them. He's quite the catch. Lucky you."

"Lucky me," I agree, and with every tidbit of my life and situation revealed, I become more determined than ever to enjoy every "lucky" moment.

And right on cue, it seems, the sexy man in question returns with a notebook computer in his hand, reclaiming his spot at the table while Marabella glances between us, a smile playing on her lips. "I should leave you two alone."

"Actually," Kayden says, "I was going to tell you to take a few days off." He glances at me. "We're set for the passport office on Thursday, so we can hibernate and let your body heal until then."

Two days to forget everything and luxuriate in this man sounds pretty darn good right now. "Hibernating sounds good."

"As does a few days off," Marabella adds, "but you must eat. I can cook in my kitchen and drop it by if you like?"

"You're going to spoil me," I say, "and soon I'll be on a diet."

"She's right," Kayden agrees. "You do spoil us. Take some real time off. We'll manage."

"All right then," Marabella agrees, "but if you need anything just call me." She winks in my direction and dashes away.

"Good grief. She thinks we're going to be naked for the next few days."

"We are," he says, "which is why we need to deal with a few issues now. David. Do you know what he looks like?"

I'm a bit stunned by how quickly he's back in attack mode, wondering what he's learned that I don't yet know. "I remember very clearly. Why?"

"Matteo did a search for all Davids that traveled to Europe from San Francisco, and there were too many to be an effective search. By cross-referencing with the California DMV he was able to narrow the pool based on age, race, and travel particulars."

"I'd also make an educated guess that a generic name wasn't an accident, and that David wasn't even his real name." He picks up the syrup and pours it over his pancakes, then sets it beside my plate. "By the time we finish eating, the files should be in my email. There are only ten, so it won't take long."

He lifts his fork and cuts his pancakes, and there is a hint of tension between us that wasn't there before and can be from only one source. David. No matter who that man was, or was not, in the recent past I was engaged to him, and it bothers Kayden.

"Kayden," I say, drawing his gaze to mine, and when he looks at me those piercing blue eyes are just a little too cold for comfort. "I'm not going to suddenly be in love with David."

"You were going to marry him."

"I can't explain what my mind hasn't told me yet, but I know I didn't love him."

He studies me for several seconds, his gaze probing, intense, as if he is trying to look into my soul and see my past and my future. "I believe you," he finally says.

And since Kayden doesn't say anything he doesn't mean, I believe *him*. "I'm glad," I whisper, and the tension uncurls in my shoulders as a breath I did not realize I was holding escapes my lips.

I reach for the syrup and his hand comes down on mine. "You're mine to lose—not his to take."

Mine to lose. The proclamation implies he has to work to keep me, not that he owns me, and it hits a nerve in a good way. "I was never his to take, Kayden."

"Either way," he says, "I still have to make sure that you don't forget me." He motions to my plate. "Eat. You're going to need your energy." And just like that, he is back to being playful and fun.

"What happened to resting and healing?" I ask, picking up my fork.

"I'll be gentle. For now. Speaking of getting naked again, you need to call Nathan about that doctor's appointment we discussed."

"I'll call him today." A thought hits me. "You know, I wonder if Giada might need an appointment, too. She's eighteen and dating."

Kayden freezes with a bite near his mouth. "Are we seriously talking about Giada and birth control?"

"Better now than when she's pregnant. She was so drunk the other night, she couldn't remember how to get into the castle. And frankly, Adriel doesn't seem like the motherly type."

"Good point," he says, looking utterly horrified at the idea. "Get her an appointment."

I laugh at his reaction and take a bite of my food, a sweet, buttery taste filling my mouth. "That's not Bisquick. That's terrific."

"Everything Marabella makes is," he assures me, devouring a bite himself while I dig in for more.

"I'm stuffed," I finally say, shoving aside my half-empty plate and watching Kayden fight through to the second half of his tall stack. "She's been with you since you moved here?"

He sips his coffee. "That's right. She outdates me by a few years. Her husband was here when I arrived as well."

"What happened to him?"

"Heart attack about seven years ago. They'd been together for fifteen years. She had a rough patch, but taking care of the castle seems to make her happy."

"She can't possibly care for this giant place alone. Just dusting must be a full-time job."

"I have a team of people come in at various times." He chuckles and sets down his cup. "She loves bossing them all around."

"Two control freaks in one house."

"Used to be three when Kevin was alive. The two of them had a lot to do with defining my character."

"Dare I say that Marabella's your second mother?"

"Dare away. That's exactly what she is. I was hoping she might be the same to Giada, but there's a difference between being ten like I was when I arrived and sixteen when Giada moved in, and it's huge."

"Ten," I say, and the idea of just how young he'd been when he'd hidden in that closet is simply devastating. "It's amazing you're as well rounded as you are."

"Well rounded. I've been called a lot of things, including beautiful, but never that."

I smile at the memory he's apparently never going to let me forget, and go all in. "You *are* beautiful," I say, giving him no time to turn that into a blush-worthy moment by quickly asking, "Did you go to public school?"

"I had tutors all the way through junior high, but Kevin insisted I go to public school for high school, and said he wouldn't make me a full-time Hunter until I finished college. He thought it prepared me for life."

"Was it weird going to public school after all of those years of tutoring?"

"Hell yeah. I skipped all the time, and when I was at school, I was in detention. The school said I had 'anger issues.' And Kevin was damn quick to call them on it, too."

"He defended you."

"Hell no. He said I had 'asshole' issues." He laughs. "Then he proceeded to kick my ass and I straightened out."

I laugh. "He was good to you."

"He was my hero."

A random image of my mother pops into my head, gone before I can fully appreciate it. "I think my mother was my hero, and I'm not quite sure what I thought of my father." Shaking off the thought before I get emotional, I refocus on Kayden. "Tell me more about Kevin."

"He was a total badass. No one crossed him without getting their teeth kicked in, but at the same time, he was the first one to be by anyone's side if they needed help. He would've willingly bled for every single Hunter he looked after."

"Like you."

"Ella—"

"It's okay, Kayden," I say, holding up a hand. "I know I can't have it both ways."

"Meaning what?"

"If you were a jerk who didn't protect your people, I wouldn't be in your bed or your house. I'd find another way to survive."

"I believe you would."

"I would, and since it's how you are that makes me want to stay, I have to embrace that and your world."

His chest expands, and he shoves aside his empty plate. "I want to take you to the shooting range and find out how well you can really handle a gun."

"Very. I promise you."

"Humor me."

I think of Elizabeth and wonder if this request is about peace of mind for him. "I'm fine with going to the range but I can promise you, you'll be impressed." Which makes me think of Giada again. "Does Giada know how to shoot?"

"Hell no, and I don't want her anywhere near a gun."

"You want her here, in Hunter central, but you don't want her to be able to shoot."

"I've lost three Hunters in five years, Ella, and that includes Kevin."

While I'm relieved the number is lower than I'd expected, death is death, and I stay focused on my agenda. "She needs to know how to protect herself. Let's get her in classes or let me teach her. Maybe it will make her feel empowered and in control. I know you, of all people, understand how that helps a person cope."

"You aren't going to let this go, are you?"

"I really think she needs to know how to protect herself."

"You're going to have to convince Adriel."

"She's eighteen."

"Like I said. You're going to have to convince Adriel."

"She lives under your roof, so I will ask you but not Adriel. Is it okay with you if I teach her to shoot, Kayden?"

He considers me a moment. "Yes. Teach her."

"Thank you." I hesitate and he arches his brow. "Adriel," I breathe out.

"What about Adriel?"

"He told me you two don't agree on much of anything."

"Did he, now?"

"I'm worried he's not as loyal to you as you are to him."

"That's an interesting assessment."

What's interesting is that he isn't defending Adriel.

His phone beeps on the table, and he presses a button to read a message. "Matteo just sent us the passport photos." He opens the MacBook he'd brought to the table earlier and powers it up.

I finish off my coffee and set the cup aside, finding it interesting that I feel none of the dread about these photos that I do about the ones of Niccolo's crew. "I hope this tells us something."

"I'm ninety-nine percent sure it won't, but I never ignore a possibility. Which is why I'm a damn good Hunter." He punches a couple of buttons and slides his chair over so that we are side by side. "Give them a look."

I scan the photos on the screen that Matteo has aligned in two rows, and no one looks familiar. To be certain, I start at number one and slowly inspect all ten, one by one.

"Nothing?" Kayden asks.

I shake my head. "Nothing. What I don't get is why he needed me, if we traveled together. Unless, maybe I met him in Italy?"

"Most likely you traveled together. Couples get less attention." He closes the MacBook and sets it aside. "I know a guy who used to be a sketch artist for the FBI in the States. Are you okay with having him sketch David for us?"

"Yes. That's great. When can he do it?"

"Not until Thursday. We can hit the consulate and then meet up with him." He drags the photo album forward. "Unless, by some crazy chance, David is in these photos."

"You think David works for Niccolo?"

"Niccolo is involved, so yes. I think it's possible."

"I feel like an idiot for being targeted. I can't imagine myself being that stupid." And suddenly my dread is far less than my need to know the truth. I open the book and start looking at the shots, each photo taking up a page. Nothing is familiar, and I'm frustrated until the last shot, which sends chills straight to my bones.

"Who is this?" I ask, pointing at the regal-looking man with thick, raven hair streaked with auburn.

"Is he familiar?"

Kayden's tone is cautious and I look at him. "Who is he?"

"That's Niccolo, Ella."

"This looks nothing like the photo you showed me before."

"Yes. It does. Are you telling me he's familiar now, and he wasn't then?"

"Let me see the other shot."

He grabs his phone and hits a few buttons before bringing up the image he showed me when we were at Matteo's house. I set the phone down next to the picture in the notebook. "They don't look like the same man." I tap the image on his phone. "This man has shorter, darker hair than the one in the photo."

"They're both Niccolo, so let's be clear. You know Niccolo."

"Yes," I whisper, my chest tightening. "I know him. I might have tried to kill him." I stand and Kayden stands with me. "I have to go. I have to leave the castle. You can't have me here. I'll get you all killed."

His hands come down on my shoulders. "Deep breath, sweetheart. We already knew he was looking for you. Our plan is still good, but I need to know if it's Niccolo who you keep having flashbacks about."

"I don't know, Kayden. The man in my flashbacks is still without an identity."

"Everything is still as it should be."

"A mobster is after me, so no. Nothing is as it should be. How do I even get out of this?"

"You don't." His hands frame my face. "I'll get you out of this. I need you to trust me. Can you do that?"

"I do, but—"

He kisses me, hard and fast. "I've got this, and you. Now,

let's put him behind us. I don't remember the last time I shut everything out and just relaxed. Do that with me now."

"You can't shut everything out with Enzo missing."

"I have people looking for him and they know how to reach me. Let's take a time-out, Ella." He links the fingers of both our hands together. "Let's go into the bedroom, get naked, have lots of sex, and I'll talk you into a Marvel movie binge. *Iron Man. The Avengers. Thor*." He starts walking backward, leading me around the table.

"Superheroes?" I ask, a bit of my tension easing.

"What's wrong with superheroes?"

"Nothing," I say, deciding to embrace being "lucky" with Kayden while I still can. "Nothing at all."

"Good. Then *The Avengers* it is." He scoops me up and starts walking to the bedroom, once again carrying me, and I know it's his way of carrying me beyond this place and time.

But he's not a superhero. He can die, and I won't let that happen. Not because of me.

twenty

I blink awake Thursday morning to find Kayden lying next to me, staring at the ceiling. The room is warm and cozy with the fireplace lit and his leg is aligned with mine. I roll to him, curling to his side, settling my hand over his heart. "Penny for your thoughts."

He strokes a lock of hair from my eyes. "I'm glad you're here."

"Me too. These past two days . . ."

His lips quirk. "I made you love Iron Man, right?"

More like he made me start falling in love with him, but I don't dare say that. "You made me love Thor."

"You just like him because he has a big hammer."

I poke his chest. "That was a *horrible* joke."

"We guys love our horrible jokes." He kisses my forehead. "I'm going to take a quick shower and check for any update on Enzo." He grabs his watch from the nightstand and glances at it. "Holy hell, it's already ten o'clock. We need to leave here by eleven-thirty to make our appointment, and I have to make a few calls in advance."

It's our appointment at the consulate, where Niccolo will

likely be looking for me. Our relaxed days of naked talks, laughter, orgasms, and TV have officially ended. "I'm nervous."

He kisses my temple. "Don't be. I have a plan."

I smile, but it's not as heartfelt as the many smiles we've shared these past two days. "You always have a plan."

"You're learning."

"Good teacher."

"Your lessons haven't even begun," he assures me, no doubt referencing his vow to put "dirty" in a box and keep it there while I fully heal. "How's your head this morning?"

"Good. Really good, actually. And I'm almost done with my medicine."

"Then let's do some shopping today. You need a real wardrobe, not the few things you found to fit in the collection everyone else picked out." He slides his hand over my naked waist and hip and gives me a wickedly hot look. "Though I prefer you without clothes. And on that note, I had better go before I forget why we need to leave."

He throws off the blankets and stands, and I raise up on my elbows to watch every moment of that gorgeous, tight ass of his as it leaves the room. I sigh, hating the end of two days of bliss, and the reality that means I have to think about the implications of knowing Niccolo that I've managed to suppress. The truth is, I've barely thought about the ruthless mobster during our little interlude, nor have I had a flashback, a true testament to just how all-consuming Kayden can be. Or . . . maybe it's my mind going into overdrive to block out what I know I'm close to revealing. I don't like that idea one little bit.

The shower echoes from the other room and I down a

pain pill with the water I have by the bed. I consider joining Kayden, but decide I'll only delay his calls. Decision made to give him space, I grab my journal from the bedside, determined to force my memories to ignite again. I start scribbling the butterfly again and make a concerted effort to actually create a drawing of the necklace. I shut my eyes and force my mind back to that hotel room, to the moment after I'd torn the pendant from my neck, and when I'd gone to my knees and picked it up. In my mind's eye, I can see that note hanging from the edge of the center stone, as if hidden there, but the handwriting is not in English. I open my eyes with this realization. Considering my preference for English, this seems to indicate that the piece of paper wasn't a love note. Rather than drawing the butterfly, I start writing down details:

—Sapphire stones cover raised wings

—The center is a ruby that is quite large. That's where the note was

—White gold setting

—Large. About two inches wide

Grimacing, I tap the pencil on the paper. Does this even matter? The note must be what matters and I'll never figure it out. I set the journal aside and lie down, shutting my eyes and trying to picture that piece of paper, hoping I can make out something that makes a little sense. Instead, I'm transported back to a familiar house. My house when I was a teenager. I inhale, and the scent of chocolate chip cookies is so real I can almost taste them.

"*What's the occasion?*" *I ask, entering the small, square kitchen to find my mother in an apron, scooping the just-out-of-the-oven cookies off the hot tray and onto a plate.*

"*You know how your father loves sweets.*" *She glances at her watch.* "*He should be back from the shooting range in the next fifteen minutes.*" *Her hands plant on her slender hips, her red hair falling in waves around her face.* "*I noticed you dodged going along with him.*"

"*Dance rehearsal.*" *I sink into a chair at the simple round wooden table.* "*And you know how intense he is right after he returns from a mission.*"

She sits down with me and brings the plate of cookies. "*His life is in danger constantly. He sees horrible things. It's hard to come down from that.*"

"*What horrible things, Mom?*"

"*You know this unit he's in is top secret and elite. He can't tell us what he does or where, but he has nightmares, honey. I think he pushes you because he's always afraid he won't come back and there will be no one to take care of you. He wants to be sure you can take care of yourself.*"

"*And you. He always tells me to take care of you.*"

She smiles. "*Good man.*" *She hands me a cookie.* "*Good cookie.*"

"Ella."

I blink to find Kayden leaning over me, the light blue shirt he's wearing turning the gorgeous in his eyes up a notch. "I love your eyes."

He smiles, and it's really a wonderful smile. "Thank you, sweetheart. Why were you lying here smiling?"

I take a deep breath and let it out. "Chocolate chip cookies."

He laughs. "What?"

"A memory of my mother baking cookies. Do you think Marabella could make some?"

"She'd be beside herself to get a special request from you." He pulls me to a sitting position. "Go get ready. We have to leave in forty-five minutes."

"*Danger, Will Robinson!* We must face our world of danger."

He arches a brow. "Isn't that from a movie?"

"*Lost in Space*, and don't ask me how I know that. It was way before my time." I frown. "Or maybe there was a re-make?"

He clunks my chin. "Get dressed, silly woman, and I'm going to leave the room before you do or I might not let you. I'll make coffee. Hurry before I drink it all."

"And you will," I tease, having witnessed him down about two pots yesterday.

"That's right, so like I said, hurry the hell up." He heads for the door and I sit up to watch the way he owns his walk and everything around him, deciding he makes jeans and boots look like sex, when my hand hits the journal, and my memory jolts.

"Kayden." He stops at the door and turns to me. "I remembered something while you were in the shower," I say. "The note in the necklace wasn't written in English. I couldn't read it."

His chest expands and he gives me a barely there nod, facing the door again, but he hesitates with his back to me, as if he wants to say something more. I wait, adrenaline rushing through me, and I'm not sure why, but he doesn't speak. He just . . . leaves.

⤜∞⤛

I dress in black slacks, boots, and an emerald-green sweater, and take extra time with my makeup and hair, because a girl wants to look good if she's going to be assassinated by a mobster at the consulate's office. The burn of that fear is only slightly cooled by my ending up in a sexy ice-blue F-TYPE two-seater Jaguar and discovering that the wall of the garage moves to allow our exit. A sexy car and a sexy man is as sweet as it gets, but there is nothing sexy about my worry that Kayden shouldn't be seen with me at the consulate. The problem disappears when I discover we're meeting the consulate agent at a coffee shop, which means neither I nor Kayden will be spotted by Niccolo. Even better, the meeting is a good distance away in the Piazza di Spagna region of the city, which turns out to be an absolutely delightful area where cobblestone streets are lined with shops, food, and history, like the Spanish Steps I can't wait to explore. Surprisingly the meeting is short and easy, and Kayden explains the paperwork to me while I nibble a pastry. Once we're done, Kayden hands the agent a thick envelope that the man inspects before grinning ear to ear.

A few minutes later, Kayden and I exit the coffee shop into a chilly day, our arms linked, me in my trench coat with a scarf, him in his fitted black leather jacket with a scarf as well.

"The envelope you gave that man had a ton of cash in it, didn't it?" I ask as we pass a horse and carriage.

"Convenience has a price. That meeting otherwise could have taken hours, and the good news, as I explained inside, is that one of those forms extended your stay in Italy for a year. You just have to agree not to work."

I stop and look at him. "You didn't tell me I can't work. I can't just stay here and do nothing."

"You don't need to work. I have more money than I know what to do with."

"*You* do. Not me."

He reaches in his pocket and holds up a credit card. "Now you do, too. This has your new name on it, and it's impossible to max it out."

"I'm not taking that."

"*Yes.* You are." He shoves it in my coat pocket. "Whatever you want or need is yours."

"Kayden—"

He kisses me. "I'm taking care of you, whether you like it or not." He links our arms together and launches us into a stroll again.

"Then you have to let me help you with something you do to make money. Research, maybe? Or whatever I can do. Please, Kayden. I need to have a purpose. And not only do I not want to live off you, I don't want you to feel I am, either."

"I don't, and I don't want you to feel that way."

"Then let me help you in some way."

"I don't want you involved in The Underground."

I step in front of him, forcing him to halt. "You *are* The Underground. There is no way I can be in your life and not have it be in my life. And besides, how dangerous can research be?"

He studies me, his expression an impassive mask. "This really matters to you."

Like he does, and I wonder if he knows that, or if I should tell him. I want to tell him. Instead I say, "Very much so."

He kisses my forehead. "We'll figure something out."

He tries to move me and put us in motion, but I plant my hands on his chest, heat radiating up my arms, his credit card burning a hole in my pocket. "Just to be clear. That means we'll figure something out."

He laughs. "That is what I said. Now." He turns me to face our left and the Spanish Steps that seem to climb a mile high.

"Wow. They're magnificent."

"Like you," he murmurs near my ear, and it is becoming clear he has as much charm as sex appeal. "During the warmer season they have flowers everywhere," he adds. "Do you want to walk up them?"

I face him. "That would be fun. Probably exhausting, but fun."

He closes my hand around his. "Better now than when we have shopping bags."

We spend a good hour milling around the steps before starting our door-to-door shopping expedition, and I soon learn the man is truly determined to spend his money on me.

We end up with so many bags we have to drop some off at the car. "You know," I say as we exit a little pizza joint where we've just had marvelous pizza, my hand stuffed in *his* pocket, a confession on my lips I've had on my mind for hours, "when I realized I knew about Niccolo, my first thought was to run."

"And now?"

"I don't want to run."

He turns me to face him. "Running isn't the answer anyway. I've told you that."

"The idea of anyone else getting hurt because of me guts me, Kayden."

"You know me well enough to know that I've taken precautions. You need to stay in one place, and that place is here with me. Every time you move around is a chance to be seen by the wrong people."

"What about when they look here?"

"There is no red-haired Ella to be found here. Besides, I have a man inside Niccolo's operation. I'm going to find out why he's after you. If you were a carrier, I might be able to pay for your freedom and give my guarantee of your silence as the Hawk for The Underground."

"I don't even know what to say to that. What about your man's safety?"

"He's a mole in Niccolo's operation, not a Hunter, and he doesn't even know it's me paying him. We're okay there."

I slide my arms under his leather jacket and tilt my chin up to whisper, "Thank you."

He leans in and kisses me. "Thank me when we get back to the castle. And be creative about it. That's an order."

I laugh and assure him, "I'm more creative than you might think."

"I can't wait to find out," he replies, draping his arm around my neck as we fall into step together, and I am thinking about how he says "the castle," rarely calling it "home."

I crave home. He has to as well, and some part of me thinks it's not the walls that make that word meaningful. It's people, and maybe we can be "home" to each other. For some reason, that stirs a few flickering images of me with my friend Sara and a knot forms in my chest.

"I'm concerned about my friend Sara, Kayden. My gut feeling is that she would file a missing persons report. What if she finds out my existence was wiped out and she starts digging?"

"That's doubtful. Once she files a report it goes in a computer, and a grown woman who apparently eloped isn't likely to get attention over the long list of missing children in the world."

"But if she was to push, she'd be in danger, right?"

"Doubtful, but possible."

"We have to find her, and I'll make up some happy story to keep her from digging around."

"We're trying to find her. But we have to tread cautiously, or we could bring attention to her ourselves."

My gaze catches on a sign hanging above a store, and my thoughts shift abruptly. "La Perla," I say, tugging Kayden forward. "That's the lingerie I was wearing when you found me. I want to see if it strikes a memory in me."

"You won't get any complaints from me," he says. "As long as you promise to buy something."

I don't laugh, focused on one thing: that store, and remembering who I am and how I got here. If anything helps me protect Sara and everyone else around me, it's that. "I'll stay out here and make some phone calls," Kayden says at the door.

I nod and enter the store, noticing mannequins here and there, and long leather benches separating rows. It's not even slightly familiar. I browse the store and choose several bras, panties, and a few sexy outfits I think Kayden will like, before pulling that credit card he'd given me from my pocket. I stare at the name. *Rae Eleana Ward.* This is me now. Ella doesn't exist. I shake off the whirlwind of emotion threatening me and hand the card to the clerk, making this the first time I have freely spent Kayden's money. I console my guilt over doing so with the idea of him enjoying the purchases I'm making.

After completing my transaction, I step outside the store to find Kayden leaning on a pole, iPhone to his ear, in what appears to be a deep conversation. My gaze shifts from him and lands on a store directly across from us with a ballerina logo on the window, and my stomach somersaults, my throat thickening.

Dance. I am drawn to dance.

I close the distance between me and Kayden, tapping his arm and pointing to the store. He nods and leans down, kissing my temple, and that easy show of affection I know he has shown so few people these past five years steals my breath and curves my lips. I cross the narrow street and enter the store.

"*Ciao!*" the clerk greets me, and I murmur the same reply, but I am already distracted by a row of shoes in the back of the store.

I weave through the racks of clothes and reach the display of ballet slippers. I reach for the classic pink I've always loved and freeze. *Always loved.* Images flicker in my mind and I shut my eyes. I am on a stage, rows of empty seats before me as I perform, while a line of judges sits at a table front and center. It's an audition for a school, I think, and my mom is there. I can't see her, but I feel her support and nerves. She is excited for me and proud of my accomplishments. It's a good memory. A happy time, but as I choose my size of ballet slippers to purchase, the warmth of moments before is gone and a cold, dark sensation rolls through me, a warning of what is to come, and even the hair on my arms stands on end.

My eyes start to blur, spots forming in my vision, and I grab a garment off a rack and rush to the dressing-room area. At the back I open a door and shut it behind me, my hand shaking so hard I can't get it to lock. I give up and walk to the farthest wall, leaning against it and clutching the slippers to me. Images start to flicker in my mind and I squeeze my eyes shut. I'm back in the kitchen with my mom, and I've just finished a cookie when my father walks in.

"There are my two girls."

I glance up as he enters, and he is big and broad, his hair buzzed, his green Army T-shirt a second skin. It's weird when he's home and empty when he's gone, which was six long months this time. He's intimidating, a hero who expects me to be more than I often think I can be. And I love him. He sits between me and my mom. "Hi, Dad. I was just sampling your cookies. Making sure they were up to standard."

"I'll have to test them myself," he says, snapping one up and *tasting it, giving a thumbs-up before kissing my mom, who glows when he's around. He shifts his attention back to me.* "You skipped out on me today at the gun range."

"Dance rehearsal," I say.

He grimaces, proving he's still not a fan of my dancing, and yet, he'd married a dance teacher. Sometimes I think he wants me to be the son he never had. "Have you been going to the gun range while I was gone?" *he asks.*

"Twice a week," my mother assures him.

He arches a brow. "That means once a week, right?"

"Some weeks," I admit.

A glass shatters somewhere in the house, and my father is on his feet in an instant. "Get in the pantry," he orders softly.

"Dad—"

"Do it," he hisses, pulling a gun from under his pant leg that I didn't even know he carried, and judging from the stunned look on my mother's face, she didn't either.

She grabs my arm and drags me with her to the pantry and inside, shutting the door. We huddle together. "Mom—" I start, but she covers my mouth. Once she knows I'm quiet, she digs her phone from her apron and dials 911 but doesn't speak. She sticks the phone back in her pocket, no doubt hoping someone comes.

There are crashing sounds and muffled gunfire, like a silencer is being used, and my mother and I both jump. And then there is silence. Oh God, the silence is deafening and I wait for my father to come to us, but he does not. I can't take it anymore. I jerk away from my mother, every instinct I own telling me my father needs help. I open the door and gasp at the sight of him lying in a puddle of blood. I dash forward and fall to my knees.

"Dad. Dad."

My mother drops down beside me, bursting into tears as she starts begging him to stay alive. "Gun," my father murmurs. "Ella . . . Get . . . gun."

I look down to find it at his fingers and I take it. "I have it."

"Two . . . men."

The kitchen door bursts open, a man in a mask and all black appearing, and my father hisses, "Shoot," and instinct takes over. I raise the gun and fire at the man in black, and he tumbles forward. Another man follows him and I fire again. And again. He drops to

his knees and falls face first. Sirens begin to sound and my mother is
shaking my father.

"*Wake up!*" *she shouts.* "*Wake up!*"

"Ella. Ella. Holy hell!"

Kayden's worried voice brings me back to the present and
I blink to find myself sitting on the floor of the dressing room,
clutching the ballerina slippers to my chest, Kayden squatting
in front of me. "I'm okay," I rasp out, but I'm trembling all
over, deep, hard shakes that I feel clear to my soul.

Kayden doesn't hear me though. He's on his phone. "Nathan," he says. "Ella passed out. She's—"

I grab the phone and put it to my ear. "Okay. She's . . . I'm
okay. Don't worry." I drop the phone, dampness clinging to
my cheeks. "I'm okay."

His hands pat my arms. "You scared the shit out of me.
Your teeth are chattering."

"It was a . . . flashback. I just . . . I . . . It was bad. Give
me . . . a moment to get past it." I inhale, and I swear the
breath feels like glass cutting my throat.

"We need to get you out of here," Kayden says. "Can you
stand?"

I grab his shirt and twist it in my fingers. "I need to tell
you what I remembered. I just . . . I need to say it so I don't
forget it. Well . . . no. I won't forget it. I just need to say it."

"I'm right here, sweetheart. I'm listening."

"My father . . ." I inhale and try to calm the trembling
running through my body. "Military. He was military, but I
think some sort of special unit." My words are stronger now.
I feel the edge easing. "The memory," I continue. "My father
was home for once. I was seventeen." I swipe at a tear drip-

ping down my cheek and a cold, cold calmness begins to roll through me. "Men came into the house and my father made me and my mother hide in the pantry, like you hid in the closet, Kayden. No wonder you're so familiar."

He cups my cheek and I lean into the touch as he says, "You were right. We do know each other. You don't have to talk about this now."

"I need to. I can't explain it, but I need to." I pause to let the images solidify in my mind. "I heard the struggle between my father and the men in our house. There were shots, but they were muffled. Silencers. I knew they used silencers. After that, there was quiet, and I had the feeling my father needed me. I fought my mother to be free of her hold and I got out of the pantry and he was lying on the ground, bleeding. Dying." My fingers dig into Kayden's arms, which I didn't even realize I was holding. "My father was holding a gun, and the two men who attacked him were still in the house." My eyes meet Kayden's. "I killed them, and my only regret is I didn't do it sooner." I push to my feet and Kayden follows. "I don't regret it, the way you said you wouldn't regret it if you found the people who killed Kevin and Elizabeth."

His arm wraps my waist, and only then do I realize I was wobbling and he's kept me from falling. "You saved your mother's life."

"But not his. Not my father's."

"And no one knows what that feels like more than me." He wipes the tears from my cheeks. "Let's go *home*."

Home. Now he says *home* and I want to be happy about that, but there is the ball in my chest that demands answers and actions. "We're supposed to see the profiler."

"It can wait, sweetheart."

"It *can't* wait. My father raised a fighter, and I'm going to fight." I shove against him. "Let go. I need to stand on my own."

He hesitates, but he releases me and I'm steady now, rejecting all weakness. I hold up the slippers. "I need these. Apparently I'm good with a gun and in ballet slippers. And I want to go to the shooting range, Kayden. Can the profiler meet us there?"

"Ella, I don't think—"

My hand flattens on his chest. "I *need* to do this now. Please."

His hand covers mine, his look probing, concerned, and whatever he sees, the result is his agreement. "I'll have him meet us there."

❦

Thirty minutes later, after a silent drive to the outskirts of the city, in which I replay my father's death far too many times, we arrive at the shooting range and sit at a small cafeteria-style table in the snack area. Tyler, a good-looking thirty-something blond American man, sits across from us.

"I'm ready when you're ready," Tyler says, opening his sketch pad, and it's then that I notice the tattoo on his arm. "You're a Hunter," I say.

He glances at Kayden, who replies for him. "He transferred from a division in America."

"And now you have resources inside the FBI," I assume, shocked at just how far The Underground's reach truly is.

"We always have," Kayden surprises me by saying. "That's

how I met Tyler in the first place. Let's get this drawing done."

"Tell me about the shape of David's face," Tyler instructs, and I hesitate, suddenly reminded of how much Kayden hates the topic of my ex-fiancé, or whatever David was.

Kayden's hand settles on my leg, a silent show of unity and understanding, just as his silence on the ride over here had been strength and comfort, rather than demand and questions. "Square," I say. "Or his jaw was square and his cheekbones very defined."

I watch as Tyler starts drawing, showing me his efforts, and when I give an approving nod, he asks, "Nose?"

"Straight, but not large."

We go on like this for fifteen minutes, until I am staring at a picture of the man from my memory. I glance at Kayden. "That's him."

Kayden eyes Tyler. "Scan that and send it to Matteo."

"Will do, boss." Tyler pushes to his feet.

"Wait," I urge. "Can you draw a necklace if I describe it?"

Kayden gives him a nod and he sits back down. "I'm ready."

I describe the butterfly, and in a matter of minutes he's drafted an exact duplication of my memories. I am cold inside. So very cold, and the pulse in my temple seems to grow faster and deeper.

"The necklace is the key to everything," I say, staring at it, not at either of the men. "Find it, and you'll find out why Niccolo is after me." I stand and walk to the shooting range's registration counter, filling out my paperwork with one of the few English-speaking attendants.

"Gun preference?" the man asks when I return the forms to him.

There is no hesitation in my reply. "Do you have a Ruger LC9?" It's the gun my father had me practice with.

"We do, and I must say that's an excellent choice for a petite woman like yourself."

I don't reply, remembering a similar comment from my father. The attendant hands me earphones, safety glasses, and a small box with my weapon inside, and while I am aware of Kayden's continued absence, I am focused on one thing. I need a gun in my hands. Adrenaline surges through me, and with it, a whirlwind of dark, edgy emotions. Anger. Loss. Guilt. More anger. I walk to the shooting area and stop at the first booth available, setting my box down and putting on my glasses and earphones.

Kayden steps behind me, but I don't turn. I grasp the gun and aim at the target, and for a moment I'm back in that kitchen, firing at those men. I picture the man in black falling face first. I picture my father lying in his own blood with my mother sobbing over him. My finger comes down on the trigger and I empty the gun, every shot hitting within target range.

Then I settle the gun back inside the case, seal the lid, and take off my gear, tossing it into a basket next to me.

I face Kayden. "Is that accurate enough for you?" I don't wait for an answer. "I'm done being afraid. I'm going to get answers about who I am, and I'm going to do it with whatever force is necessary."

"I'm taking care of this for you," he insists.

"Not anymore. You can stand by my side, step aside, or

try to lock me up—but you'd better be sure I don't have a gun if you do." I shove the box at him and take off walking. He falls into step with me but doesn't speak, dropping the gun off at the counter as we head to the door. We exit the building, gravel crunching under our boots, neither of us in a coat. I barely feel the rapidly dropping temperature, but I am aware of the unison of our steps. I stop at my side of the Jag and he opens my door, but before I can enter, he pulls me against him.

"I'm standing in front of you, protecting you, whether you like it or not." He releases me and all but sets me in the car, shutting me inside.

My heart is racing, a new rush of adrenaline assaulting my body, and the instant he is in the car, the door sealed, we whirl on each other, our gazes colliding in a battle of wills. "I don't need you to protect me," I grind out through clenched teeth.

"Too fucking bad."

"I am not your responsibility."

"Yes. You are."

"Says you."

"That's right. Says me. And if you think that because you can handle a gun, you can handle the mob, you're sadly mistaken. You're running on heartache and adrenaline right now. And you need to come down."

"I just remembered killing two men, and watching my father die in a pool of his own blood. How the hell am I supposed to come down?"

"The same way I do. Sex." His fingers twine in my hair and he drags my mouth to his, his tongue licking into my mouth, a hot rasp of demand. I lean into the kiss, needing the outlet, needing it so damn bad.

"Don't you *dare* coddle me," I hiss when his mouth leaves mine.

"You want dirty, sweetheart, I'll give you dirty." He releases me and starts the car.

twenty-one

K ayden and I enter the castle without speaking, sexual tension crackling between us, and he is right. I need to come down from the adrenaline rush. I need the escape I know he can give me and that he claims sex can deliver. Sex *with him*. And it's not just about the escape. It's about honesty and choice, about the freedom for him to be him and me to be whatever I feel I need to be right here and now with him. We climb the stairs side by side and he doesn't touch me. I know it's to drive anticipation, a way to claim control, and I'd rather he have it than I have this firestorm of emotions inside. With every step we take, the promise of an experience that will be dark, erotic, and all-consuming echoes through me.

My pulse races as we approach the door to his bedroom, *our* bedroom, and Kayden is at my back, reaching around me to open it, and still he does not touch me. I cross the threshold and he is quick to follow, a wolf at my back, and I am most definitely his willing prey. I whirl around to face him, and he kicks the door shut. "Get naked," he orders, tearing his shirt over his head, giving me a wicked, hot view of taut skin over lean, hard muscle.

I wet my lips and turn away, walking to the rug in front of the fireplace as it flickers to life. There is no hesitation in me as I undress, and oh how I feel the heat of his stare, a heavy caress that might as well be his tongue for the way it licks every intimate part of me. I toss away my bra and step out of my panties, but when I'm about to face him again, his hand comes down on my back.

"On your knees," he commands, his voice low, sultry in its demand, but the order stirs a memory I try to reject. *On my knees.* A tight knot forms in my chest as my mind takes me back to that night in the club. To the woman tied up. To me tied up and the punishment, and the pain, that followed. But this is not then *or him.* This is Kayden. This is a man I think I'm falling in love with, who I trust. He won't hurt me. There is no question of this in my mind or heart, and it infuriates me that the monster of my past has invaded this night.

Rebelling against my own weakness, I lower myself to my knees, but Kayden doesn't follow. Seconds tick by, and I listen for every sound that does not come, waiting for a touch I desperately crave, goose bumps rising on my skin that have nothing to do with being cold, and everything to do with how much I want Kayden. It is amazing to me how alive my nerve endings are, how my nipples tighten and my sex clenches, when he has done nothing but issue a command. That is the power of this man over me, but there is no fear. There is only arousal. And the promise of pleasure.

Finally, though, he kneels in front of me, naked, magnificently male, his thick shaft at my hip. There is power in knowing I arouse him, and that no matter what control I give him, it is never all his.

His finger slides under my chin, that one touch shivering through me and tightening my nipples, his gorgeous, pale blue eyes glinting with what manages to be lust and tenderness, when I never knew two such things could coexist. "The things I want to do to you are many, and not enough. But tonight, I have only one purpose. One goal. I want you to conquer a fear tonight."

"I'm not afraid."

"Not of me, but this isn't about me, now, is it? It's about a past you might not fully realize, but it affects you and us."

"You're talking about *him*—and he doesn't belong here with us."

"He, like Elizabeth, has to be here, because those pieces of us we can't escape. We shouldn't try. They're part of who we are, separately and together. We can't pretend the things they make us feel don't impact who we are."

As much as I wish to reject this idea, Kayden is right, and he is only trying to make me, and us, stronger. "What are you suggesting?"

"I have no intention of destroying us, Ella. Just the opposite. I want to give you a memory of being tied up that isn't about punishment, but trust and pleasure. I want to bind your wrists." He holds up a black silk sash. "This is your choice, though. Say yes or say no. It changes nothing and it does not mean we won't try again later. There is no pressure. This isn't our only night together."

My chest is tight with the magnitude of this moment and the mix of nerves, arousal, and tenderness this man stirs in me. "Yes is my answer," I whisper, but as sure as I am as I issue my reply, a dark memory tears at the back of my mind, words finding my lips that I did not even know existed. "But I will *never* call you Master."

Surprise registers on his handsome face, his arm circling my waist, molding me close to him, that silk sash dangling at my hip, teasing my skin. "How do you even know that word?"

The question is a soft demand I can't really answer. "It just came to me. I think . . . I *know* he made me call him that."

"*Made you?* I've played around in that world, Ella, and you don't *make* someone call you Master. It's a choice. The submissive is ultimately in control, and I have no interest in your being my submissive. Because I like control during sex doesn't make me your Master. You call me Kayden, or asshole; I don't care. I care about your pleasure and your safety." His tone is vehement, anger barely contained in its depths, and I can feel the thunder of his heart beneath my palm where my hand has settled. "Tell me you understand."

"Yes. And it matters to me in ways I'm not sure I even understand yet. I don't want to say no to you, Kayden."

"But you can. Even after you say yes." He cups my face and repeats those words. "Even after you say yes."

"I know."

"Now your promise."

"I promise."

He kisses me, a deep caress of his tongue against mine that entices, seduces, but I taste the gentleness in him, the worry, that places him, and us, so far from his version of "dirty" I am not sure we can find it again. "Don't you dare coddle me," I demand, shoving against his chest and grabbing the silk sash he's allowed to fall to the floor. "Tie me up."

"Not tonight."

"Yes, damn it. Tonight. You promised me a new memory, and I want it. Don't take that from me."

"Ella—"

"I *need* to face my fears. I need to know he doesn't win."

His expression tightens, his eyes probing mine, searching. I hold out my wrists. "Trust," I say. "I'm giving it to you. Take it."

"I want far more trust than I'm sure you should give me."

"What does that mean?"

His chest expands, thick lashes lowering, forming dark circles on his cheeks, my eyes lingering there a moment, and I think . . . I think the past he's talked about being a part of us has found its place in this moment, and for him that is guilt, and mistrust of himself.

"I trust you," I whisper, holding out my hands.

He doesn't look at me but he shackles my wrists, easily holding them with one hand while he twines the silk around them with the other. And when his gaze finally collides with mine, the man I want and need is back within reach, darker flecks of blue heating the pale blue of his stare. "It's loose enough that you can slide out of it if you absolutely want to. Next time it won't be."

The way he says 'next time it won't be' sends an erotic thrill down my spine. I don't know why or how it is possible, but being at Kayden Wilkens's mercy is sexy and exciting, not terrifying. Not about fear and degradation. "Understand?" he asks, and it's more than a question. It's a clear opportunity for me to use the word *no* he has stressed is mine to own and control.

"Yes," I say, choosing the word to send a message. I'm making my choice, and trusting him is that choice.

"Be clear, Ella. I'm going to push tonight. Not the way I'm capable of pushing you, but you won't argue with me on that." He tightens his grip around my hands. "You will not win that war. Now you say 'yes.'"

"Yes," I whisper, the absoluteness in him too intense to fight.

"That time will come, and I'm not ready yet to find out how you'll react. Not because of some man in your past. Because of me. Because right now, I don't deserve that kind of trust."

"Kayden—"

He kisses me, fingers twining roughly, erotically in my hair, and I taste the demons of his past, the inner war he battles but will not fully allow me to fight with him. I lean into him, trying to feel him close, but he is quick to deny me that touch, and almost as if he is punishing me for trying, he tears his mouth from mine, leaving me panting for the more that is now out of reach.

He moves behind me, the thick ridge of his erection nestling between my thighs, pressing into the silky wet heat of my sex, teasing me with how easily he could be inside me. And I want him inside me. His hands caress up and down my sides, leaving me cold where he is not touching and hot where he is. I arch into him, my breasts thrusting in the air, a silent plea for his hands, but I am granted only a side brush, a light tease of fingers on my pebbled nipples. A soft brush of fingers on my clit never fully realized.

"Kayden," I whisper, squeezing my thighs around his

shaft, the need for everything when he gives me so little pure torture I can do nothing to resolve.

"Lean forward," he urges, a command in his voice. "Elbows on the rug." He doesn't give me time to digest the order, pressing me forward, hand flattening on my back, the position thrusting my backside into the air, leaving me vulnerable and exposed, but there is no time to think of what might happen. He cups my backside, caressing me over and over, and his words play in my mind. *I will tease you. Bite you. Spank you.* As if he is in my head, his palm lifts and comes back down with a fast smack that is not painful, but shocking, and has me yelping and trying to sit up. But that hand of his is back on my spine, holding me down.

"Trust," he says. "Do I have it or not?"

I bite my bottom lip, willing my heart rate to calm. He hasn't hurt me. Not even close, and I whisper, "Yes. Yes. Yes."

He smacks the other cheek. Not a spanking. No pain. Just a slight sting that delivers an erotic thrill and the promise of so much more, if not now, soon. Too soon. Not soon enough. My sex clenches fiercely and I want the hidden part of him he still denies, but I *know* he will not give it to me tonight. He will not rush this and as much as I want to change that, there is safety, there is *trust* I can give him, in knowing he is being cautious with me.

His hands drag up and down my sides, and then finally, his body curves around mine, and he is hot and hard between my thighs, sliding the head of his cock along the slick line of my sex. "I need—"

"I know what you need," he promises, but he does not give it to me. He slides his shaft back and forth, the nerve endings he is touching lighting up like the fire burning in front of me. I sink lower into the rug, weaker with need, and finally, finally, he presses into me, driving deep and fast, his cock finding the farthest part of me and staying there. He isn't moving, and I am panting to the point I can barely breathe when finally he pulls back and thrusts hard into me. And *oh God*, that one hard pump and already I am on the edge of orgasm. Another thrust and I push against him, his only reply his hand bracing my hips, his cock nudging left, right, deeper, before he starts a fast, hard pumping rhythm. I lose time. I lose the room. The rug. The silk at my hands. I climb that peak of pleasure and tip over far too fast, all but collapsing as my body clenches around him. His hand flattens on my belly, holding me up, and then he is shaking, shattering with me, the deep, guttural sound he makes a sexy, erotic charge that ripples through me.

I shut my eyes, riding his pleasure with him, sighing with the way he slowly relaxes against me, his fingers softening at my hips, and then he folds himself around me, holding me in the most intimate of ways. "You okay?" he murmurs near my ear.

My lips curve at what is becoming our little question to each other. "Yes. Are you okay?"

He laughs, low and sexy. I really love his laugh. I think I can really love this man. "You're naked," he says. "Of course I'm okay. Let me get rid of this condom and I'll untie you."

He pulls out of me and I gasp, which earns me another one of those sexy laughs. "The feeling's mutual," he says of my reaction.

A smile on my lips, I sit up, my eyes lifting to the fireplace, and I don't know why, but I see the past in those flames. I flash back to the club. I am there, living it again, afraid. So afraid.

He shoves me to my knees and I try to get up, but he holds me while the woman in leather ties me up, stretching one arm to the side and roping it, then the other. I fight. I fight as hard as I can but he, he holds me down and then I am bound, a prisoner, and he moves away. I hear her speak to him. "How badly do you want her bruised?"

He squats in front of me, caressing my lips, and I try to bite him. Fury radiates off him and he stands. "Don't leave scars."

I blink the fireplace back into view. "Kayden! Kayden!" I try to free my hands, but I'm shaking so hard I can't get them free. "Untie me. Untie me now! Please! Now!"

Kayden kneels in front of me, ripping away the silk in a flash. "Sweetheart. I'm sorry." He cups my face. "I would never—"

I grab his arms. "It's not you. We . . . we are good. He . . . he tied me up. He had me whipped. That's what woke me up yesterday, but I didn't want to tell you, and—"

"He fucking *beat* you? Tell me it's Niccolo and I will go there, beat him, and kill him, tonight."

"I still don't know. And you don't get to beat him and kill him—I do. Do you hear me? *I do!* And now I've made it so you can't be you with me. Tie me back up. Tie me back up now."

He takes us down on the rug, pulling me close, his legs twined with mine. "I'm not tying you back up."

"Kayden—"

"No." His tone is absolute. "Fuck, Ella. I teased you with a possible spanking, and now you tell me he beat you? I should never have let this happen tonight, when you just remembered your father's death."

"I'm right. You're going to be afraid with me."

"No. I'm not, but the timing of this was wrong." He strokes my hair behind my ear, his voice softening. "We will get by this and we will be okay together. I promise you." He molds me to him, into the cocoon of his body. "Tell me about dancing."

I blink at the sudden change of topic. "Dancing?"

"Yes. I want to hear about dancing. I want to know about what you love. Who you are. What you want from life."

My fingers tease a loose silky strand of his light brown hair, tears prickling my eyes. "You're amazing, Kayden Wilkens."

"The feeling's mutual, sweetheart." He kisses my knuckles. "Now. Tell me. You danced. You *dance.*"

Tension uncurls inside me, replaced by an image of my mother smiling as she watches me dance, both of us in ballet slippers, a piece of the past coming back to me. "My mom was a dance teacher, and I took it seriously enough to audition for either a big production or an elite school. I think it was a school. It was important to me and to her. Her gift to me was dance. My father's was the ability to protect myself. I'm eager to see if I remember dancing as well as I remember shooting a gun."

"A woman who can dance and shoot. Sexy, sweetheart."

I smile. "Let's wait and see if I can actually dance."

"We both know you can." He lifts up on one elbow. "The school thing is interesting."

"What do you mean?"

"There can't be that many elite dance schools."

Hope rises inside me. "You think you can find me that way?"

"It's a long shot, but everything is worth trying." He stands and takes me with him.

"What are we doing?"

"I want to show you something." He snatches his shirt and hands it to me. "Put that on, and socks or slippers. The castle floors are cold."

I pull it over my head and he drags on his jeans commando style, not bothering to zip them. I stuff my feet in my slippers. "Where are we going?"

He smiles and shakes his head, a long lock of light brown hair teasing his forehead. "It's a surprise." He motions me to the door and holds it open, and I follow him into the hallway, shivering with the cold, deciding I should have bought a robe today. Kayden hits a button on the wall and a panel opens. I grin. "I love this castle."

"I'm glad you do." He waves me forward and I step inside a small foyer to find a path with heavy stone steps wide enough for both of us. Kayden steps to my side and we start the climb that halfway up forks left, right, or straight.

"Straight up," he says, but I am curious about every direction.

"I'm exploring tomorrow. That's all there is to it."

"After the doctor. I meant to tell you. Nathan called while you were in the lingerie store. He got you an appointment tomorrow afternoon."

"For Giada, too?"

"Oh, yeah. Her too. The idea of her pregnant was enough to get my attention."

I laugh, and it hits me that it's truly a miracle I can laugh after all that has happened today, and it's because of Kayden. I can only hope I do the same for him. Finally, at the top of the stairs, we enter an incredible, well-equipped gym with moonlight peeking through a giant, arched floor-to-ceiling window. "Are you trying to tell me something?"

"Are you kidding? One mention of the gym and Marabella will be feeding you gallons of ice cream. She's convinced you're too skinny."

"She just wants an excuse to feed us all," I say as he walks to the far right wall and punches a button; with no surprise at this point, it slides open and reveals a secret room. He waves me forward, and ever so curious, I enter to find a long, empty rectangular room with hardwood floors. "What is this room?"

He leans on the door frame. "Your new dance studio, if you want it to be."

A dance studio. The idea hits a nerve, a piece of my past I don't know but feel. I hug him, tilting my chin up to look at him. "This is the sweetest thing ever."

"Something no one else would ever call me." He wraps an arm around my waist, sealing us together, one hand cupping my face. "And *he*, whoever he is, will not think I'm sweet when I am done with him. That absolutely is *a promise*."

∞∞

The next morning, Kayden has some sort of lead on Enzo. He doesn't seem eager to talk about it, but the result is him calling a meeting with a group of local Hunters to be held in his "War Room" in the central tower. In light of this event, he lines up Nathan to escort Giada and me to the doctor, despite my insisting we can handle it on our own. I'm not sure if that means I'm less safe than he's claimed or if he's just being his protective self, both of which are easy to believe.

Whatever the case, Giada and I meet in the main foyer and laugh as we come face to face in almost the same outfit of skinny black jeans, black sweaters, and boots. The only difference is her black leather coat and my trench coat.

"Twinkies," she claims, and we exit the castle to find Nathan's black Mercedes waiting on us. Even his car screams Mr. *GQ* Doctor and I relax a little. If Kayden were really worried about my safety, he'd have sent someone else with us.

Nathan steps out of the car and motions us forward, his brown hair fluttering in a cold breeze. "He's so damn sexy," Giada murmurs. "I get the front seat."

"He's at least fourteen years older than you," I remind her.

"And a doctor. That's hot." She dashes down the stairs and manages to be inside the car before I even reach the vehicle.

Nathan lingers where he is, speaking to me over the hood of the car. "How are you?"

"I'm fine. Thank you."

"That call I got last night did not sound fine. We need to talk about that when we get a moment alone."

I give him a quick nod and climb into the backseat, rethinking my assessment of Nathan as our escort. Kayden's worried all right, but not about strangers attacking us. It's about the way my past is attacking me, and us. "How far is the doctor's office from here?"

"Only about ten minutes," Nathan says, maneuvering us onto the narrow roadway, and since I really don't want to spend the ride fearing for my life, I sink low in the seat.

Giada has no such issues, chatting away with Nathan. He is courteous but reserved, and I'd be disappointed in him otherwise. He also keeps eyeing his mirror, and there's that hint of hardness beneath his surface I'd seen the day in the store. He's The Undergound's doctor, and something tells me he's as lethal as he is a healer.

Once we're at the doctor's office, Giada and I are taken into exam rooms at the same time, and my checkup is pretty painless. The result is a birth control injection I'll have to repeat every three months. When I'm done I join Nathan back in the lobby, sitting next to him.

"You want to tell me about yesterday?" he asks.

"Amnesia is hell. When I remember things that are painful, it's like I'm experiencing them all over again. Instead of having years of healing behind me, the process starts all over again."

"Are you sleeping?"

"I am, but I wake up to some pretty crappy memories sometimes."

"I can give you something to knock you out."

"As much as I appreciate that, there are far more reasons to remember than to forget, and drugs are only going to delay the process. And right now it seems the memories are starting to really flow."

"That's a good thing."

We're silent for a little while, and I finally broach a subject I've been worrying about. "How often are you needed by The Underground?"

He gives me a direct look. "That's not your real question. What do you really want to know?"

"How often do they get hurt?"

"You're worried about Kayden."

"How can I not be? You told me he takes the dangerous jobs."

"You need to have this conversation with Kayden."

"You can't give me an answer I like, so you aren't going to give me one at all."

"Talk to Kayden."

His phone beeps with a text and he pulls it from his pocket, glancing at the screen with a frown. "How about checking on Giada? Kayden wants me in the meeting he's holding after all, and I have a patient who was just admitted into the hospital. Not a good combination."

I want to ask for details, but he's already standing and stepping into the hallway, probably to make a call.

Fortunately, Giada comes into the lobby just then, looking irritated. "We need to hurry back. Adriel's in a pissy mood for me to get back and run the store."

So Kayden wants Adriel in the meeting, too. I don't say that to Giada, who believes he's retired from hunting. Whatever the case, I'm officially worried.

∽∾∽∾∽

I try to call Kayden but he doesn't answer, and the minute the car halts in front of the castle, I'm out of the door and darting for the steps. I'm just keying in the code when the door opens and Kayden appears. "What's going on?" I ask.

"Walk with me upstairs and we'll talk."

"You're scaring me," I say as we hurry through the open door to our tower and up the stairs.

"Enzo's being held captive," he explains. "I have to free him."

"Who has him?" I ask as we reach the main level.

"The cartel he tried to steal from."

"Oh God," I murmur, following him down the hallway to our room. "Tell me no."

He opens the bedroom door. "I wish I could." He heads inside and makes a beeline for the security room.

I follow and once I'm in the doorway, I ask, "How can I help?"

"Stay here until I get back, so I know you're safe. I can't worry about my men and you, too." He holds out the chair for me. "Sit down; I need to show you some things."

I do as he says and he kneels beside me. "A quick lesson." He punches a key and the visual on the security feed changes. "Every time you punch it, you alter the location of the view. You can see every single part of the castle if you need to." He indicates yet another key. "That turns on the volume. The only places you can't see and hear are the private bedrooms and the War Room. Got it?"

"Yes. Got it."

"Good." He stands and walks to the wall in one corner and hits a button. A panel rotates and displays a selection of guns, two of which he attaches to various parts of his body, and a sick feeling forms in my belly.

He turns to face me and he must read the terror I feel for him, because he kneels in front of me again. "I told you I walk the line of legal and illegal. You don't deal with a cartel without crossing lines. Not even the FBI and CIA manage that, I promise you."

"I didn't say anything."

"You didn't have to. But I will do whatever is necessary to save my men, just like I will for you."

I cup his cheek. "I know. I can handle this."

He draws my hand in his. "If you call, I'll answer, so don't call unless it's an emergency. Matteo is staying here in the War Room as field support and in case you need him. We won't make a move to retrieve Enzo until nightfall, so don't worry when I'm not back until late." He pushes to his feet and takes me with him. "I'll text you if I can to check in, but I can't promise." He leans in and kisses me. "I'm crazy about you. You know that, right?"

I grab his shirt, balling my fingers around the cotton. "Prove it and come back safe."

He gives me a nod—no promise, no words—and I move to the doorway to watch him stride across the bedroom and disappear. I inhale and face the panel of guns, and turn away. I can't think about guns and death right now. I need to do something to stay busy. I cross to the bathroom, place my purse on the vanity, then shrug out of my coat, which I toss on the edge of the tub.

I stare at myself in the mirror a minute, starting to get used to this me. I'm not sure if that's good or bad, but if it involves Kayden, I vote good. My mind flickers back to those last happy moments with my mother, and I dig my phone out of my purse and dial Marabella.

"Ella," she says. "Are you okay?"

"Yes. I was just wondering if you wanted to come bake chocolate chip cookies with me."

"I would love to bake cookies with you. I'll run to the corner store and be in the kitchen in half an hour."

"Perfect. Thank you." I set my phone down and head into the closet, where I exchange my boots for flats, throw on a hoodie, and head to the kitchen. There I make coffee and stand at the window Kayden favors, staring at the amazing view of a church with high steeples and stunning architecture.

Fifteen minutes later Marabella breezes into the kitchen, and my mood lightens with her infectious happiness. I help her bake, and we both decide it's not my thing, though we get some good laughs at my efforts. Baking complete, we settle at the table and I tell her what I remember about my mother, and listen to her stories of Kevin, Kayden, and her husband.

Eventually though, our tongues are tired, the sun has set, and she sighs and stands. "I'm tired, honey. I need to rest. Are you okay here alone?"

"I am. Thank you for the cookies and the great conversation."

It's then that she says what has been in the air but not discussed. "This is his life. He needs you. I see it in his eyes, but be sure you can handle this before you do something like fall in love with him."

Love. It's a big word, and it's not the first time I've wondered if that is where I'm headed with Kayden. "I can handle it. I just might need cookies and talk sessions here or there."

She smiles her approval. "Cookies and conversations I can

do." She waves, and just like Kayden, she is gone, and I'm alone inside the tower.

I sit there and don't move for quite some time. Just blank. No memories. No real thoughts. I think I am blocking it all out. Oh, how my mind likes to protect me and then turn around and destroy me.

An idea hits me and I stand, rushing to the bedroom closet, where I dig out my ballet slippers. Excited to give them a try, I hurry back to the hallway and open the panel leading to the gym. I all but run until I hit the fork in the path again and stop dead in my tracks, curiosity killing me. I have lots of time to kill, and exploring would be fun. So, *hmmmm*. Which way to go?

I choose left, and a short hallway leads me to a door. I open it and find an office with a giant, curved blond wood desk in the center, a fancy etched design in the wood, with two tan leather chairs, and bookshelves framing it. I inhale and smile; the sweet, spicy scent of Kayden is everywhere. I'm definitely staying a while. I move forward, rounding the desk to sit down, placing my slippers on the shiny surface, trailing my hands over the smooth wood and admiring the knobs that are in the shape of hawks. "The Hawk," I whisper. "Kayden is The Hawk. He has to protect his people."

I rest my elbows on the leather desk pad, thinking of what that kind of responsibility must feel like, my eyes catching on a file sticking out that reads *Gallo*. Frowning, I grab it and flip it open to find every piece of Gallo's life since childhood inside. It's very personal, and I feel like I'm invading his privacy by reading it. I shut it and set it aside. Why would Kayden have this? Unless . . . he's planning something involving

Gallo? Maybe he just wants to know the man who's clearly out to get him. That, I can see for sure.

Then I see another file, one that reads *Ella* on the front. My breath hitches and a sense of foreboding washes over me that I don't understand. Of course he has a file on me. He's trying to figure out who I am.

Still, I have to inhale a calming breath, air trickling from my lips as I open it. My heart begins to race, charging so fast, it feels like it might explode from my chest. There's only one thing in the file: a snapshot of the butterfly necklace.

Not a drawing. An actual photo.

I only just told him about the necklace, and why would he have Tyler draw it, if he knew what it looked like?

Kayden knew about the necklace but didn't tell me.

I tell myself there's a good reason, but I can't think of what that can be.

I stand up, barely able to breathe. I need air. I need space. I run out of the room and down the stairs, and don't stop until my purse is over my shoulder. I leave my coat behind, needing the realness of the cold. I need to decide whether I talk to Kayden about this or dig for answers on my own. I'm also reminded that he felt familiar from day one. Why? *Why?* And *damn it*, I do not want to doubt the one person I have trusted, the man I feel so connected to.

But I can't be a fool, either. The idea drives me forward, and my mind and emotions are so jumbled that I blink—I am at the front door of the castle and don't even remember the walk. I reach for the knob and it bursts open. I back up and watch in disbelief as the men from the bar last night carry a bleeding man inside.

Kayden follows, speaking into his phone. "Why the fuck aren't you here already, Nathan? Hurry the hell up." He ends the call and the men charge toward the center tower steps, blood dripping everywhere, and a series of images flashes through my mind. My father was a medic in the army, and he taught me about that, too.

"Stop!" I shout, racing after them. "Put him down before you make him lose too much blood, or put him into shock!"

The men pause and look at Kayden, who I feel at my back.

I whirl around. "Put him down if you want him to live."

Kayden doesn't hesitate. "Do it!" he orders.

They lower the man, who I assume is Enzo, to the floor and I drop to my knees next to him, applying pressure to the wound in his chest, but he's bleeding from his arm, too. He's not moving and pale.

Kayden kneels across from me and applies pressure to his arm, checking his pulse as he does. "It's weak."

"He's losing too much blood," I say, eyeing one of the men. "I need you to hold where I'm holding."

The man swiftly joins me on the ground, replacing my hands with his, but before I fully release my hold, I warn, "Don't let go or he'll die."

Then I climb over Enzo to get to Kayden, unhook his belt, and pull it from the loops. "I need your shirt to wrap the wound. I'll keep pressure on his arm while you take it off."

My hand replaces his and he yanks his shirt over his head. "You wrap his arm," he says, "and I'll belt it."

"Good. Belt it really tight."

He gives me a nod, and in a blur of movement, we have

the tourniquet on. Enzo moans, and as far as I'm concerned, that's a good sign.

"I'm here!" Nathan shouts, entering with Matteo, both men carrying bags, and just the sight of him is relief. Then he's taking my spot. "I need to start an IV; he needs blood. Get me blood now!"

I don't even want to know where they're going to get that. No longer needed, I turn and start walking, so cold I'm brittle, and I barely remember reaching the main level of our tower, or when I turn toward the spare bedroom. Inside, I continue to the bathroom and turn on the shower. I then step inside fully dressed and sit down, staring at the blood pouring off of me and down the drain. My shaky hand unzips my purse and closes around my gun. It's my friend. I'm not sure who else is.

The shower door opens and Kayden steps inside, kneeling in front of me, blood washing off his pants and body as they are mine. So much blood.

"Ella." His hands settle on my shoulders and I want them there, and I don't want them there. I don't look at him and he cups my face, forcing my gaze to his. "Sweetheart. What are you doing?"

I swallow the knot in my throat, water running over my face and his. "I can handle a lot of things, Kayden. Maybe even a bloody man dying in your foyer. But I can't handle lies."

"What are you talking about?"

"I saw the photo of my necklace in your office."

His hands fall away, his withdrawal proving the betrayal I'd prayed wasn't true. What else did he know that he hasn't told me?

The certainty that too much with this man hasn't been what it seems hurts, cutting like a jagged-edged knife through my heart. I want answers. I want the lies to end.

I pull my gun from my purse and point it at him. "Who are you to me, Kayden? Who am I?"

To be continued in the next book in the Careless Whispers series, *Demand*!